Jon Stock is a freelance journalist and writes for a variety of national newspapers. He is also London correspondent of *The Week* magazine in India. He lives with his wife in Greenwich.

Other Mask Noir titles

Alex Abella	*The Killing of the Saints*
Susan Wittig Albert	*Thyme of Death*
Gopal Baratham	*Moonrise, Sunset*
Pieke Biermann	*Violetta*
Nicholas Blincoe	*Acid Casuals*
	Jello Salad
Ken Bruen	*Rilke on Black*
Agnes Bushell	*The Enumerator*
Charlotte Carter	*Rhode Island Red*
Jerome Charyn	*Maria's Girls*
Didier Daeninckx	*Murder in Memoriam*
	A Very Profitable War
John Dale	*Dark Angel*
Stella Duffy	*Beneath the Blonde*
	Calendar Girl
	Wavewalker
Graeme Gordon	*Bayswater Bodycount*
Gar Anthony Haywood	*You Can Die Trying*
Maxim Jakubowski (ed)	*London Noir*
Russell James	*Count Me Out*
Elsa Lewin	*I, Anna*
Walter Mosley	*Black Betty*
	Devil in a Blue Dress
	A Little Yellow Dog
	A Red Death
	White Butterfly
George P. Pelecanos	*Down by the River Where the Dead Men Go*
	A Firing Offense
Julian Rathbone	*Accidents Will Happen*
	Sand Blind
Derek Raymond	*The Crust on Its Uppers*
	A State of Denmark
Sam Reaves	*Fear Will Do It*
	A Long Cold Fall
Manuel Vazquez Montalban	*The Angst-Ridden Executive*
	Murder in the Central Committee
	Off Side
	An Olympic Death
	Southern Seas
David Veronese	*Jana*
Oscar Zarate (ed)	*It's Dark in London*

THE RIOT ACT

Jon Stock

Library of Congress Catalog Card Number: 97–066230

A complete catalogue record for this book can be obtained from the
British Library on request

First published in 1997 by Serpent's Tail,
4 Blackstock Mews, London N4, and
180 Varick Street, 10th floor, New York, NY 10014
website: www.serpentstail.com

Phototypeset in 10pt ITC Century by
Intype London Ltd

Printed in Great Britain by
Mackays of Chatham plc, Chatham, Kent

For Hilary

Acknowledgements

The author would like to thank Mike D for sharing his knowledge of the City, Dinah and Stewart McLennan for the Nook in Cornwall, where this book was written, and Peggy, for her lasting generosity.

"What, he does not blow his nose on
his fingers? He has a handkerchief!
He is an aristocrat! Hang him on a lamp-post!"

Danton's Death, Georg Buchner

CHAPTER 1

Annalese was the only woman I have ever loved, the first person to betray me. I have been let down often enough, but never betrayed. Betrayal is about surprise. You expect the state to mess you about, it goes with the turf, and my family – we have held mutually low expectations of each other since the day I was born (kicking and shouting, I like to think). But Annalese? She caught me off guard, napping. I never suspected a thing.

It was a raw Christmas Eve and a fog had settled on the Thames, shifting restlessly just above the surface. The tide was high and beginning to turn, the water trapped in indecision, running both ways around the rotting jetty posts alongside our barge. It made a clean trickling sound, quite distinct from the low hum of the nearby refinery. We were moored close to the Blackwall Tunnel, in a derelict wharf used mainly as a graveyard for knackered pleasure boats. Annalese had chosen the place for its concentration of ley lines and because our boat was directly below the mother of them all, the Meridian, marked by a laser shining out from the Royal Observatory.

Despite the cold I was sitting outside in the cockpit. Above me the green beam was struggling to reach across to Docklands. (On clear nights we thought we could see it on the other side of Greenwich Park, faint after its journey around the globe.) Every few seconds a light on top of Canary Wharf brightened the dense fog, popping like a distant flashbulb. Annalese was already in bed attempting to stay warm. Quietly, I raised the wooden seat opposite, pushed a bundle of icy rope to one side and felt around in the dark. My fingers touched something smooth and cold. I had almost forgotten about the shotgun, stolen from my dad years ago. It was draped in an oil-stained muslin cloth, which snagged on the burrs at the end of the barrels as I carefully unwrapped it. (I had stumped it myself, badly, using a blunt hacksaw.) I looked briefly down the sights, towards Docklands, and cracked it open. Both chambers were loaded. Snapping it shut again, I searched under the seat until I found what I was looking for, a blue camping stove.

I set the stove up on the floor of the cockpit, out of the wind, and struck a few matches. The cylinder was almost empty and it took several attempts to light. When they finally came, the flames were pale and timid, barely enough to cast shadows. The gas roared hoarsely.

On paper, making Cat – Methcathinone if you're from the Home Office – is easier than baking bread. Take some Epsom salts, a couple of aspirin, a pinch of ephedrine, available from all good chemists if you are an asthmatic (conveniently, Annalese had suffered since a child), add some car battery acid, preferably fresh, and heat gently on a silver crucible.

I turned to my left and picked up a sheet of Kit Kat foil. The ingredients had formed into a soggy heap in the middle, making the foil sag. Resting it on the stove, I cupped my hands closely around the flames, careful not to singe the wool on my fingerless gloves. After a few minutes something appeared in the gloom, more grey than my recipe had promised. I licked my fingers, quickly removed the foil from the stove and dropped it on the seat beside me. I then turned off the gas, the tread on the tiny black handle cutting into my numb fingers. It was the coldest it had been all year and there was no more wood for the burner down below. I put my head by the closed hatch and listened guiltily.

"You awake?" I called.

"Sssshhhh. You'll wake Leafe."

Leafe was Annalese's three-year-old kid. I got on fine with him, there was no problem, except when he needed to be shopped for. All her life, as far as I could tell, Annalese had objected to certain products on moral and environmental grounds. Then Leafe came along and she changed her mind and began ordering truck-loads of dodgy baby wipes and disposable nappies. She would do anything for him. It wasn't that I cared about the environment, far from it, I just wanted her to admit that she had ditched her principles, to accept that life was easier without them.

The foil had cooled quickly and I cut the powder with a small kitchen knife. It had been a while since I'd prepared my own Cat and there was always a risk with DIY of getting the measurements wrong. Too much acid and you had a flat battery for life. A little voice was telling me that I had got them wrong, but I wasn't expecting to hear voices until I had taken the gear so I ignored it. A pity, really. I removed one of Leafe's spiral striped straws from my pocket, folded and sliced it in half, gently inserted one up each nostril, bent forward and hoovered both lines simultaneously.

Cat is an acquired taste. There is not much money in it (yet), no one deals big time in the stuff, but it has a certain homely appeal for the enthusiast, like kit beer or Blue Peter models – never as good as the ready-made version, but somehow more satisfying. It also ruins your appetite for a few days, a useful bonus when you're out of food. The authorities haven't even bothered to classify it as a controlled substance. (Those of us reduced to getting our acid from car batteries need the occasional break.) I shuddered and looked around. My head was beginning to feel draughty, ajar, as if a gale was passing through one ear and out the other, missing my brain by several yards.

I couldn't be certain, but the fog appeared to be moving towards me, slowly, as if someone was shifting a scenery wall. I looked up river and saw a pleasure boat emerging from the gloom. It was passing from left to right, like a radio-controlled model, its coloured deck lights bright and crucified. The hull was too sharply focused. It must have been thirty yards away, but it suddenly seemed like three. At the stern a large paddle wheel was scooping up glistening water into the night sky and dropping it like tinsel. People were dancing awkwardly on the deck, visible through large plate glass windows. The music sounded strangely intimate, coming and going in waves, separate from the other sounds of people laughing and talking. Their voices were disturbingly clear, each one standing out on its own, uninterrupted, upper class . . .

Curled up in the bottom of the cockpit, I took in the morning at a slant. It wasn't the ideal start to Christmas Day. My face lay soldered against a row of wooden slats. Below them a pool of oily water glistened darkly, barely an inch away, rainbow colours smudged across its surface. My neck was tight and aching, and my clothes were wet down one side. I decided to give Cat a miss for a while.

I rolled over on to my knees and stayed there for a few moments, head held low like a baying cow. The veins in my forearms were swollen. It was weird but all I could think of was a McDonald's toilet. They had recently introduced blue lighting in their Glasgow branches to make it harder for junkies to find their veins. My right shoulder was bruised and sore. I climbed to my feet, trying to slide out from under the hangover without it noticing. It must have been early because the sun was still low, a red ball somewhere above the Canning Town flyover. There was no traffic, no noise, just the refinery's incessant hum – as close to silence as the river ever got.

The tide was out and had left the mud rippled like mousse. I looked across at the row of gravel conveyor belts, stretching out into the main channel, and stepped up on to the cockpit seat. As I did so, I heard a dull thud against the side of the hull. I ignored it at first, thinking it must be a piece of driftwood, and stretched gingerly on to the shore. But I glanced down and something black caught my eye in the water, wedged in the gap between the boat and the posts running along one side of the jetty. I knew immediately that it was a body, swollen and waterlogged, the back arching limply like an exhausted seal. The head was face down but it was obviously a man, still wearing peach-soled brogues and what looked like a dinner jacket and trousers. One of the feet was pointing awkwardly sideways, broken at the ankle. I thought back to the previous night, the turning wheel, the music. I tried to recall some more but my head hurt with the effort.

Then I remembered the gun. My stomach tightened momentarily. I stepped back on to the boat, rocking it gently, and looked around. Lifting the seat, I saw the gun lying next to the rope, its barrel wrapped neatly in the muslin. I picked it up, and unfolded the material. Faint the night before, the smell of oil now seemed overpowering. Both barrels were still loaded. I smiled, and then felt a pang of disappointment. It was coming back to me now, the dancing, the voices. The boat had been a long way off, but I could have tried at least, holed her midships.

I glanced up and down the river, and bent to pick up the aluminium tender lying along the boat roof. I then lay flat on the narrow deck beside the cockpit, reached down and hooked one end of the tender under the body, by his armpit. I tried to turn him over but he wouldn't budge, bobbing instead below the surface. I pulled harder. Suddenly the tender slipped and banged against the hollow side of the boat. I froze, waiting for Annalese to call out. After ten seconds or so, I leant down and tried again, this time catching the hook under his face. It lodged in his mouth, pulling against a cheek, and the head revolved slowly.

The man had black hair, lightly curled, and the edges floated on the surface, blurred like a barber shop photo. He can't have been more than twenty. A jagged strand of wet hair stuck to his skin, breaking up the whiteness like party paint. His eyes were closed. The tender hook was distorting his mouth into a sneer. I returned the compliment, let the body turn, and sat up. There were no obvious wounds, no chunks missing. He must have fallen overboard.

I watched as he began to slide slowly down the side of the barge, disturbed from his quiet corner. The current took him past the lattice of decaying posts underneath the jetty, to the far end, where he snagged himself briefly on a solitary green post. Then he drifted out towards the centre of the river and disappeared without even a wave goodbye. Toffs had no manners anymore, no class.

I walked down to the end of the jetty and had a smoke. Beside the cement factory I could see huge steel silos lying on their sides like spent rockets. Beyond them, the Woolwich ferries were slipping past one another, momentarily hidden behind the steel sentinels of the Barrier. I turned to the old pleasure craft listing in the mud next to me. It was time for presents. Christmas had been a close call this year. I usually gave it a miss, but Annalese had talked me into it, said it was a time for lovers. Her present was sentimental, not exactly me, a compromise.

Treading carefully I stepped on to the gunwhale of the pleasure boat and dropped down on to the deck. The wood was shot through with rot and a plank split as I climbed up into the wheelhouse. The cardboard box was still there, miaowing at me as I approached. Annalese had always wanted a kitten. I had bought it from a bloke who lived on an estate near *The Cutty Sark*. (He hired out puppies for a living, leasing me his Alsatian whenever I went begging in the Greenwich foot tunnel.) I opened the lid to check he was alright. The box was lined with a couple of Annalese's old woollen hats and the kitten, ten weeks old and the runt of the litter, was shivering in one corner. At least it hadn't frozen to death.

I made my way back along the jetty, casually checking the water for more bodies. The toff might be back again when the tide turned, become a regular visitor. We could do with the company. The other boats were all sealed up for winter and people rarely strayed off the towpath.

Annalese stirred as I slid down the cabin hatch, which threw me slightly. I had some vague, embarrassing notion of placing the thing on the pillow next to her as she slept, letting it nuzzle her awake.

"What time is it?" she asked, her eyes still shut.

"Time for presents," I said, putting the box down quietly on the floor, out of sight. My breath was condensing in the cold.

"Presents?" The tone in her voice made me edgy.

"Yeah, presents." I glanced at her. She looked beautiful when she was asleep, her big eyes swollen under the skin. "It's Christmas, remember? Your idea."

There was a pause. "It's only the twenty-second, Dutchie."

"Is it?" I looked down at the box on the floor and almost kicked it. "I got you a present anyway."

She yawned and sat up, swinging her feet to the floor. It was all going wrong. She was meant to stay in bed.

"You're very sweet, Dutchie," she said sleepily, hugging herself in the cold and reaching for a jumper. "I'm touched. But can it wait? I'm a bit old-fashioned when it comes to dates."

"No. It can't wait. Do you want it or not?"

She looked up at me, sensing the change in my voice.

"When did you come to bed?" she asked quietly. "I didn't hear you."

I bent down to pick up the box.

"I got you a kitten. It's called Lamorna."

I didn't want to talk about last night. Annalese wasn't bothered if I stayed out, that was never a problem. It was the shame of it, the ignominy of revealing that I hadn't even made it off the boat.

Our barge was thirty feet long and consisted of one main room and a tiny bathroom. We had only been living in it for a couple of months and were still discovering cupboards and hatches. As you came in from the cockpit, there was a small cooker, a Fifties cream-coloured fridge and a plastic sink on the left, and a shelf on the right with a few empty jars, green ones recycled in Spain (Annalese's choice). Beyond them was a formica fold-out table, which she had painted with purple flowers. There was a bench on one side and two chairs on the other, covered in mauve and black velvet cushions sent by a friend of hers from Salem. Dark, star-patterned drapes lined the walls and windows, for privacy and warmth. Leafe was asleep on the bench, wrapped up in a blanket. At the far end was our bed which sagged dramatically down the middle.

Annalese loved Lamorna and went back to bed with her, while I tried to fix some breakfast – difficult without any food. I turned on the cooker out of habit, remembered we were out of gas and went outside to retrieve the camping stove.

"Leafe will be hungry when he wakes," Annalese said, as I returned. She was propped up on a pillow, dragging a piece of thread across the blanket in front of Lamorna's pouncing paws. I said nothing. Holding the kettle under the tap, I pumped out some brown water with my foot. The tank was almost empty.

"You said . . ." she began.

" . . . I forgot."

"I don't mind doing the shopping. You offered so I assumed . . ."

" . . . I know what you assumed. We're out of water."

I struck a match, lit the camping stove and rested the half-full kettle on top of it. We both stayed silent for a while, listening to the faint roar of the flame. Neither of us had the energy for an argument. I turned around and looked along the shelf. We were out of everything and it was freezing. All I could find was one vegetable Oxo cube, fallen down behind the clay jar we used for garlic.

"Last night," Annalese began.

"What about last night?" I snapped. She paused for a moment, genuinely taken aback. I felt stupid. She was going to talk about something else.

"Sorry," I said, leaning forward on the sink.

"Last night," she continued, "I had nightmares. Like I had the night Tom died."

Tom, her twin, had been killed in a road accident when she was twenty. Her words left me cold, then annoyed. She knew I couldn't pass over it lightly, but I managed. There was a distance between us this morning.

"I woke up and you weren't around," she continued.

"I slept out. It was a beautiful night."

We were silent for a while. "You're far away today," she said.

I didn't answer. My head was still scrambled, starting to hurt.

"Did you have nightmares, too?" she asked.

"Kind of."

"You only take it when we've rowed."

"It makes me lose my appetite."

"For shopping."

"We're skint."

"Never stopped you in the past."

It was true. I hadn't paid for anything in years. I was an

accomplished lifter, a player, but for some reason I had lost my bottle yesterday. Annalese had cast some bad runes in the morning. I didn't believe in that sort of thing, but she did and her apprehension had worried me.

I went into the bathroom to look at myself in the mirror. I felt a touch weird and needed reassurance that I hadn't swapped bodies with the man in the water. My face was as pale, a little pasty, but my eyes were black and shiny, peering out from deep-set sockets.

"Are you going to ring your dad this year?" Annalese asked from next door.

My dad? "What's the point?" I said, beginning to admire myself. I had the constitution of an ox, there was no avoiding it. A few hours earlier, I had been consuming regulation car battery acid. Few people could survive that. I felt stronger already.

"People like being rung at Christmas," she continued.

"You've never met him."

"He can't be that bad."

"He's a tosser."

I came back out of the bathroom and went over to the stove. The kettle was beginning to steam gently, barely managing a whistle. It was as close to boiling as it was going to get. I unwrapped the Oxo cube, crushed it into two mugs and poured on the water.

"Why? Are you going to ring yours?" I asked.

"If I knew where he was."

"You'd sooner kill him."

"Not at Christmas."

Her dad had run off years ago, leaving her mum to bring up Annalese. He never got in touch, but we had him to thank for the barge. One day, out of the blue, he sent Annalese a cheque. Guilt money. She had always wanted to live on a boat, so we bought one. It didn't make her feel any better about him.

"I went out for a drink with Mia and Katrina yesterday," she continued. "When I thought you were doing the shopping."

"Oh yeah? How are they?"

Mia and Katrina ran a stall next to Annalese's in Greenwich market.

"Katrina's split up with Matt," she said.

"That didn't last long."

"Six months. She's quite cut up about it."

"He was a lunchout."

"He was alright."

Annalese could never see it, but Matt liked to find cracks and tap them. He spread dark rumours, played people off against each other. Once, when we were very drunk, he had talked about Annalese, accused her of telling tales.

I took both cups of Oxo to her and sat down. Lamorna was purring. "You're all wet," she said, brushing the side of my arm. We sat in silence for a while, watching the cat. I hadn't thought about Matt recently, or what he had said. I'd never given him the time of day.

"Why don't you talk about him more?" Annalese asked.

"Who?"

"Your dad. You should."

"My dad? Nothing to say."

"That's what you said about your mum."

"She was different."

"Why?"

I didn't answer.

"Shall we go into town today?" she continued. "Drop Leafe off at mum's?"

"Could do," I said, getting up. I glanced out of the window, watched a bright orange tug head up river, and then turned to Annalese. She was staring at me, her eyes calm and transfixing. We looked at each other, as if weighing up our entire lives in a moment.

"What's the matter?" she asked quietly.

"Katrina's better off without him," I said, looking away. "Matt was a liar."

"I checked to see if you were alright last night," she said, beginning to giggle. "When I heard you fall over."

I went over to her. "Come to bed," she said, pulling me down. "It's Christmas Day, remember."

CHAPTER 2

Thomas Hardy once wrote that we all have deathdays as well as birthdays. The only difference is that we pass silently over our deathday each year, unaware of its presence. Perhaps if we knew when it was, we could celebrate, send cards, prepare ourselves better for death. I think Annalese was aware of something that morning, as we pretended it was Christmas Day. She cried after we had made love. When I asked her what was wrong, she said she didn't know, couldn't explain. Not yet, at least. She loved me, she said, whatever happened. Her friends in Cornwall claimed she was psychic. We had only ever talked about it once; her problem, she explained, was that she was only ever aware of imminent darkness, and she had no desire to scare anyone. But that wasn't it. There was something else troubling her.

We first met each other in the centre of Penzance, a few miles along the coast from the Lamorna valley, where she was born. I was down in Cornwall to take a break. The police had been steaming me, pulling me in every few days, trying to make a case, until I had finally had enough and given them the slip.

It was a spring morning and I was walking down Causeway Head towards the clock tower. I had just purchased some blow down a side street, when I came across a band playing in front of Midland Bank, on the corner. They were better than usual and I stopped to listen, standing at the back of the crowd – a mixture of Saturday morning shoppers, curious tourists, crusties. Most eyes were on the zither player, whose deft wrist movements and floating harmonies had everyone hypnotised. His head, covered in birds' feathers, nodded gently to the beat kept by a bongo player and a woman, lissome and wild, who shook a tambourine and tossed her head back in the chorus ("in the circles of the sun, turn the crystal on"). She had long, henna'd hair and olive skin. Next to her a weathered, older man was doing his own thing, extracting neanderthal noises from a didgeridoo.

My eyes moved reluctantly from the woman to the crowd. It wasn't the travellers sitting on the pavement who interested me, but the group of tourists who had just walked up the hill from the station. They were American, and all of them were sporting plump money belts about their even plumper middles. I took off my hat, green and woollen, and unrolled it. Then, with a quick glance at the band, I made my way to the back of the crowd and mingled with the Americans.

"Money for the music?" I asked. "Spare any change? Anyone want to give some money for the band?"

The words came easily – it was no different from begging – and so did the money. After a couple of minutes, I had collected enough to get me drunk, unaware that the tambourine player had broken off from the group. Suddenly I saw her, a few feet away, holding a rainbow-coloured tam-o'-shanter in one hand and a child in the other, hooked over her hip. Instinctively I closed the hat and stepped back. I watched her move amongst the crowd, smiling and chatting quietly. She exuded an intoxicating calmness, untroubled. People opened their wallets for this woman. She looked the part – how a traveller was meant to look. Hair coloured with ties and beads, horse-brown eyes the size of crystal balls, layers of richly coloured skirts. Nothing about her threatened.

"Money for the band? We're part of Tanglewood travelling theatre," she said, standing in front of me.

Shit, I thought, she was talking to me. I hadn't retreated into the shadows with the money, her money, as I would normally have done. I was caught. Without hesitating I opened my hat and poured the contents into hers. The odd collection of coins rattled accusingly as we looked at each other.

"You're very generous," she said, suspiciously. "Where you from?"

"What's it to you?"

"Just asking."

She started to move on, the child squinting up at me in the sun.

"What's the show?" I called after her.

She continued to collect money. "Midsummer Night's Dream. Seven o'clock, at the Minack," she said, her back still turned.

"See you then," I said, watching her disappear into the crowd. "I played Puck once." She turned and smiled briefly.

I was standing in a crowd again now, watching Annalese from a distance as she moved around the entrance hall of the British Museum. We had dropped Leafe off at her mum's and decided to head into town to continue our Christmas Day celebrations. First stop, the museum. I was a regular in the Reading Room – it was warm and free – and had noticed a poster for an exhibition of Egyptian pottery. Annalese had a soft spot for the Pharaohs, had done ever since she was a child. We hadn't expected to wait, but security was extra tight today. For some reason, I had been told to queue and Annalese was waved on. The story of my life, really.

I stood on the strangely quiet museum steps, waiting to be searched, and thought what a weird place the West End was at the moment. For the past three weeks London had been torn apart by a bombing campaign like no other. No one knew who the terrorists were, but the blasts had killed enough people to send the country into a state of mild hysteria. People stayed at home, too afraid to go into work. The shops had never known a quieter Christmas. It didn't bother me. I liked the space, the chance to walk down the middle of once busy roads.

I stamped my black worker's boots impatiently in the cold as the security guard searched my canvas shoulder sack, his gloved fingers clumsily rifling through a few pencils, Annalese's sketch pad, a bag of tobacco and a rag which I had emptied my nose on a few seconds earlier. He removed his sticky hands and gave me a glare. Was it the dreadlocks? Some days I thought about wearing a flashing pink neon sign on my nut saying terrorist. I might get less hassle.

"Satisfied?" I said, my arms outstretched.

"There's a war on, you know," the guard said, looking at me suspiciously as he patted the sides of my ribcage. "You're lucky this place is still open."

A war? The old geezer would be digging trenches next. I found Annalese in the corner of the entrance hall, looking through leaflets. Despite the bombings, the museum was determined to stay open. There were a few tourists milling around, but no children. The high ceiling used to echo with shrieks and shouts; now the hall was respectful, like a church.

"Let's eat here shall we?" Annalese suggested. "I'm starving."

"Christmas lunch," I said, smiling. She was looking up at a poster of a pyramid.

"How did you know this show was on?" she asked. "It wasn't advertised anywhere."

"Contacts. Me and the Pharaohs, we're like this," I said,

crossing my fingers. "Oh yeah, before we go up, I've got something to show you."

I sounded casual but I had been waiting a long time for this moment. It was the day's hidden agenda. She followed me behind the brown screens at the end of the hall into the deserted Reading Room, where I prepared to be strip-searched again. Another guard proceeded to empty the contents of my bag on to the counter. I said nothing, knowing who was about to have the last laugh.

"That's a nice badge," Annalese said impulsively, touching the guard's lapel. She had a way with authority. She seduced it. The guard watched her rub his Royal British Legion insignia between her thumb and finger, and smiled weakly, waving her through. I loved her when she was like this.

"Right," I said, catching up with her and striding over to the bank of computers. There was never a queue for them these days. I glanced down the row of empty terminals and settled for one in the middle. There can't have been more than ten people in the entire room, and only a skeleton staff was on duty. Annalese stood next to me and then began to wander, her eyes drawn to the walls of leather-bound books all around us. She walked along the shelves, dragging her fingers along the flaky bindings.

"Are you watching?" I asked, booting up the main index of books.

She wandered back, let her hand hang loosely over my chest, and kissed me noisily in my ear. As she did so, a prim woman with a soft leather satchel sat down at the far end of the row of terminals, glancing at us reproachfully. Annalese gave her a little wave.

"What have you been up to, you bad man?" she whispered, kissing me on the neck and putting her hand inside my shirt. She began to rub the hairs on my stomach, round and around, and then finger my tummy button.

"Nothing much. Keyword?"

"What?"

"You have to suggest a word, a book subject."

"Sex?"

"Read them all."

"You dirty bugger," she said, stroking me in widening circles. Her nails were beginning to hurt.

"I don't know. You suggest something."

"Shoplifting."

"Shoplifting?" she said indignantly.

"Yeah. How many books do you reckon have been written on the art of lifting?"

"Don't know. Ten?" She was losing interest, and removed her hand from my shirt. Instead she leant on the back of my shoulders, her arms folded in a pouting sulk.

I typed in "shoplifting" and pressed enter. "Twenty-four."

"So?"

"Wait. Watch this."

I had to be quick. She had an attention span of a flea when she was in this kind of mood. The details of the first entry came up on the screen. At least, they should have done. Instead, it read: "Item one has been removed from catalogue."

"Shame, that," I said. "A book on shoplifting appears to have gone walkabout."

Annalese started to giggle. I could feel her warm breath on my neck, smell the sandalwood incense on her jumper. I highlighted the second entry and the screen carried the same message: "Item two has been removed from catalogue."

"And there was me thinking you'd been educating yourself," Annalese said, standing upright and looking around. "Has anyone noticed?"

"Not yet. Impressive, eh?"

Not very, it seemed. Annalese had drifted over to the woman working on the other terminal. I scrolled through a few more entries. Each time the computer gave out the same message. It was beautiful.

"Hiya," I heard Annalese say to the woman. "What you doing? Anything interesting?"

I glanced across and saw the woman flush a deep red. I smiled. "Oh, nothing really," she stuttered. "Mary Ann Evans."

"All twenty four," I said triumphantly, getting up from the screen. "Work of genius." I was addressing no one in particular, hoping that someone might show a little interest.

"How long did it take you?" Annalese said loyally, meandering back in my direction.

"Weeks. Months."

An alarm bell suddenly started to ring above us.

"Shit," I said, looking around. People were getting up from their seats, pretending not to rush.

"What's that mean?" Annalese asked.

"They won't let us back in today. We should have gone upstairs first."

Annalese looked at me and smiled, pressing keys at random with her long fingers. "Don't worry," she said. "We can always see the Pharaohs tomorrow."

Outside in the front courtyard security guards were ushering confused academics and foreign students on to Museum Street. We cut down Coptic Street towards Centrepoint. The big junction between Tottenham Court Road and Oxford Street stood empty, an eerie sight. There was no noise and the lights were blinking their commands to invisible traffic. In one corner a vast revolving poster clicked every few seconds to reveal a new advert. The pictures were out of sync, though, creating disfigured, hybrid images of broken bottles and dislocated limbs.

Oxford Street itself was also deserted, except for the rubbish. It looked like a dried up river bed littered with urban excrement – Learn English leaflets, flattened Coke cans, dated underground tickets, copies of *Nine to Five*. No one swept the streets anymore, no one dared, and there was trash everywhere. I loved the way it levelled London, like snow, making the streets all look the same.

We walked past a boarded up store. I hadn't realised how many shops were closed. Even the dossers had pulled out of town, leaving the doorways strangely empty. I stopped to peer through a jigsawed hole in the hoardings. Inside the shelves were bare and the floor was covered with wire coathangers, latticed like cracks across the smooth white concrete.

Annalese was turning in childlike circles in the bus lane, raising the black and purple folds of her skirt. She waited for me to catch up. She took my arm, and together we walked in happy silence towards Oxford Circus. An arctic wind was blowing in our faces, sending sheets of a newspaper tumbling and folding towards us. As we passed Dean Street, I saw a police Range Rover fifty yards away, careened, two wheels up on the pavement. Officers sat silently inside. I raised my middle finger and walked on.

We stopped to look in the window of High and Mighty, one of the few shops that was still open. I was fascinated by this place, the length of the ties, the sheer girth of Y-fronts.

"I'll be looking at shoes," Annalese said, as I went inside. She had seen it all before and walked across the street toward Pied à Terre. It was true, I had an inexplicable interest in shops which catered for the "taller person", the "bigger frame". They were smart establishments and I wasn't their typical customer. Offsetting the ring in my right nostril, I had two through my left eyebrow, one in my upper lip and a total of twenty-eight arcing like slinkies around both ears – one for each year of my life. Today I was wearing a red T-shirt with cut-off sleeves, a loose leather waistcoat, a frayed jumper and matted army green trousers. There was also a Celtic armband tattoo on my right bicep and I had twisted leather thongs around my neck and wrists.

But I knew none of this would worry the two young assistants in High and Mighty. What concerned them was my size: I was short. I stood in front of a rack of suits the size of sails, and savoured the diplomatic tension. Which one was going to confront me, explain politely that I had been bonzied at birth? I began to study the jackets intently, rubbing the cloth of one, holding another up to the light. As I moved around the shop, admiring size 16 shoes made by "Magnum" and "Colossus" socks, I sensed the assistants gravitating behind the till, hovering but saying nothing. Their boss had joined them.

"Need a suit," I said finally, still facing away from them. I couldn't keep a straight face for much longer. "For a funeral."

The assistants glanced up at their elderly superior. A tall man, he stepped forward, cleared his throat. "We, um, we tend to cater for the larger end of the market, sir."

"I know," I said, turning round with an enormous scarlet suit in one hand and grinning. "I'll take this one."

At that moment the entire shop window disintegrated. The blast knocked me to the floor and sent shards of glass winking through the compressed air. A fraction of a second later there was a deafening crack, followed by a rushing sound, then silence. How long it lasted I could never remember. Gradually the air shook itself down, regaining its shape. I became aware of a pain in my left leg and a hideous cacophony in the street outside: tinkling glass mixed with screams, Annalese's screams.

Recently, in moments of crisis, I had found myself thinking of Annalese's face, with its carefree curves and muddy freckles. It was something I never thought I would do. My past life maybe, but not one person and so vivid, too. Now, as I lay on the shop floor, staring at the manager's deflated frame next to me, I saw Annalese's smile beneath her favourite velvet hat, lifted in style from Covent Garden.

I was rolled semi-conscious into an ambulance, staring across to where the shoe shop had once stood. A heavy stillness hung in the street like fog, muffling moans, absorbing the cries of the dying. Then a piece of glass fell from a high up window, echoing down a stairwell. I became aware of a burglar alarm ringing somewhere in the distance, its hammer twitching needlessly. A grey nylon anorak had been placed on something in the dust, a child perhaps.

CHAPTER 3

I turned on to Mudlark Way, the footpath by the old gas works, and saw the wharf up ahead. I was exhausted. I should have been dead. The manager had taken the full impact of the blast, shielding me from flying glass and a chunk of concrete bollard. My left leg was badly bruised, bandaged at the knee, but otherwise I seemed to be intact. The hospital had released me in the early afternoon, armed with crutches. To keep away the pain they had filled me with pethidine. I had since consumed a couple of cans of Special Brew, just to make sure. A bad idea. As I picked my way clumsily through the ropes and twisted iron, one of my crutches jammed between two jetty planks. I freed it with effort but lost the rubber nozzle at the end. I stumbled on. Annalese had built a garden of sorts near the towpath: plants tumbled bravely out of ancient funnels and rusting paint pots, and a broken anchor, wrapped in plastic ivy, was propped up against a small bench.

Then I saw the flowers, a stockpile of colour, heaped up on the quayside and on the barge roof. There were messages on bits of paper, flapping in the cabin door and trapped under stones. I stood swaying, trying to focus on the scene, and took another swig of beer. A couple of women were sitting on the edge of the quay, backs turned. They looked around as I approached. One of them got up. It was Katrina from the market. Her eyes were black and hollow, smudged by tears. She hugged me and started to sob. I tried to hold her, but the crutches made it difficult. Instead I looked out across the water. A tug was towing rubbish towards Dartford.

"She loved you, Dutchie, she really loved you," Katrina said, sniffing. "It wasn't true what they said."

What who said? I couldn't think about her words and concentrate on standing at the same time. I felt myself deflating in her arms. Her cheeks were wet and salty. My own eyes were moist, tears beginning to refract my already blurred vision. Until now, Annalese's death had only happened to me; I was able to dispute my own evidence, question whether there had been a bomb at all. On the train home, walking back from the station, people had given me strange looks but they had known nothing of her death. I hung on to their indifference, trusted their ignorance. Now I realised that other people – she had so many friends – were mourning too, complicating things, making it harder to doubt what had happened. Katrina disentangled herself to read some of the messages, leaving me leaning precariously in the wind. The other woman, Mia, was still sitting on the quayside.

"We thought it was Christmas Day," I began, apologetically. Why was I apologising? The river and sky were merging into a greyness, absorbing my words almost before I had spoken them. I felt unable to say anymore and stepped on to the side of the boat, levering myself awkwardly into the cockpit and dropping a crutch. I put a hand on the hatch to steady myself. The women exchanged looks.

"I'm alright, just need a kip," I said, and sank slowly to the floor.

Hungover but happy I lay staring at the low ceiling, reassured by the barge's familiar smell of kerosene, its imperceptible lilt. My dreams had been of Cornwall, of heady times with Annalese, swimming naked below the cliffs at Treen. The clock by the bed said half past eleven. Propping myself on one elbow, I picked up a packet of Rizlas and looked around for some puff. Instinctively I put my hand to my breast pocket. Why was I still wearing a shirt? I took a sharp, involuntary breath. Slowly, I closed my eyes and sunk back into the pillow. My leg began to burn.

Katrina and Mia had left a note telling me to come round and chat in the morning if I wanted. I didn't feel like talking to anyone. Their presence earlier had been unambiguous: Annalese was dead. Silence kept her alive. I got up slowly and tried to light a cigarette on the stove, kicking its base when it didn't ignite. I sat down at the narrow table. The boat rocked slightly as I manoeuvred my leg on to a chair. It wasn't just my leg that hurt. I had a churning feeling in my stomach, like permanent butterflies. Each time I thought of Annalese they swarmed.

It was approaching midnight rather than midday. A tanker was making its way quietly out to sea having unburdened its huge rolls of newsprint at Deptford. The wake lapped noisily against the concrete wharf along the towpath. It had lapped this morning, as we celebrated Christmas. I thought back to the afternoon, to the mortuary. I had to go there after leaving hospital to identify the body. According to one of the doctors, Annalese's mum was too distraught.

"Take your time," the man had said, tucking a clipboard under his arm. Barely twenty years old, he had looked like a medical student, fresh-faced, too at ease around death. A packet of Marlboro was clearly visible in the breast pocket of his white coat. "Please, there's no rush," he continued. Of course there wasn't. She was hardly going to get up and run away. She had no legs, arsehole. I very nearly hit him. Instead, I pressed my lips together until they hurt and focused on a small oval stain on the white, breeze-blocked wall. Blood? The man stood awkwardly for a moment, too concerned, then walked away.

The room was cold and whitewashed. The man's shoes

squeaked noisily on the plastic tiled floor. I didn't look up but I sensed him pausing before leaving, looking at me again. I kept staring ahead at the opaque plastic curtain. I hadn't been allowed to see my mum's body. For years a part of me had been able to say she had never died. It was only as the evidence mounted, slowly and incontrovertibly (the quietness in the kitchen, my dad beginning to talk about girlfriends), that the indifference wore off and I began to believe she was dead. The two of them would have got on. For a moment I imagined her lying next to Annalese, chatting, as if nothing was wrong. Second time around and I was doing better. I actually felt something, sadness, guilt, terror, I wasn't sure, but it was an improvement.

I stepped forward, pushing the rings back along the cheap metal rail. Annalese looked like she was wearing a mask. Her skin was yellower than usual, almost waxed, and her hairline seemed more pronounced, stitched even. Then I saw her facial wounds. Strange that I hadn't noticed them first. Large black blotches beneath the cheek skin, grated cuts criss-crossing her forehead and nose. Her left ear had gone. Instead, there was a grey dent. Below her waist, supports pressed up against the sheet like tent poles. I squinted, searching for the whole. This was the first woman I had loved. Had she known that? Did I ever tell her? I leant forward and kissed her gently on the lips. They were as hard as marble.

I reached for a scarf on the windowsill and inhaled. It always amazed me how the barge became untidy within hours, even minutes of her leaving, buried beneath cans and ash. This time, however, she had been gone barely twelve hours and the boat remained exactly as she had left it. I was determined to keep it that way. The kitten asleep on the bed, bottled unguents lined up like soldiers in the bathroom, the sign by the window – "plants like water", written in her italic hand – the velvet hat hung up by the hatch. (I had found the barnacled hook at low tide and spent a whole day cleaning it up for her birthday.) Nothing had changed. If I walked down the river tomorrow, passed Lovell's Wharf, *The Cutty Sark* and on through to the market into Greenwich, she would be at her stall selling jewellery, pieces like the beads above the mirror.

Then I heard the explosion again, the implosion of silence.

I grabbed a crutch and cleared the table with a clumsy sweep. A gas lamp toppled and fell, enriching the smell of kerosene. It was the formaldehyde at the mortuary that had shocked me the most – so antiseptic and final. I hauled the table over, knocking a plant into the wicker bin. Her beads slunk from the mirror to the floor. Already her presence was ebbing. I moved awkwardly to the sink and spat down the plughole. Then, as an afterthought, I pulled the drying rack off the wall, plates smashing to the floor. Lamorna had long since departed.

Annalese felt very close as I cleared up. Her silence now was familiar, reassuring. She had never commented on my anger, not directly anyway. "When you've done, we'll be in the caff. And don't forget to water the plants," she had said once, when I was trashing the place. I had just gone for an audition at a community theatre in Lewisham – her idea – and beaten up the director. (He was fresh out of drama school and we had spent the first hour being trees. "Where are your leaves, Dutchie? Anyone would think it's autumn.")

Sometimes she would stay in the boat if Leafe wasn't around. She didn't like violence, but I knew it fascinated her. The day I mellowed she would have left me. I smiled as I picked up the beads. Then it hit me again, like a poisoned chaser. Had she died instantly? (The doctors said yes, but they would, wouldn't they?) Or had the glass wheedled its way slowly into her flesh like fiery maggots?

From the moment I woke I wondered what Annalese's killers looked like. There was no early morning respite, no break from the grief. It was better this way, I thought, a more coherent start to the day. Something easy and uncomplicated had nudged my grief to one side and I could do nothing about it. I needed a face, an image to replace her own. I wanted to tell her killers what sort of person she was, show them her jewellery, let them know of her innocence. (I was the guilty one.) Then I would kill them. I was certain of that. Annalese wouldn't like it, but she was dead now.

For the next two days I barely left the boat, venturing out into Charlton only to nick newspapers from the public library. When people knocked on the barge's frosted up windows I hid behind the cupboard or lay on the floor out of sight, watching them leave flowers, write clumsy notes with numb fingers. Events like death were too big for my own world, I accepted that now. They spilled over into another, one which I could only observe from a distance.

Detached, I digested every detail of the bombing campaign, from the first, febrile headlines in *The Evening Standard*, to longer pieces in the Sunday papers. The lump in the street hadn't been a child, it was Annalese. A bit of her, anyway. It was the third blast that week. "The Bomb That Sliced New Age Traveller in Half", as *The News of the World* delicately put it, had killed eight people. The week before had been worse. Who was behind the violence remained a mystery. Terrorist organisations queued up to deny their involvement and people believed them. MI5 announced that everything possible was being done to find the faceless terrorists and were believed less. Day after day the bombs continued to detonate, quarry blasts in the middle of crowded cities.

Everyone had their theories. *The Daily Star* blamed Class War, which made me laugh. They wouldn't know a block of semtex if someone stuck it down their trousers. Personally,

I hadn't given the bombings much thought. On principle, of course, I welcomed the chaos. The resumption of violence was a business opportunity – my Christmas bonus. It didn't take a genius to work out that when eight hundred people tried to get out of a train in a hurry, there was a fair chance that a few briefcases would be left behind. It was the same with office evacuations (computers, bottles, more briefcases).

But that was before Annalese died.

I picked up another newspaper, a local one, and there she was, staring back up at me, anemones in her hair. The picture had been taken around the time I met her in Cornwall. The butterflies beat against my stomach wall. I tried to reason with myself. She meant little to me; if she had been special, her death would have been unbearable. As it was, the loss was sad, nothing more. People come and go. She had come into my life a year earlier and now she had gone, like the others. I'd get over it. We hardly knew each other. I tried to be detached, to tap the void like I used to, but I tore out the picture and stuck it above the bed. Then I started reading again, drawn to what I thought was a small misprint. It didn't strike me as odd at first, but gradually, as I devoured more and more papers, an idea took root in my fertile mind. I checked and double-checked the accounts of the Oxford Street bombing, cross-referencing the death tallies. There was a flaw, I was sure of it, a discrepancy in the reporting. It wasn't much, but I needed to tell someone.

For the first time in five years I headed home.

CHAPTER 4

It was Christmas Day, the real one, and a crisp frost sharpened the edges of the deep Hampshire hedgerows. All colour had been sucked from the hills, leaving them empty and white, and the vaulting sky was a brilliant, darkened blue. As the narrow road dropped down a hill, twisting sharply, I cut the ignition (the car had been thoughtfully abandoned on someone's driveway in Charlton), wound down the windows and free-wheeled. I hadn't passed any other vehicles since coming off the motorway and the freezing air rushed silently past. I drew up in the middle of the road and listened. The whole world, it seemed, had been stilled by the cold.

My dad lived in one of the small villages outside Portsmouth which was popular with retired naval officers. It had a cricket pitch and a pond, which was iced over, and a pub which I had been banned from years ago. I slowed down as I passed it to look at the name above the door, but it was partially obscured by some ivy. The only blot on the rural idyll was the concrete shell of a derelict petrol garage, up ahead, opposite the post office. It looked like a bombed out temple, the vast awning cracked and peeled.

The turning into my dad's road was up on the left. I slowed and took a deep breath. It annoyed me that I felt nervous. A car hooted behind me. I wound down my window and gave it the finger. Then I pulled out after it, accelerating into the turning fast enough to make the tyres whine and give the other driver a shock. My dad's road was lined with barren cherry trees which pushed up the paving stones. The houses were set back in their own land. Most of them were modern, mock Tudor buildings. At the far end, up a steep hill, they became older, hidden out of sight down longer driveways.

I drove up the road, looking at the coloured lights in the windows, the Christmas trees in manicured front gardens. Heavy oak doors were cloaked in ivy. Then, up ahead, I saw something strange. It was my dad's Volvo, I was certain, but it seemed to be reversing, driving forwards, reversing then driving forwards again, all within the space of a few yards. The old git had finally lost it. I approached cautiously, winding down the passenger seat window as I drew level with his car.

"Alright?" I asked.

My dad pulled up hard on the handbrake and looked at me briefly, his eyes widening.

"Christ Almighty!" he shouted. "The last of the Mohicans."

Releasing the handbrake, he let the car roll down the hill two yards, and then drove forward, drawing level with me again.

"You owe me money," he said aggressively.

"What you doing?" I asked. There were more creases at the side of his eyes. I glanced down at the black cable lying across the road like a flattened worm.

"Do you have any idea how much it cost me?" he continued loudly, and then paused, wiping one of the dials on the dashboard with the back of his hand. We were silent for a couple of moments, acknowledging each other's presence, letting the formal bluster die down.

"You can afford it," I said quietly. "What's going on?" I nodded again at the cable.

"Bloody council. They're planning to close off the end of this road. Not being used enough."

"It isn't."

"That's not the bloody point. If they close it, we'll have to drive half way round Hampshire to get to the shops."

"The golf course."

"That too."

"You could walk."

"What?"

He had slipped back two yards, out of earshot. He drove forward again, conning the cable with another car. When the council came back to check the traffic frequency, they would write in their reports that the entire M25 had been diverted down his road. I left him to it, drove on ahead, parking my car in front of the house. It was the only genuinely old one in the whole road. Nelson, no less, had spent a night in it, as my dad insisted on telling everyone. But it had never felt like home. It was where I had stayed in between terms. I watched dad walk across the gravel towards me, picking out a weed from the stones and throwing it on to the lawn. The house might have to be sold if Lloyd's didn't cough up. Crying shame, that.

"Thought you were the man from the water board," he said, wheezing passed me into the kitchen. His sandy hair was still all there, but his face was too rubied, even for a sailor. The dents above his eyes were deep, giving him an air of being permanently surprised. His eyebrows had once curved normally, but the longer hairs now failed to turn the corner, forming little wings or handles like the tuft on a peewit's head.

"Try that," he said, passing me a half-empty gin and tonic. "I put the ice in and it's ruined. I told them it tastes like the bloody swimming pool."

I sniffed it and put it down on the tiled sideboard. I didn't want to hang around for long. I was expecting him to be with someone on Christmas morning, one of the many middle-aged divorcees who had come knocking at his door within months of mum dying, but he appeared to be on his own. There were no signs of Christmas about the house, except for a small, balding tree propped up against the wall in the corner of the hall. It was in a plastic red bucket and hadn't been decorated.

"I was living with a woman called Annalese," I began bluntly. "On a barge. We were very happy. She was killed last week, by a bomb."

My dad grunted and walked over to the fridge. He was a big man, well stacked. "Beer?" he asked, his head still in the fridge.

"Ta."

He never used to look at me if there was the faintest whiff of emotion in the air. Now was no exception. His back turned, I slid a packet of cigarettes off the table into my pocket.

"A bomb you say?" he said, pulling at the can with his fat fingers. I knew he was feeling awkward about how little he knew. I let him suffer.

"Last Tuesday. Oxford Street."

"That was a big one."

"500lbs."

"I haven't been into town this year. Too damn risky. At least with the IRA you knew who the enemy were."

"Are you still friendly with Walter?"

"Walter? Saw him only last week. Why?"

"I need to talk to him."

"Not quite your sort is he?"

"He's my godfather."

"Is he? Never knew that."

"Nor did I. Is he still working?"

"About to retire, I think. Of course you never really know with him."

My mysterious godfather was an American, from the West Coast, but he had spent most of his life in London, and was as good as English. He worked in some capacity for the security services, though nobody knew exactly what he did. There were various rumours along the lines that he was employed by the CIA to keep an eye on the British, but most assumed he was here because he preferred the English to his fellow countrymen. "Talk to Walter if he talks to you," mum used to say.

"What's he do again?" I asked.

"Don't know. Don't ask. Not much these days."

"I need to talk with him."

"The last time he saw you, you were wearing a decent set of clothes and could speak properly. Does that lot set off the metal detectors?" he asked, motioning towards my earrings.

I walked into the sitting room at the back of the house to drink my beer. I could hear him fiddling around in the kitchen, pretending to clear up. Too much had happened for a reconciliation. Our last encounter captured the unique flavour of our relationship. He was one of the first to drive through the newly opened bypass at Twyford Down (he had queued at 6 a.m. for the privilege) and I was there to greet him, shouting "scum" through the window of his Volvo estate, pouring acid on the roof and running a Stanley knife along the nearside panel.

Later, when I was arrested, the police contacted him about pressing charges. He declined. Even I was surprised. Deep down, I figured, he felt responsible for the way I had turned out. We had never talked about my mum's death. I was back at boarding school within the week, sitting in a maths lesson wondering what all the fuss had been about. My world hadn't changed. The only clue that she had died was a small piece in the *Portsmouth Evening News* which he sent me. (No letter, just the cutting, the date written usefully at the top in case I wanted to file it.)

"What did you say she was called?" he asked, joining me in front of the patio windows. He worked his faded plum trousers sideways then upwards. Emotions were looming again.

"Annalese."

"Unusual."

"Yeah. She was."

There was a pause as we both looked out on to the blanched lawn.

"Needs weeding," he said. "Look, if I give him a call, he'll ask me what it's about."

"Tell him I have got some information about the bombings and I can't risk talking to anyone else," I replied, and started walking to the car.

CHAPTER 5

The evening after I had seen Annalese playing in the band, I hitched a lift with a farmer down to Porthcurno beach, and walked up the cliffs to the Minack, cut into the rocks like a Roman amphitheatre. The performance had already started and I stood on the path above, listening to the laughter and the sea. It was a warm evening and the show had sold out. I didn't have any money anyway. Then I heard the tambourine being shaken. I tried to imagine her face and was frustrated that I couldn't see it. I walked around to the front of the theatre and dropped down below the path on to some gorse-covered rocks. The sea was swelling below me. On the far side of the bay, Atlantic rollers were throwing themselves against a granite outcrop. There was a hidden thud as each wave disintegrated, but the spray seemed to explode silently, the plumes hanging in the air too long.

I looked the other way, towards Land's End. The sun had recently set and the wounded sky was scorched a deep red. It had all the ingredients of a spiritual moment, but there were voices growing louder above me, bays of rich laughter staining the night air. I sat down on a rock, still out of sight, and lost my appetite to go any further. I reminded myself I hadn't come here to fight. I tried to ignore the voices (there wasn't a Cornish one among them) but it was impossible. It was the corporate crew who really got my goat, the ones who thought Shakespeare was full of clichés. The last time I had gone to the theatre I had managed to smuggle myself into a hospitality box as a waiter. I poured one drink down a Laura Ashley dress, another over a draft business proposal,

and placed a small incendiary device in the managing director's cigar box. The MD's giggling tart of a secretary was so
drunk when it exploded that she thought it was part of the
show. She applauded wildly, until she noticed her boss was
unconscious.

I was still smiling at the memory when a small child came
tottering down the path on his own towards me. I looked
up, wondering where his mother was, and then I saw her
strolling around the corner a few yards behind. She had an
easy gait, loose-limbed, taller than I remembered.

"Alright?" she said, her smile tinted with recognition. I
tossed a stone into the dust and looked ahead.

"I want to throw up."

"Come here Leafe, back from the edge," she said, taking
the boy's hand. She started swinging his arm backwards and
forwards, enough to make him giggle. "What's the matter
then?" she asked, turning to me.

"I hope they pay you well," I said, nodding up at the
theatre above us.

"Enough, why?"

"I wouldn't stand in front of them for nothing."

"Where you from, London?" she asked, bending down to
look at a piece of purple quartz in a rock. She stroked it,
and Leafe did the same. She was wearing a silver ring on
her thumb, and her nails were painted black.

"Came down last week."

"What for?"

"What for?" I said, turning to her. Her question surprised
me. I hadn't planned on telling anyone what I was doing in
Cornwall.

"It's a long way to come."

"I had to leave in a hurry. Kept going, I suppose."

She looked at me, scrutinising my face for more information. I wanted to tell her everything.

"You running away, then?" she asked after a while.

"Taking a break."

"What from?"

"This and that."

"A woman?"

"Where's his dad?" I said, nodding at Leafe. I didn't like her questions.

"No idea. Left the next morning. No, that's not quite true."

"What was his name?"

"His name?"

"I might know him."

" 'Tree'. He spent most of his time falling out of one."

The name rang a bell. He was a protester, famous for constructing walkways high up in the canopies of theatened forests.

"And you prefered tambourines."

There was no answer as she bent down next to Leafe. She wasn't wearing anything beneath her loose purple vest. Leafe was still bewitched by the quartz. "I see him occasionally, on the telly. He believes in what he's doing. What's your name?" she asked, not looking up.

"Dutchie," I replied, breaking another promise.

We looked at each other for a moment, and then she stood up.

"It's easy to lose yourself round here, if you need to," she said. A bell was rung somewhere above us. "I've got to go."

"Tambourine solo?"

"Flute. Three notes, but they're long notes. Come."

"How do I get in?"

"You can sit in the dressing room," she said, smiling. "With Leafe."

I walked back up the path with them. Leafe held my hand and wanted to swing between us. We swung him until our arms ached, and were only saved when Bottom walked passed us into the dressing room wearing an ass's head. Leafe must have seen it a hundred times, but he laughed and laughed and so did I. For the first time in months I felt good inside. Tree demos weren't really my kind of thing – they attracted the wrong sort, the non-violent, fluffy sort – but it was an encouraging start.

The following evening I saw the whole show and went with her and some of the cast down to Treen beach, where we swam in the moonlit sea. It was a warm night and our clothes were piled in a heap on the sand. Annalese and I concentrated on Leafe, but he was little more than a conduit. Back on the shore, we traced each other's shadows in the sand with sticks. They were comically long and thin, cast by the low moon.

"Careful," I said, as she pulled the stick up my twelve-foot-long leg. She looked up at me and smiled. We were still naked and I felt small in the cold. I pulled on my cock when she glanced away at Leafe; unfortunately my shadow did the same.

"Wasn't sure you even had one," she said, tracing my groin. The others were sitting on the rocks fifty yards away, smoking and drinking. I began to feel turned on, watching the arc of her spine disappear into darkness.

"One of the cast reckons you were involved with Class War," she said, taking me by surprise. Her tone was brittle.

"And if I was?" I said, shifting awkwardly.

"Stand still. Doesn't bother me." She was slipping slowly down my other leg. "Were you?" she asked again.

I studied her for a moment. She was incandescent in the moonlight, untouchable.

"I wasn't with them for long. Too organised for kosher anarchists like me," I grinned. "They started having AGMs, taking votes."

"There, finished," she said, coming towards me. "I'm cold."

"Who recognised me?" I asked, as I passed her a T-shirt.

"Charlie. You know, with the didgeridoo?"

"Never seen him before."

"He's alright," she said, wrapping a skirt around her. Her manner had changed a little; the intimacy of the swimming had slipped. I walked over towards the water's edge on my own, carrying my boots. I could talk politics all night, but I was hoping for something else. I found her sudden changes in tempo unsettling. One moment she was grabbing my cock under the water, pulling me towards her, the next she was withdrawn, releasing sudden, unexpected questions.

"Do you remember the battle of the beanfield?" she asked more warmly. She had come across to join me and was looking out to sea. The moonlight picked out the white surf like ultraviolet.

"Bit before my time."

"I'd just turned fifteen. The police that day, they were crazy, out of their heads. We saw them shooting up behind the Stones and then running out, clubbing whoever they met. I watched a child, he can't have been more than ten, being chased through a field and beaten around the head."

"That's what we're up against," I said, encouraged by her concern. "It was easy then, when it was just the cops. The state's less focused now, more disguised."

We watched a wave reach the shore, impeded by the one before. The pebbles applauded as it was sucked away.

"Are you still fighting, then?" she asked, linking her arm in mine.

"Always."

"Me too."

I drove straight back to London after visiting my dad, and spent the rest of Christmas Day on the barge, in bed as Annalese had suggested. I hadn't been able to get away from him quick enough, not because he had been particularly hostile, but because he was showing signs of wanting to talk, and I couldn't handle that. I waited two days before ringing him and he spoke quietly on the phone, his voice showing the same restraint as it had when we had parted. Walter was happy to see me on the 29th, he said, and then he paused, trying to bring himself to say something more, or perhaps to extract a few words from me. I hung up.

Walter was fatter than I remembered, much fatter. He was wearing round, fusewire glasses, half hidden in the fleshy folds of his face. A few more weeks and they would be absorbed altogether. To my surprise, he wanted to meet at a side entrance of the Security Services building at the south end of Vauxhall Bridge. (It used to be occupied solely by MI6 but the new Labour government had forced them to share it with MI5.) Bypassing the main body of the building, he took me in a side lift to the fourth floor, where there was a canteen, with a balcony looking out across the Thames.

The place was like any other office canteen, except for the eerie, diffuse light streaming in through a row of thick green windows, and a scanner shaped like an arch which everyone had to pass through. (I didn't set any alarms off. As a gesture of goodwill, I had removed all my studs and earrings except for the one through my lower lip.) There was also a disproportionate number of security guards checking passes. Walter walked towards the arch and began to reach for something in his pocket but the guards waved him through. He turned to wait for me. For the first time in my life I wasn't searched either.

"They were expecting you," Walter said, as we joined the queue. "Visitors are welcome these days, well kind of, anyway. Who did you vote for?"

"I didn't," I said, looking around. I felt edgy. I had been in too much trouble to be ignored by places like this.

"It was the PM's idea," he continued. "A delayed reaction to glasnost, I guess. You must be one of the first visitors in here. Hey, there's even an open day next week. You should come along. It'll be fun."

I wasn't listening. People nodded and smiled at Walter as they passed us with their food. Walter scrutinised each tray as it went by, piecing together the day's menu.

"No cookies today?" he said to one woman as she passed. "Too bad." He turned around and gave me a tray. "No cookies. Have what you want, kid, on the state."

I took the tray, trying to ignore being called a kid. I wanted to know what sort of person worked so consciously for authority. They looked a pretty mundane bunch, more women than men, sporting sensible skirts and white blouses with long sleeves. It was probably just another job for them. The only men I saw were wearing grey shoes. No one seemed to be looking directly at me. They probably knew everything there was to know anyway. My file couldn't be far away.

We were served our coffee and headed towards a row of heavy green doors, behind which was a smooth brown pillar and a balcony. Walter insisted I should see the view. He was carrying two coffees and three large sticky buns on a tray, which he balanced precariously in one hand. He struggled with the door and I stepped forward to prop it open for him. As he passed I noticed a small bead of sweat forming on his brow.

It was chilly outside and we were the only people braving the cold, but the sky was clear and London was shining in the weak winter sunlight. Walter walked over to the metal table nearest the river and sat down on a thin seat, his fleshy sides spilling over the edges. The size of his distended stomach forced him to sit leaning backwards, legs spread apart. His fly zip was open several inches at the top. I sat down opposite him and watched as he tucked into one of the buns. Behind him I could see Big Ben, tanned and wealthy. We sat in silence for a while as he ate two of the donuts in quick succession.

"I've got something for you," he said finally, his mouth

still full. "I bought it in a bookshop in Oxford a few years ago."

He wiped his sticky hand on a paper napkin and pulled out a small hardback book from his breast pocket. It was a copy of *When We Were Six* by A.A. Milne. I shifted awkwardly in my seat.

"I never was much of a godfather, but you were a pretty lousy godson, too. To hell with dates, Happy twenty-first."

I tried to look at some of the pictures but I suddenly wanted to go. He had once read the book to me when I was a child. My mouth was filling with the unpleasant taste of family. The choice of rendezvous was also getting to me. If it was a test of some kind, I was failing it.

"It's not a first edition, but it's beautiful, isn't it?" he continued.

I flicked through the pages and said nothing.

"How old are you now, anyway?" he asked, hesitating a moment before picking up the third donut. I put the book down on the metal table harder than I meant to.

"Does it matter?"

"Not to me. Don't you want it?" he asked, nodding at the book. I ignored him and looked around, wondering who preened the conical fir trees on each ledge of the building. A security guard was walking past on one of the levels above us, talking into a radio. Below us two joggers were running along the river front, moving wide when they saw a drunk asleep on a bench.

"Your dad was exaggerating," Walter said after a pause. "I was expecting some kind of wild animal."

"Yeah?"

The comment annoyed me and I sucked on the ring in my lip. How far would I get, I wondered, if I just got up and walked away? I would be arrested within seconds. "They think it was a mistake, by the way," he continued, licking his sugary fingers. "Not enough people around."

"Who's they?" I asked, nettled.

"The Security Services."

"I thought that was you."

"Me? No," he said, laughing at the suggestion. "I just make up the numbers."

He began to blink. I wished I hadn't come. He always blinked a lot when he told crap jokes after Christmas lunch. He was a show-off, a frustrated performer. His blinking had turned into a kind of circus drum roll. Unsettling if the joke wasn't obvious. He was blinking a lot now.

"What are you doing here, then?" I asked aggressively.

"I told you. Making up the numbers. Codes."

So there it was. This year's crap Christmas joke.

"I lost someone once," he started, tilting his head back as he dredged the remains of his cappuccino. "We were engaged. She was run over in LA, crossing the road with some groceries. I couldn't understand why the whole world didn't stop. The goddam truck didn't even stop."

"What did you do?"

"Do? I made a lot of noise. Wailed my arse off and dialled the police."

It was hard to imagine him making a lot of noise. It was harder still imagining him with a woman. He seemed sexless somehow, as if bloated by castration.

"I want you to find the people who killed Annalese," I continued.

"Sure you do. The whole country does. But it's not so easy. These guys are pretty smart, smarter than us."

"You must know something."

"Sure, we know something."

I paused and found myself swallowing.

"If I gave you information, would you let me help?"

"Help?"

"I want to be there, when they're brought in."

Walter looked at me for a moment then got up and walked

to the edge of the terrace, staring down the river towards Westminster.

"Do you have any idea how these things work?" he asked, turning. "It's not like running around the countryside with a large butterfly net in one hand and a book of mugshots in the other. Heck, if it was that easy I'd be out there, doing it myself, believe me. It takes months of work finding these people, sometimes years."

"I know."

I managed a grin, but my mouth was drying. In the moment I had heard myself asking him, I knew it was all for real. The muscles at the side of my mouth tightened.

"It's tough when you lose someone," Walter continued. "You feel all kinds of things, love, guilt, anger, a lot of anger. Perhaps you should take a break some place, where it's hot. Get away from all this . . ."

" . . . I'm not registered with the Social. The only people who know I exist are M15."

"Don't count on it."

I looked out on to the river for inspiration. It was time to play my only card.

"How many people were killed in the Oxford Street bomb?" I asked.

"Oxford Street? Eight, wasn't it. I would need to look it up."

"The papers all said eight. Everyone said eight, the news, politicians, the cops."

"Okay, so it was eight. Eight too many."

"I was at the morgue. To identify Annalese. There were nine bodies, not eight."

Walter looked at me for a moment, then pushed his lower lip out and his chin up, dimpling it like a peach stone.

"You serious?"

"Yeah. I'm serious."

CHAPTER 6

It was late and I was heading west towards places pregnant with memories. Annalese's funeral was tomorrow and I was trying to order my thoughts. Whether it was a cover-up, or just a mistake by the hospital, I wasn't sure. The ninth body could have been an MP, anyone whose death would have lowered national morale. (A dead MP would have raised my morale, but no one was consulting me.) In truth, I didn't expect to hear from Walter again, unless he turned me over.

I pulled in for a coffee at a service station. A teenager was playing on a car game in the deserted foyer, rattling the loose steering wheel backwards and forwards. Behind him a plant was dying. The restaurant was empty except for a young, ginger-haired waiter who was standing by the coffee machine, one hand tapping to Abba, his ring clicking against the stainless steel. He glanced up at me as I came in and moved towards the food counter, his eyes avoiding mine.

I looked around the restaurant as he made me a coffee. There was a children's area in one corner, cheerful and plastic, and a mop propped up against the door of the ladies' lavatory.

"What time do you close?" I asked.

"We don't," he said, pushing the coffee towards me. He had a faint Somerset accent.

"Just you tonight, then?" I asked.

He looked at me nervously and managed a weak smile. "We stop serving hot food at ten."

I wasn't in the mood to jump him. There wouldn't be much in the till anyway. I picked up a waterproof menu from one of the tables. "It says here," I began, "'for the widest choice of food and drink on the roadside'."

"Where it belongs," he said, smiling more confidently. "You didn't miss much."

He gave me a stale donut on the house. I went over to the large plate-glass windows, and sat down on a seat bolted to the floor. The road was out of sight, but the tops of headlight beams lit up the embankment as cars passed below. On the far side I could see another service station, a mirror image of this one. The building's harsh lights spilled out into the night, creating a pool of daylight in the darkness. A waiter was wiping down empty tables.

No one here knew Annalese was dead. I wasn't convinced that I knew. I wrote down on a paper napkin a chronological list of important dates in my life. Then I added "Annalese died" at the end. It looked so incongruous, like a piece of irrelevant graffiti. I didn't feel sad, just angry. Then I felt guilty because somewhere inside me I knew there was a pang of relief.

From the day I had met her, a year ago, my life had thickened, become more complicated. She had brought to the surface feelings which I thought were buried with my mother. She had made me discuss her, the effect her death had on me. I had felt nothing at the funeral; instead, in the months and years that followed, I had watched myself like a neutral observer. I had explored my own numbness, probed its limits. Detachment meant no guilt, no checks on behaviour. No regrets. Annalese reminded me of consequences.

Life had been quieter, too. She believed in the struggle, she said, but something always seemed to stop her. Like a child standing too close to the fire, she would suddenly step back, shocked by its heat. We had once tried to go on a march together, but she wanted to stay at the back, away from the bricks and the milk bottle Molotovs and the javelin poles. We had argued all the way home. I hadn't been on a day out since, didn't dare. My reputation was in tatters.

As Penzance drew closer, the car slowed and stammered. It had broken down three times already. There was always a risk when siphoning petrol from other people's cars that it was unleaded or, worse still, super unleaded. The last tankload, from a Honda in a lay-by near Stonehenge, had been far too green. I crawled into the town, passed Causeway Head, and parked on the promenade in time for dawn. The sea was grey and choppy. A fishing boat from Newlyn was pushing out to sea. On the horizon, an HM Customs boat was riding the tide, probably waiting for Charlie. I pushed the seat back with a jerk. I was too tired to sleep and decided to drive on. Rubbing my fists in my eyes, I yanked the chair forward again. It was only another four or five miles.

Annalese was being cremated in a private ceremony at nine o'clock. At ten, everyone was meeting at the Merry Maiden stones to watch her ashes being thrown to the four winds. There were going to be a lot of people I hadn't seen for a while, friends of Annalese who had never liked me.

I drove up through Newlyn and on towards Lamorna. The circle of stones came into sight above the hedgerow. I had been here a few times and preferred the one lump of rock on its own at the far end of the field, banished from the rest. I parked the car in the muddy lay-by and tried to sleep again. The light was so different from London: the sun bounced off the sea around the large, open skies. Annalese said it was the peninsula effect.

I was just drifting off when there was a knock on the passenger door window. I thought I was dreaming, but there, standing in the field looking sceptically across at the stones, was Walter. The fat profile couldn't belong to anyone else. Behind me a dark Daimler was ticking over, its driver looking impassively ahead. It was one of those moments when I knew my life would never be the same again. Walter turned around and came across. I slid down the window.

"Get out the car, Dutchie," he said coolly. "We've got to be back in London by noon."

I sat silently in the back of the Daimler with Walter, relieved to be missing the ceremony. We were travelling fast along the dual carriageway. The sight of Walter standing in a remote Cornish field had shocked me, but I knew what it meant: I was being taken seriously. We were now destined for Clapham, that's all I had been told. Curiosity and the suggestion that I might be able to do something about Annalese's killers had subdued any desire to run, at least for the time being.

"I'm sorry about the funeral, really I am," Walter said quietly. "It was unavoidable." He opened a briefcase and passed me a photograph of a man in a white coat. "Was that the doc at the mortuary?"

The face was familiar.

"Yeah, that's him."

"He died yesterday. A hit and run accident. Too bad."

I wondered what I was supposed to feel. I had only met the man once.

"He was the one who told you, about the number of people killed?" Walter asked, anxiety creeping into his voice.

"Yes."

"Did he tell anyone else?"

"How do I know?"

I could feel my pulse begin to pick up.

"Did anyone hear him tell you? Was there anybody else around? It's kind of important."

"No," I said, my mind racing. It had just been a clerical cock-up, hadn't it? Nine, eight, what did it matter? Over fifty had died in the past fortnight.

"Was I right then?" I asked, failing to conceal my enthusiasm.

"Let me put it this way," he said. "You were told something you weren't meant to hear."

"There was a cover-up."

"One of the corpses was removed from the mortuary before they began identifying them."

"Who took it?"

"We certainly didn't."

"How do you know it was taken, then?"

"I checked out the mortuary after our conversation. He was a nice kid, shouldn't have died. When I asked him to show me the deceased, he pulled out eight corpses and one empty box."

"Was he surprised?"

"Speechless."

"Then he was run over."

"Correct."

"But not by you."

"Dutchie, a little respect, please."

"So who took the body?"

"We're not sure. Maybe the terrorists. Maybe not."

Walter looked at me directly for the first time. I turned away. I didn't know what to think. It had never occurred to me that the missing body might have been one of the terror-ists. I had assumed they were professional operators, cold and efficient. But they'd screwed up.

"It's not so easy to walk out of a mortuary with a body tucked under your arm and no one notice," Walter con-tinued.

"No," I replied vaguely. I had taken a step towards finding Annalese's killers. Walter's words sounded distant.

"I'm going to come clean with you, Dutchie. We know more about these terrorists than we're letting on. You prob-ably figured that. We don't know who they are exactly, but we know what they do when they're not blowing people away."

"What?"

He held up the white palm of his flabby hand, checking me.

"We've got an idea what the ninth person looked like. There was a security camera in the street."

"Did you see Annalese?"

"We did. That reminds me. She would have been arrested for shoplifting. I'm sorry. Two pairs of boots, some leather cleaner, a pair of espadrilles. I thought you should know." Walter paused. He was beginning to blink. "Hey, what were you doing in High and Mighty anyway?"

"Shopping."

"But it's for big people, fatsos like me. You nearly lost your head in there."

I didn't want to be reminded. The manager, one moment taut, the next limp and lifeless, the air so rudely let out of him. Walter passed me another photo, black and white this time. The date was printed in yellow over the bottom of the image. It was a still, the outside of Pied A Terre. Security cameras were built like black boxes these days. They had to be. A couple of people were looking at the window display; a third, circled in red ink, was walking briskly from right to left.

"That's her, the ninth victim."

"A woman?"

"I hope so. Nicole Farhi dress. Gucci shoes. Smart babe."

The circled figure was in her late twenties, tall and slight. Her hair was close-cropped. The stride was confident, her face muscles relaxed. She looked in charge of her life. And she was attractive, Walter was right; fresh-faced, a rich bitch.

"We've run a check on her, matched her face with company files and our own. Her name's Samantha West. She worked for a firm in the City called Jensen Klein Abrahall, foreign exchange dealer, Deutsche Marks."

"Does she have a criminal record?" I asked, still looking at the photo.

"Nothing on our files. We've checked with everyone. She's a clean-skin."

"There must have been cameras outside the hospital, in the mortuary."

"That's the clever part. All switched off. They moved quickly, these guys. As soon as the bomb went off, they were looking for ways to get the body back. My guess is there was more than one bomber at the scene. Maybe watching."

"Are you sure she's a terrorist?" I asked, passing the photo back. I couldn't believe she had it in her.

"No, we're not sure. But she's special enough not to die."

I looked around at the fitted kitchen: a cream-coloured Aga, the beechwood sideboard, a slender bottle of olive oil, a stone sink, sunken halogen lamps, dried herbs in baskets, an RNLI calendar pinned to the farmhouse dresser. A Persian blue cat sat patiently on the terracotta-tiled floor, looking up at Walter, who was making a mess of opening a tin. Through the doorway I could see the warm glow of the sitting room, oriental rugs, an antique bureau, large paintings of horses, sashay curtains. I didn't feel at home.

"Dutchie, Saturday 31st March 1990, remember what you were doing?" Walter asked.

I knew exactly what I was doing.

"Take a look in the folder."

I leant across the pine table and opened it. It was full of photographs, black and white A4. I looked closer, smiling. Crowd shots in Trafalgar Square. The Poll Tax riot. Who could forget it? £6 million of damage, the most violent scenes of civil disorder this century. One photo showed me with my teeth bared, challenging a row of policemen in riot gear. It had been taken from behind the line and the green initials, MP, on the back of the helmets were clearly visible, their numbers below. A flash had been used and my forehead had a slight sheen to it, making me look sweaty. But I liked the expression, uncompromising, on fire. Others were of me hard at work, punching, gobbing, screaming.

"Who took these? They're good," I said, proudly spreading them out on the table.

"Hell, I don't know. They're just file shots. We probably seized them from the press. Our guys are useless unless they're shooting round corners."

"It was a good crack that day."

"Hey, who needs terrorists when you've got Class War?"

I ignored him and sifted through some more photos. Stop the City, 29th March 1986. That had been a laugh, too, gone like a dream. Running down Fenchurch Street, I had come across a lorryload of bricks, *behind* the police lines. After posting them through various stockbrokers' windows, I had legged it, somehow avoiding arrest.

"The English get so uptight about class," Walter continued. "Only in England would you get an organisation calling itself Class War."

"Brightling Sea," I muttered. January 1995.

"Can I keep one of these?" I asked.

"We might need them."

I got up from the table. The pictures were making me restless, reminding me of my recent inactivity. "I've got to go," I said.

"Go? Where?"

"Out, anywhere. I'm bored."

I leant against the table with my arms folded, knowing Walter still had something more to say. Sure enough, he stopped trying to open the cat food and turned to me, wiping his hands on a towel.

"You came to me two days ago with a useful piece of information," he began. "You took a risk, I appreciate that. You're a wanted man. You also said you would like to find Annalese's killers, 'to help in some way' – I think that's how you put it."

"Yeah. So what's with the pictures?"

"Would you be prepared to turn your absurd, English hatred of the rich to some good?"

"I doubt it. Good's a bad word, it makes me nervous."

"If it helped find Annalese's killers?"

I remained silent.

"There's every indication that these terrorists have day jobs in the City. We think they are working as foreign exchange dealers, we don't know for sure."

"There's a surprise. Rich wanking bastards. What do you want me to do? Organise a riot and hope they get pole-axed?"

"Not quite." He paused. "I want you to work in the City."

I looked at him, my eyes slowly widening, waiting for him to blink. But he didn't.

"Did you have a particular job in mind?" I asked. "Chairman of the Bank of England? Chancellor of the fucking Exchequer?"

"You would be in the same firm as the terrorist who was killed. Foreign exchange. Derivatives. I've spoken with the chairman, he's an old buddy. You won't have to do much. Just turn up on time, don't mess up and find out what you can."

Walter was still not blinking. Did he know about Henley, the time I had dressed as a toff, bluffed my way into the private members enclosure and started a small war over the strawberries? (I wouldn't have minded seeing a photo of that.) I had a reputation for cover work, but I was never under for long; just enough to crash posh parties. He had to be joking.

"How much will you pay me?" I asked, trying to assimilate what he was saying.

"I won't pay you a dime. I thought the scheme might appeal to your warped vision of the world, that's all." He paused. "I'm serious, Dutchie. You'll earn a salary, like everyone else, if you're good."

"A salary? How much?"

"Jesus, I don't know. The going rate. Does it matter?"

I walked around the table, thinking fast. Where was the catch?

"Do I have a choice?" I asked. He ignored me, and returned to opening the tin. Within seconds he had nicked his thumb on the jagged lid.

"Damn," he said, sucking the cut and pulling out a handkerchief. "This is where you would live."

"Here?"

"Here. In this house. Do you have a problem with that?"

Yes, I did. A big problem. I didn't like Walter's tone. It didn't sound like there was an alternative. And this was Clapham for fucksake. I had a reputation to think about.

"The place is yours," Walter continued. "Your room's upstairs, across the landing. But please, try to use the back door until you've got a haircut. It would be a pity if the neighbours mistook you for a squatter."

He put a key on the table and a white envelope, a wad of notes clearly visible. I stared at the purple money.

"Chop it all off and buy yourself a suit," he added.

I glanced briefly around the kitchen, looked at the money again and tried to think clearly.

"What if I decide I don't want to do this?" I asked.

Walter appeared genuinely hurt. He put the opener down on the sideboard but he still had his back to me.

"Would you mind saying that again?" he asked.

"I said, I might not want to live in Clapham, work in the City. In fact, I know I don't."

The idea sounded even more absurd when I repeated it back to him.

"I don't think you quite get it," he said, turning. His voice was on a level, but there was more behind it, greater depth. "Sit down Dutchie, take a seat."

I hesitated, then reluctantly leant against the table, wanting to know more. Walter adjusted the hankerchief. He had wrapped it loosely around his thumb, making it look enormous.

"You came to me wanting to 'help'," he started. "Well, I'm giving you that chance. But I'm telling you Dutchie, I don't warm to ingratitude. The police have enough information to put you away for life, do you know that? But for some reason, I've watched your file over the years, kept it thin. Maybe it's because I like your father."

"You're blackmailing me," I said, stopping him. These were serious allegations he was making. I didn't get arrested because I never got caught, not because of family favours.

"I wouldn't call it blackmail, exactly." He paused. "I'm giving you a break. Discover who the terrorists are, and you can be around when we bring them in. Have a few minutes on your own. Introduce yourself."

CHAPTER 7

I turned on to the river and walked towards the wharf. To my right, a pile-driver was squeezing a concrete post inch by inch into the earth, the double knock echoing across the water and back again. To my left, a rusty barge was listing on the mud, abandoned by the cruel tide to balance a load of steel piping. Beyond it seagulls were pecking at something in the shallow water. For a moment I thought it was the toff, back to see us, then I realised it was a cat, stiff-legged and bloated, like a set of bagpipes.

Walter wanted an answer by six. I sensed it was a formality, to humour me. There was something suspicious about his relaxed manner, the lack of concern as I had left the house with his money. I tried to weigh up the options. The notion of me, of all people, working in the City was ridiculous, a non-starter, strangely appealing. It brought my revenge into focus, made it easier. Annalese's killers were rich bastards. It didn't matter that they were living a lie. I could lie too, then kill them. Perhaps Walter knew that. There was something of the Trojan horse in the plan, entering the heart of the establishment by the front door. Apart from my few brief stints undercover, I had always been on the wrong side of the barriers, running, circling; here was a chance to hit them from within. Who knows? After I had found the bombers, I could have some fun, wipe off a few millions, a few smiles.

As I drew close to the jetty, I could smell the refinery further down stream. It supplied sugar to brewers. On some days, when the wind was from the east, our barge smelt of nothing else. I used to tell Annalese that was why South London was so full of alcoholics. The slightest whiff had everyone diving for the nearest pub.

I couldn't see the barge from the path – it was tucked behind a carcass once used to ferry passengers up to Charing Cross – but as I approached, something struck me immediately as wrong. I walked up to the Portakabin where Vic, the wharf foreman, usually sat. I could see the top of a head, but it wasn't Victor's. His son sometimes covered but it wasn't his head either.

"Alright?" I said. The stranger pushed open the sliding window. He had a crew-cut and a dense, soldier's moustache.

"Yes mate, can I help you?"

I looked over towards the barge. I could normally see the stern from where I was standing, but there was nothing there. I felt my stomach twisting into a tight ball. Glancing at the unfamiliar face again, I walked past the Portakabin.

"Oi! Where do you think you are going?" he said. I could hear him pushing back his metal chair.

"Go fuck yourself," I said quietly. I was running now. The boat had definitely gone. There was no trace of it. I even had difficulty trying to work out where it had been moored. The boats had been moved about. Two new ones had come in – a crabber and an old tug – and our neighbour's boat had also disappeared.

I looked around. The new foreman was walking briskly towards me. He seemed bigger now, more thick-set, a large beer gut hanging over his jeans. He was too big to take out, and in his left hand he had a thin metal bar, about two feet long.

"Where's my boat?" I asked, turning to meet him.

"What boat?"

"My fucking boat. It's been moored here for the last six months."

"I ain't seen you or your boat before."

I stared incredulously at the man. My mind was humming, checking through the possibilities. It had to be Walter.

"Now get off the site," he said, raising the bar a fraction. I didn't wait around. As I was leaving, a flash of colour caught my eye. I bent down and retrieved something from the mud without stopping. It was a small card, partially sealed in seethrough plastic. One side was blank. On the other it had a picture of flowers and some blurred biro writing, distorted by water. I could just make out Annalese's name.

CHAPTER 8

I stood at the front door, knocked and waited, pulling nervously on the cuffs of my jacket. My shoes were ridiculously shiny, like two little pools of still water. I could hear someone walking down the hall.

"I thought I said the back," Walter said, fiddling with the chain. His voice tailed off as he opened the door.

"Jesus . . ."

"One rich bastard," I said coldly, and tugged at my cuffs again. Walter stood there admiring his new creation. All my earrings had gone and my dreadlocks had been cut off. My head was completely shaved. The suit was double-breasted, dark and lightly herringboned. My tie was sober blue and patterned with bubbles shaped like quotation marks.

"All you need now is a copy of the *FT*," he said quietly. "Come in, come in."

I squeezed past Walter, who remained standing in the doorway, his right arm outstretched, directing traffic. There was a whiff of sweet sherry on his breath. It was a familiar smell, rushing me back twenty years to when I used to stand on his toes, hold his outstretched hands and lean back, pretending to water-ski. For a moment, I wanted to turn around and run past him into the night. But the warmth of the kitchen drew me in. The lighting was low and the room smelt of baked potatoes, burning onions, home. Walter came in behind me, went straight to the microwave and removed a lump of grey, sweating meat.

"I'm off the pace. Pour yourself a drink," he said, and

began chopping carrots with a blunt knife. "Are you hungry? You look hungry."

"It depends. I don't eat meat."

"You don't eat meat? Of course you do. How can you be English and not like meat? You used to like it. I got a piece of beef in specially, just like old times."

I ignored him. Since the bomb I had been unable to walk past a butcher's. There were two bulging suitcases in the hall, green with brown leather straps and brass buckles. A bottle of Californian red wine was standing on the table, uncorked. I picked it up, had a sniff and replaced it too hard. Pulling a chair out from under the table, I sat down, splaying my legs out in front of me. I then opened my suit jacket, removed a can of Special Brew and peeled it open.

"Where's my barge?" I asked.

Walter turned around, squinted over the top of his glasses and resumed chopping. A pan on the stove started to smoke purposefully.

"Safe enough. There's some Merlot on the table. Wash that pigswill down the sink and pour yourself a glass."

I wasn't too concerned about the barge. In fact, its disappearance had swayed me, made me get a haircut and buy a suit. It showed Walter had resources, that he was serious. Barges were hard things to lose.

Walter's cooking was painful to watch. He took the pan off the red-hot ring and waved the smoke away. Then he dipped a fat finger into another pan, licked it and tipped some wine from his glass into it. The smoke alarm went off, making us both jump.

"Damn thing," Walter said, shuffling over to the corner. He picked up a broom and tried to knock the red button on the alarm above the doorway. I watched him miss a few times. He was almost falling over with the effort. The alarm was piercing.

"Here, I'll do it," I said.

Reluctantly, I stood and pulled a chair over to the door, scraping it across the tiles. I climbed up and turned the alarm off.

"Goddam thing," he said, a faint asthmatic wheeze thickening his breath. "It's so unforgiving! Wouldn't even let me cook toast this morning."

Walter looked ridiculous, standing there with an upturned brush in his hand, and sweat glistening on his brow. He must have been bullied as a child, taunted for his fatness, forced to go on cross-country runs. I was in danger of feeling sorry for him when the doorbell went. "That'll be your partner," he said, and turned back to the sideboard.

"My partner?"

"Charlotte. Your handler."

"I'm not a dog."

"She'll be staying here with you. Lay the table, would you mind?"

I took a swig of Special Brew and watched Walter wipe his hands on a tea-cloth. As he went into the hallway, the cloth slid off its hook and caught on the leaves of a yucca plant below. Events were moving too quickly. I felt a slight draught as the front door opened. I could smell the tangy night air – exhaust fumes mingled with rain. Again, I had a sudden urge to run. I glanced around the room for another way out, and then checked myself, listening for the sound of my partner's voice. For some reason I expected to hear Annalese. There was silence. The door closed and I saw Walter coming towards me, followed by a woman, hidden behind his frame.

"Charlotte, meet Douglas," he said. Douglas? I turned on Walter.

"My name's Dutchie," I said, ignoring Charlotte's outstretched hand and taking another swig of lager.

"Not anymore it isn't," Walter said. "Did I forget to tell you? No one's called Dutchie in the City. It's too . . ."

"Too what?"

"Too . . . unlikely. Hey, Douglas is a nice enough name. It's the one you were born with, for Chrissake. Pour yourself a drink. Charlotte, make yourself at home."

Charlotte had been watching our tense exchange awkwardly, gradually letting her outstretched arm drop. She put her shoulder bag down by the door and went over to the stove to see what was cooking.

"Mmm, smells good," she said, trying to lighten the mood.

"Scottish roast beef with Yorkshire pudding. And Dutchie eats plants."

She glanced at me but I was consciously looking elsewhere. She leant with her back against the sideboard, turning sideways towards Walter.

"Nice place you have here Walter," she said. "I was expecting something more . . . Manhattan."

"There's a loft conversion."

"Really? But no views of Central Park."

"Just good old Clapham Common. It'll do for now."

She looked across at me again. I had sat down, wrong-footed by the new woman in my life. Charlotte was immaculately dressed in dark brown jacket and trousers. Her hair was blonde and bobbed, rocks sparkled from her ears. She had a strong, muscular physique, about my height, perhaps a little taller. Not my type at all.

"The suit. Did you buy it today?" she asked, nodding at my chest.

"Yeah," I said, putting a cigarette to my lips and letting it hang limply. I didn't want to open my mouth until I had calculated the effect my new appearance had on others. Before, people either crossed the street or gave me money.

"It's a nice cut," she said, smiling.

"How much has he told you?" I asked, lighting the cigarette and gesturing vaguely in Walter's direction.

"She knows that's not the accent you were born with,"

Walter said, removing another smoking pan from the stove. "Got that broom ready?"

"I've seen your file," she said. "That's all."

"I'm doing this for Annalese," I said, exaggerating my accent. It had taken me years to shake off the one I had been born with. "I don't usually wear suits. Or go to dinner parties in Clapham. Or work in the City."

"Relax," she said, pulling a chair out and sitting down opposite me. I looked at her intently, forcing her to look away. Her jaw was broad, masculine in its sweep, but she had a slight, tidy nose, and her lips were full. I got up and walked around the kitchen. She watched me cautiously.

"I know about Annalese," she said. "I'm sorry. We all are. She was a very special woman."

She glanced briefly at Walter for support. How dare she talk about Annalese? She had never even met her.

"You can trust her," Walter said. "She's here to take care of things, help you out."

"What sort of help?" I asked.

"Advice, information," she said.

"I'm not interested in information. I'm finding Annalese's killers then I'm . . ."

" . . . I know," she said. "We're all in this together."

"It's important you don't go after the wrong people, that's all," Walter added.

Charlotte turned the can of lager around on the table and read the label. "Nine per cent. Ouch. Do they drink this stuff in the City?"

I came back to the table and retrieved the can. "I don't give a fuck what they drink in the City."

"The terrorists will kill you if they suspect anything," she said bluntly.

Her words surprised me but I tried to ignore them. I finished the lager in one long draught, leaning my head back further than necessary. I then jolted it forward and looked

at her. I could feel the alcohol begin to dissolve my brain.
Charlotte's eyes were striking, not the irises, which seemed
grey and indeterminate, but the white around them,
blanched and vivid, just like her teeth.

"Do we get to sleep together?" I asked as I crumpled the
can.

"Regrettably, no," she said, looking away.

"Shame."

"Best not mix business with pleasure," she said, smiling.

"Anyone for tomato soup?" Walter had arrived between
us, holding two lukewarm bowls. Charlotte pushed her chair
back and opened a drawer. She pulled out a sheaf of silver
spoons and dropped them in the middle of the table. "Will
you excuse me for a moment," she said.

She got up and went down the corridor to the bathroom,
taking her bag with her. Her hips were supple, confident.
Cigarette in one hand, I spread the cutlery out into three
rough places. The lager was taking the edge off my unease.

"Don't think about her that way, Dutchie," Walter said,
blinking. "Think of her as a man."

He put the last bowl of soup down on the table, spilling
it a little. It was always a surprise when Walter spoke with
a broken voice. In fact, he talked softly in deep West Coast
tones, a lisp curling the edge of occasional words.

"Never crossed my tiny mind," I said.

That wasn't quite true. For a moment, I had imagined her
sitting astride me on the kitchen floor, her skirt hitched up,
but I dismissed it when Annalese walked in on us, jealous,
mutilated. There would be too much to explain.

We both sat down. Walter produced three white linen
napkins and tucked a corner of one of them in amongst his
family of chins. He glanced awkwardly over his shoulder
and then leant forward.

"She's a dyke, really. You wouldn't think so, looking at
her. Sexy, no?"

This time Annalese and Charlotte were on the floor together. Walter smiled mischievously, blinking again. I had never heard him raise the subject of sex before. His lisp, more pronounced when he was drunk, chose to turn "sexy" into "theckthee". The door opened at the end of the corridor.

"Don't wait for me," Charlotte called, walking in and sitting down. She leant back and ran one hand breezily through her hair.

"You're a wonderful cook, Walter. The best," she said, joining the conspiracy. His face sweated with pride.

"You're too kind. Now, when do we start?" He picked up the bottle of wine and poured Charlotte a glass.

"I suggest we go through the mechanics of the City tomorrow," Charlotte said, looking at me. "I've brought some books for you to read."

"Kids' stuff," Walter said. "Honestly. People see the City as some kind of holy labyrinth, shrouded in myth and ritual. It's not. It's a place where people make money. Simple as that."

"It's full of rich arseholes," I said. The soup was barely warm.

"True," Walter said.

"Bourgeois, elitist, Tory arseholes."

"Also true."

"Then on Sunday, we run through your new biography," Charlotte added, looking at both of us in turn.

Walter poured wine into my glass and raised his own into the middle of the table. "To Douglas. Your life as it might have been."

I didn't join in the toast.

"Actually, your life's fairly straightforward," Charlotte said, putting her glass down. She had already drunk half of it. I hoped I was making her nervous.

"Ha! If only," Walter said.

"One or two areas worry me, though," she continued.

"Jesus, his whole damn life worries me," Walter added.

"Like what?" I asked. The desire to headbutt Walter was suddenly becoming irresistible.

"University. Have you ever been to Cambridge, visited the city?" Charlotte asked.

"Once."

"A remarkable place for bookshops," Walter chipped in. "At least it was. I once found a first edition of Lear's *Nonsense* near the market. Just sitting there in a box on the sidewalk."

"You were there for three years," Charlotte said.

"I was?" I asked.

"Uh huh."

"It wasn't mint. For fifty bucks, hey, who's complaining?" No one was listening to Walter.

"And if I meet someone who was there at the same time as me?" I asked.

"You were at Trinity, a big college. It's possible no one knew you. You kept to yourself, stayed in your rooms."

"What sort of degree does he get? A Desmond Tutu?" Walter asked, laughing before he had finished.

"Douglas Hurd, I'm afraid," Charlotte said, looking at me with sympathy.

"Too bad. Still, I was reading the other day that some British companies make a point of only employing people with thirds. It takes impeccable judgment to know how little work you can get by on and still make the grade."

I listened to them both with growing contempt. As details of the plan unfolded, the pressure began to build inside me. I reminded myself why I was doing this. Annalese was dead. Killed by a bomb. The Bombers work in the City. I join the City to find bombers. Kill bombers. I could go back to the barge after that. Burn the suit, grow my hair. Maybe come back and torch Clapham, too.

"I've had a word with a crammer in Oxford," Charlotte

continued. "You completed your A levels there. One B and two Cs."

"But I ran away."

"Dutchie ran away. Douglas, on the other hand, did just fine," Walter said, pouring himself another glass. "Can I ask you something, Dutchie?" he said, not waiting for an answer. "If you had your life to live again, would you do anything different?"

"No," I said immediately, before I had time to consider.

"You'd still run away? Still throw scaffolding poles at policemen?"

"Yeah," I said. There was an awkward pause. Just when Charlotte was about to fill it, I asked Walter the same question. "Would you? Would you do anything different?"

"Hey, I can't. Unlike you. No point in even thinking about it. It's an unusual situation you're in. Enviable even."

"That right?"

"Sure. You've got a wonderful chance to start all over again. To wipe the slate clean."

"I don't see it that way."

"Most of us, we mess things up, and we have to live with the consequences."

"Who said anything about messing up?"

"Oh come on Dutchie. You've screwed up. We all know that."

"Screwed up. You really believe that, don't you?"

"It's not just me. Your father . . ."

"Fuck him."

"Your mother."

I paused, then sucked at a spoonful of soup. "Fuck her."

"Douglas doesn't have to disappear when all this is finished," Charlotte said. "That's all he's saying. We can destroy your old file. Providing everything works out."

"I'm staying as Dutchie."

Charlotte looked across at Walter. He dabbed at the

corner of his mouth with the napkin, leaving an orange smudge on the linen.

"That might not be so smart," he said. "According to our files, Dutchie's wanted on seven accounts of shoplifting, attempting to defraud the DSS, jumping bail, assaulting a policeman . . ."

" . . . fuck you," I said, interrupting him.

" . . . causing criminal damage."

" . . . shut it."

" . . . breaking and entering."

"Shut the fuck up."

" . . . arson."

I couldn't hear any more and lunged across the table. I grabbed Walter by the throat with both hands, knocking his glasses on to the table. His neck was clammy, malleable. A moment later I was conscious of Charlotte's arm clamped around my own throat. Everyone struggled for a few seconds, locked into an awkward triangle. Walter was trying desperately to pull my hands away, the maroon skin on his face darkening all the time. His eyes were moist in the corners and beginning to widen unnaturally. A few more seconds and he would be dead. The thought was hypnotic. Then I felt the lock around my own neck tighten dramatically and I realised I was close to passing out. I could smell Charlotte's perfume: clean apples. Her presence was strangely reassuring, professional. I released the folds of Walter's throat and slunk back into the chair. I felt better, much better.

"You alright?" Charlotte asked, releasing me and moving around to Walter. His tie askew, he looked warily in my direction, panting hard. He bent his head down close to the table and looked for his glasses. Charlotte reached across, picked them up and gave them to him.

"You take it too far, Dutchie, way too far," Walter wheezed, and bent the wire of his glasses around his tiny, shiny ears. His hands were shaking. I said nothing and lit a cigarette, watching Charlotte clear the soup plates. I rubbed my neck. Somewhere, deep inside me, a bud of guilt spread itself open. Walter was too fat, too fey to fight.

"It was me who came to you," I said, for my own benefit. "Remember that. I was the one who spotted the mistake."

"And we want to help you," Charlotte said, sliding the bowls into the sink. I was suddenly annoyed that she had intervened.

"Is that how you see it?" I asked, getting up from the table and walking over to her. "Part of the job? Putting people back on the straight and narrow? A slice of state correction? Since when was Stella Rimington a fucking social worker?"

"It was just a thought, a friendly offer," she said, not even bothering to look up at me.

"That's not what this is about," I said. "It's to do with Annalese, not me. Why bring me into this?"

"Forget it. It's not important."

"It is to him," I said, nodding at Walter, who held his palms up in mock defence. "You said you'd hand me over if I didn't cooperate. I'm cooperating. I'll find the terrorists. But then Douglas dies. End of story."

CHAPTER 9

Supper finished peacefully enough, given the circumstances. I listened quietly as Walter outlined further details, and made more jokes about my expendability. He kept repeating that the chairman of JKA was an old friend, that I wouldn't actually have to do anything on the exchange floor. Still, why me? There must have been other people he could have recruited, or blackmailed, who were more qualified. Walter knew my background, knew that I had rejected it utterly. I began to doubt who had initiated the whole idea. Perhaps Walter had been waiting for me to make contact? Hampered by wine and Special Brew, I struggled to think clearly. I had spotted the mistake about the bodies, I had gone to them. Working in the City was their plan, devised in response to my information. There was no confusion, no hidden agenda. I was still in control. But Charlotte's words – "The terrorists will kill you if they suspect anything" – wouldn't go away.

Upstairs I ran a bath, rolled a joint. Before Charlotte arrived, I had begun to imagine myself operating on my own, answerable to no one. Walter's plan was bearable in those terms. Now I had a partner. Charlotte – it couldn't have been worse. Almost as bad as Douglas. But a dyke? She was too much of a headgirl, a man's woman. Perhaps Walter's clumsy advances had been rejected once. She was necessary, though. I had to look credible. Clapham was full of Charlottes. I just wished the whole scheme didn't give Walter such a kick.

There was a knock on the bathroom door.

"I didn't think the great unwashed had baths." It was her. "Are you going to be long?" she asked.

"A couple of days," I said, sliding under the bubbles. The next moment Charlotte was standing in the middle of the room. I sat up suddenly, sending a small tidal wave over the edge of the bath.

"Pathetic," she said and went over to the basin.

I stared at her as she started to brush her teeth. She was wearing a crimson towelling dressing gown, the cord tied firmly around her waist. Without tights, her calves were as white as veal.

"Walter was out of order tonight," she said spitting into the basin. "Drunk and tactless."

Evidently she was staying. Despite myself, I liked that.

"He's rather quaint in his beliefs," she continued. "Thinks MI5 is the custodian of the nation's morals."

"And what do you think?" I asked, watching her buttocks shimmer with the effort of brushing.

"About MI5? It's a useful weapon in the fight against terrorism and organised crime."

"Nothing to do with morals, then?"

"I don't believe someone has the right to go around blowing innocent people up."

She dried her face with a towel and went over to the lavatory. For a moment I thought she was about to pee in it. Instead, she closed the lid and sat down.

"Mind if I build one?"

I looked up and saw her holding a small plastic bag which I had left on the shelf above the roll holder.

"Help yourself." The absurdity of the scene appealed. I sat forward awkwardly, retrieving my own joint from the milky soapdish. Wet and soggy, it took a while to re-light.

"I bet you smoke a bit, all you agents. Gear you've nicked," I said, beginning to relax.

"If only."

"You know what? I think the old Bill should hold dope auctions, like they do with stolen bikes. That would be alright, wouldn't it?"

"Lot 48, three kilos of high grade hashish, seized in the English Channel, provenance Pakistan. Any offers? I can't really see it."

"Want a light?"

She nodded, the joint angled from her mouth. I threw my lighter across the room. It landed on the edge of a pink rug which didn't quite fit around the base of the lavatory. I watched her pick it up and saw a flash of breast, faintly shocking in its whiteness. She lit her spliff and inhaled deeply, blowing the smoke into the middle of the room. I leant back, resting my head on the rim of the bath. From where she was sitting, she could see my head and shoulders, nothing more, but it felt provocative.

"What are you doing working for a bunch of tossers like MI5?" I asked.

"There are lots of misconceptions about what the security services do," she said, beginning to cough.

"You sound just like Stella Rimington."

"I'm flattered."

"Why? She was a fascist."

"You see, there you go again. She was a very decent woman. It's a tragedy she's left the service."

I sat up and started to wash my neck. Her tone had changed. I was suddenly bored, angry at being taken in.

"That right?" I said, unconvinced.

"If you only read *The Guardian*, you'd think she was some kind of witch. She did a difficult job well."

"Bollocks. Why did she put people on my back then?"

"Yours?"

"You've seen the file."

"The company you chose to live in, perhaps."

"And what's wrong with them?"

"MI5's job is to counter threats to national security."

"And anyone who decides to live outside society poses a threat?"

"I wouldn't describe climbing over the gates of Downing Street as the action of a hermit, would you?"

I had heard enough. "Could you leave. I'm having a bath."

She got up, went to the door and stopped.

"We'll start at nine. Breakfast at eight. Thanks." She waved the joint in the air and left.

I lay there confused. I had never met anyone like her before. She was hard to place. Full of the trite rhetoric I would expect from someone working for the state, and yet there was a coldness of heart, an inscrutable confidence which I found attractive. It made me want to peel away her convictions.

CHAPTER 10

I woke early the next morning and went downstairs to make a coffee. As I was waiting for the kettle to boil, I heard a noise, a faint moan, in the sitting room. I walked over to the door and opened it gently. There on the sofa, half on it, half off, was Walter, still in his suit and snoring loudly. A hand was hangling limply in the air. His mouth was open, falling away to one side. On the table was an empty bottle of red wine. A glass lay capsized on the carpet, a dark, funnelled stain spreading like an oil slick.

I closed the door quietly and looked down the corridor. The papers had arrived: a copy of *The Financial Times*, no doubt for the weekend lessons, and *The Daily Telegraph*. I picked them up and was just about to dump them on the kitchen table when a small headline on the front page of *The Daily Telegraph* caught my eye: "Police issue warning to protesters". I only bothered reading half the article, forgot about the coffee and climbed the stairs silently and swiftly.

School was cancelled for the day, no question. It was my last chance before starting in the City. The only problem was what to wear. All I had was a suit, although Walter had said that there were some casual clothes in the wardrobe. I slid open a drawer and discovered a couple of patterned jumpers, a pair of brown cords and some stripey shirts. I wouldn't last five minutes. In the bottom drawer I found a T-shirt, some black jeans and an inoffensive bottle-green jumper. They would have to do.

I went over to the sink and removed a blade from the razor. Laying the trousers flat on the bed, I made a few small incisions in the legs, which I then ripped open with my hands. I did the same with the jersey, holing it in two places. All that was left were my nose and ear rings, which were in my suit trouser pocket. There wasn't time to put them all in, so I settled on five in the ear, two in my nose.

Outside in the street I closed the heavy oak door quietly and looked up at the front of the house. One of Charlotte's windows was open, but her curtains were still closed. I walked briskly down the road to the end, where it joined Clapham Southside, and broke into a run.

"Leggit, it's me, Dutchie."

"Dutchie! Where've you been all my life?"

"Can't talk now. Anything cooking today?"

"A fest, mate, fucking fest. You in?"

"Yeah."

"The George at eleven. Get in some decent dipping."

"Eleven."

"You still with that fluffy bint?"

I closed my eyes. "No."

"Good."

I put the phone down and held on to the receiver for a few seconds. I hadn't seen Leggit since I had been with Annalese. Even talking to him now felt like a betrayal. He lived in a famous road near the Elephant and Castle where someone from every household could be counted on to turn up at all the major riots. It was a local profession, a cottage industry. After a day out, everyone would return to the St George's Tavern at the end of the road where the barman would count them back in, like spitfire pilots. I had first met them years ago when I came up from Bath for an anti-apartheid demo. I was impressed with the level of organis-ation. In case of arrest, we were all issued with the number of a solicitor who specialised in public order offences.

"Don't mess about with the duty solicitors," Leggit had warned. "They're with the pigs."

I had written the number proudly on the back of my hand, admiring it like the entrance stamp for an exclusive nightclub.

Pocketing a couple of calling cards from the phone booth, I walked towards the tube at Clapham South, glancing occasionally back down the road. A woman in a red tracksuit was having an early morning tennis lesson with an instructor on one of the courts by Nightingale Lane. Her Golf GTI was parked up on the curb. Foolishly she had left the roof down. As I passed I spat wholesomely on the tanned driving seat. I felt lightheaded, de-mob happy, the first time since Anna-lese had died.

There was something about a riot which induced the same exhilarating feelings I had experienced when I had run away from school. Of course there was the adrenalin, the anticipation of human conflict. And being out of your head in the middle of mayhem, amphetamined, paranoid, striking out at everyone around you – that was fun in its way. But it was the purity of expression, the unambiguity, which appealed to me most. Eyeballing a terrified copper through his scratched visor, screaming at him at the top of your voice, abusing him for working for the State, telling him he was going to die – my life came together in moments like that.

As I approached the tube station entrance I stopped suddenly and moved in close to the wall. Charlotte was standing in the doorway of a newsagent's, just inside the station foyer. She was talking into a mobile phone and looking around anxiously, her coat pressed against her by the wind from the escalator shaft. The bitch. What was I playing at last night? Turning around, I walked across the grass, partially hidden by trees, and kept my head low. Had she seen me? I broke into a run and crossed a side road stacked up with traffic. New shoes biting, I kept running until I reached the glass domes of Clapham Common underground. Down one subway and up the other, I jumped on to a bus heading for the Elephant and Castle. I looked back. Charlotte was nowhere to be seen.

The George was heaving, reassuring. It had been over a year since I had been here and nothing much had changed. Sky Sports was on high up in the corner, volume turned down in deference to a juke box belting out music by Crass. It was like a living time capsule, a souvenir of anti-Thatcher insurrection. On the walls there were newspaper cuttings about famous riots: Brixton, Toxteth, Stop The City, Poll Tax, Welling, Broadwater Farm, Luton airport. When I was squatting in Bath, this place had become a second home, the first place I would visit whenever I was in town. It was aggressive, hot, catalytic, in tune with the mood. A good location, too. Westminster was within easy striking distance, but the pub was not too close to be shut down on riot days.

I saw the place differently when I made the mistake of bringing Annalese along, shortly after we had moved to London. I saw myself differently. She pointed out the obvious: the barmaid was the only woman in the room, everyone was white, out of their heads, and the place stank of body odour. I tried to give reasons, talked about means justifying ends, said that everyone was really anti-racist, pro women, despite appearances, but her visit changed my view of the place irreparably.

Today, however, was pure nostalgia. I pushed my way to the bar, squeezing past tight T-shirts and tattooed forearms, and ordered two pints of Tennants. It was half past eleven and I had some catching up to do. I looked around, recognising faces. Anarchists to a man, the lot of them. It felt good to be back. A hunt saboteur from the Brixton Group nodded from the doorway, grinning. A mixture of squatters and sabs, the group had enjoyed its finest hour at Trafalgar Square. Red Action were around, too, comparing notes.

I spotted Leggit in the corner, talking to an old man I knew as Jean Paul, and three other people I hadn't seen before. Jean Paul was a Frenchman and far too old to fight, but he always came along, waiting for others to floor policemen before kicking them with short, stubby thrusts, more like a scuff of the heels. He was a refugee from the Sixties, an old-school anarchist who would have preferred to hang out in smoke filled salons in Paris. Instead he had to make do with South London and places like the George. Life was tough.

Leggit was different. A fast-talking street trader (he was known as Leggit because of the speed with which he could pack up his stall), he had done two spells in Parkhurst for ringing motors, and spoke proudly of numerous robberies. He had never stolen from his own, mind, and liked to style himself as a decent, natural criminal. I had met him through Class War, when it was in its heyday. Together we had stamped on BMWs in Docklands, superglued people into their Range Rovers, wandered the streets in search of dinner parties to crash (usually with a dustbin through the window, although Leggit once achieved a famous double when he joyrode someone's Mercedes into their front room just as the port was being served). But, like him, I had grown disillusioned. Class War became organised, factionalised, and Leggit went off to run his own firm.

"Bugger me, I hope you didn't pay for that," he said, as I approached.

"Chemotherapy," I replied, rubbing my head.

"Don't boast. Where've you been? Still living in your fucking teepee?"

"No."

"We all make mistakes my son, and yours was Cornish. I always had my doubts about her. Let me introduce you to the family. Changed a bit since you was last here. This is Danny; Danny, Dutchie, Dutchie, Danny; Rick, Martin and you know Jean Paul. This man might be short, gents, and a slaphead now – Jesus you look ugly – but he's warrior, believe me. Spikey as they come."

I drank deeply on my lager and stared at the pub's misted up windows, taking in the elaborate gilt borders. When I knew Leggit was looking elsewhere, I glanced at him. He was tall, thin-lipped, and his retreating, silver hair was slicked forward into a jagged fringe. He liked me because I'd shown a bit of form at Poll Tax. Four policemen were trying to drag him into a Maria but I managed to free him with a fist blizzard I have never been able to repeat since.

"How long have the doctors given you?" Martin asked. His face was unfamiliar. I looked at him for a second, fearing that he might not be joking. No one cared what you looked like at The George. You could turn up dressed as Father Christmas, providing your sack was full of the right kind of presents. I glanced at Leggit, whose smile had gone.

"Today's my last fling," I said.

"Mere anarchy loosed upon the world," Jean Paul added thickly. He had been on the sherbert and his English was barely intelligible.

"Are you up to this, Martin?" Leggit asked. "It's the big one today, and you're fucking scaring me with your crass fucking questions."

I was taken aback by Leggit's sudden change of tone. I looked around at the others, who seemed less surprised.

"'Course I'm up to it, guv," Martin said. "One more for the road everyone?"

Waving a glass in the air, Martin was doing his best to look cheerful, but his mouth was tense, too scared for smiling. His face was short and square, like the rest of his body, rough cast with a large forehead. He looked at people as if from under an overhang, never lifting his head high enough to stare them in the eye. It made him seem shy, shifty.

"A double," Leggit said, looking sideways at Martin, mockingly, almost as if he was a buxom blonde. "Malt."

As Martin walked past, he peered out at me, raising his eyebrows. "Tennants?"

I nodded. There was something strange going on, an unease. Martin's eyes had rested on me a moment longer than was natural. They looked scared, beseeching. Once he was out of earshot Leggit moved over to me and stood too close.

"We've got ourselves a tiny problem, Dutchie. Someone here isn't who he says he is."

"Is that right?" I tried to move back a pace, but felt the wall behind me. The white fur on Leggit's camel coat lapels was stained in several places. It never used to be stained.

"Someone pretending to be one of us, but who isn't. Someone saying they're from the working classes, but he ain't."

I twisted my fingers into the palm of my hand.

"How can you tell?" I asked.

"By their skin. Their pretty boy skin. You see that man standing at the bar?"

"Martin?"

"Is it? Is that his name? Bollocks it is."

"Who is he then?"

"Ask him. Ask him when he comes back. He'll tell you he's called Martin Denton, lives in Bow, works for the council housing department."

"But he's not."

"He's a copper."

"A copper?"

"Keep it down. This place is crawling with them. We don't want anyone coming to the rescue."

I glanced around the pub, looked at the back of Martin's granite head, bobbing at a barmaid's joke.

"Bastard," I said without much conviction. A part of me felt sorry for him.

"Things aren't what they used to be, Dutchie," Leggit said. "Old Bill are all over us. I'm not kidding. There are probably more undercover cops in this pub than brew crew. You missed fuck at Hyde Park. We were reduced to bystanders, watching Special Branch throw stones at each other. It was a joke."

Martin came back, wobbling with a tray of drinks. He was wearing a cheap black leather jacket, blue jeans and trainers. It suddenly all seemed very obvious. Leggit took his whisky, knocked it back and replaced it far too heavily on the tray. Martin tried to keep the pint glasses level, but beer had gone everywhere.

"You wouldn't ever serve us short, would you Martin?" Leggit asked.

I had never met anyone more at ease with violence than Leggit. His skull seemed too close to the surface, trying to push through. Martin attempted to ignore him and offered the pints around.

"We should drink up. Kick off's at twelve," he said.

"Drink up then," Leggit said.

Martin looked around him. Everyone was quiet, watching him. He knew his number was up. He downed his pint in one, keeping his eyes on Leggit as he tilted back his head.

"No one else coming?" he asked, wiping his mouth with the back of his hand.

"We're coming," Leggit said.

"I'll see you in the car park, then. Just have a slash." He hesitated a moment, looking at the ground, almost waiting to see if anyone had believed him. He then walked away towards the Gents.

"With him," Leggit said to me, and threw a nod across the room.

I cleared my pint and eased through the crowd. Was Leggit testing me? Did he suspect something? I should just walk away from the pub. The riot wasn't part of the plan. It was an indulgence, nothing more.

As I pushed open the Gents door, I heard the sound of smashing glass. I walked to the middle of the room, treading carefully. One of the urinals was blocked and the floor was covered in pools of watery piss. Another piece of glass cracked behind a locked cubicle. I pushed open the door next to it and saw a wire-meshed window high up on the back wall. It was small, too tight for Martin to squeeze through. The man was desperate, trapped.

I paused. I hated policemen. If I was in there and a copper was standing out here, I'd be nicked. Kicked then nicked. This had nothing to do with Annalese. I wasn't undercover yet. I went to the main door, kept it open with my foot and caught Leggit's attention. There was another sound from behind the door. I signalled to Leggit to go outside, around to the car park. It took a few moments for him to understand, then he put his thumb up and left the bar.

I let the door swing closed, and then had a slash myself.

"Martin, what you doing in there?" I asked, still standing at the urinal.

I heard a scuffle, a muffled scream. Was he stuck?

"So what's it like then, going undercover?"

Silence. Then a muted groan.

"When you become mates with people, real mates. Is it easy stitching them up?"

There was no answer. I went out to the car park.

Leggit and the others were out of sight from the pub entrance, standing in a small semi-circle behind the outside wall of the Gents. Martin had managed to squeeze himself through the broken window, and was lying in a crumpled heap on the ground, surrounded by glass. The jagged edges of the window had cut him badly, particularly his arms and the top of his legs. He was alive, but losing a lot of blood.

"We haven't finished with this piece of scum yet," Leggit said, and kicked Martin hard in the stomach. He moaned, and pulled his knees further up towards him. "You driving, Jean Paul?"

The old Frenchman nodded and shuffled off pigeon-toed towards a white Ford Transit. When he was halfway across the car park he turned around and walked back again. People sensed what he was returning to do, and they made way for him. He stood beside Martin, holding a cigarette away from him in a camp gesture, and gave the body a short kick in the chest. "You piece of filthy shit piss," he said quietly, almost like a mantra. The rest of us laughed, nervously, and then began laying into Martin too. Everyone except me. I followed Jean Paul back to the van and sat in my old seat, behind the driver.

"You not with them?" Jean Paul asked, adjusting the mirror to look at me. His hand was shaking.

"Saving my best till later," I lied, managing a grin. In truth, I didn't know why I wasn't kicking Martin into the next world. The man was going to bleed to death anyway, but my mixed feelings were annoying. Perhaps it was the element of doubt. I didn't know Martin, hadn't personally been betrayed by him like the others. And the man wasn't wearing a police uniform. It sounded stupid, but that mattered.

Jean Paul started to hum the Marseillaise.

Staring across the dusty ground at the others, their legs still swinging in sudden arcs, I wondered whether I was up to confronting Annalese's killers. They would be dressed like normal people, just like Martin was, just like the woman in the photo. They weren't going to make it easy for me by wearing uniforms.

Revenge was such a fragile thing, easily lost in other emotions. I had to remain clear-headed. Whenever I remembered the anorak in Oxford Street, I felt it, pure and distilled. Someone had taken away the woman I loved, and they would have to pay the ultimate price, just like she had. I felt better when I thought like that, knowing that once they were dead, I could start mourning for her. But I didn't always think like that. It had been an impulsive reaction to turn to Walter, to offer him my services. I didn't know what else to do. Now I realised there was no turning back. Walter had taken up my offer and returned it with interest. If I backed out, he would turn me over. I just had to keep moving forwards. Face to face with her killers, I would know what to do. I only wished it would happen now rather than later.

CHAPTER 11

As Jean Paul drove the van along Waterloo Road, his fragile hair blowing in unintended directions, I began to enjoy myself. It was cold, and the skies were clear, sharpening the edges of tall buildings. In the distance I could see the Nat West Tower, and beyond it, Canary Wharf. The City would have to wait. I looked around at the assembled crew, forgot about Martin and smiled. The van, stolen by Leggit in the morning, had no suspension, and jarred with every blemish in the tarmac. The plastic seats had all been slashed, their aero filling yellowed and spilling, and there was a hole in the rusted floor. Above the din of the blurred black-top rushing beneath us we could all hear the tripping beat of Danny's walkman. He was lost in his own world at the back of the bus, jogging hood up, head nodding. Occasionally he would shout out a word, letting it linger and fade into a long drawn-out moan. He was seventeen, maybe eighteen and had hollowed-out cheeks, as if the flesh had been sucked from under the skin.

Leggit was sitting two seats in front of him, his back to the window, looking lordly. These people were nothing without him, and he knew it. Feet set wide apart to steady himself, he pulled out a brown paper bag of speed from deep within his coat and handed it to Rick, who licked his fat finger and dipped it clumsily into the bag.

"Rick," Leggit said, snatching the bag back. "Leave it out. You're like a big baby."

Rick weighed twenty stone, lived with his mother and had no neck. He watched Leggit fold the bag into his coat pocket, his brow furrowed with dismay. He licked his finger again, and then cheered up as Leggit produced a bottle of whisky. After drinking deeply, Leggit waved it in the air. Rick's eyes followed the bottle, but Leggit held on to it.

"Coming up on your right," he said, pointing with the top of the bottle, "the Security Services building. Two hundred million quid, and they can't even use the front door."

"Why not?" Rick asked.

"In case the Russians are watching, Rick. Only there aren't any Ruskies anymore. Just us." He grinned. No one had ever told him that he had terrible teeth. No one dared. "They've built themselves a tunnel to get in. Clever, that. And they wonder why the place is full of fucking moles."

"Where's the tunnel start?" I asked, beginning to laugh. I had forgotten how much I liked Leggit's company.

"Start? Vauxhall tube."

Leggit slid the whisky down over Jean Paul's shoulder. He took a swig, steering with one hand, and passed the bottle back.

"A knackered lift-shaft, apparently," Leggit continued. "Take a few wrong turnings and you're in."

"Need a travelcard?" I asked, as he gave me the bottle.

"Ah, we've missed you Dutchie," he said, grinning.

I knew he hadn't. Leggit never missed anyone. But if you wanted to have a good crack, he was your man. He made sure you got home. Then, two weeks later, two months even, he would turn up and ask an awkward favour. He had appeared at the barge once, knocked on the window at three in the morning, and told me to run some skag up to a club in Bermondsey. It wasn't worth arguing.

"What's that all about, then?" he asked, nodding at my head. "Joined the Foreign Legion?"

"Someone flamed me," I said.

"No scars," he replied flatly. It was less an observation than a challenge. He knew I was lying.

"Suits you, it does," he continued. "Makes you look hard."

He mocked me with the last word, let it hang in the noisy air long enough for it to sound anything but. I had gone soft since meeting Annalese and he wasn't going to let me forget it. Fortunately he was distracted as we approached the Security Services building. Lining either side of the road were coaches full of riot police, helmets on laps, minds focused. It wasn't the usual collection of iron-grilled Marias. Rusting pantechnicons had been hauled out of forgotten garages, painted in faded greens and cream. Coaches hired from Oxford, Brighton and Birmingham sparkled in the sunlight. As Leggit predicted, this was the big one.

"Must be over five thousand of them," he said quietly, standing to take a closer look. Danny looked up to see what all the fuss was about.

"Cunts! Fascist cunts," he suddenly shouted, and started to slap the back window like a trapped marlin. We had stopped at traffic lights, alongside one of the coaches. Jean Paul leant out of his window and spat at the doors. His lime phlegm slid down the glass, stopping at the black rubber seal. Rick lurched heavily to the right of the van, pulling a slow face at the expressionless police. Then one of the officers gave Danny a little wave, no more than a knuckle ripple. Incensed, Danny slid back the window next to me and leant out of the van, one knee digging into my thigh. I moved over, watching nostalgically. From his overcoat sleeve he pulled out an eighteen-inch metal bar and smacked the coach window. A crack cobwebbed across the glass. The policeman sat back, startled. Others turned around, stood up, talked into radios.

"You stupid fucker, Danny," Leggit shouted. "Can't you wait? Floor it, Jean Paul."

Jean Paul looked around briefly then pulled out of the queue of cars, drove up to the red lights and crossed them, hooted all the way by other drivers. He turned right over

Vauxhall Bridge, narrowly missing a Danish Bacon jugger-
naut (there were pigs everywhere) and roared up Vauxhall
Bridge Road, smoke pouring out of the cindered exhaust.
Danny still had his head out the window, shouting wildly.

"Shut him up, Dutchie," Leggit said. "Turn left here, by
the pub."

I pulled Danny from the window just as Jean Paul was
braking. We fell to the floor together, our faces suddenly as
close as lovers. Danny's eyes were glazed, naive. "Raise your
game, dickhead," I said. "And whatever you've taken, next
time wait for the rest of us. We might not think you're so
fucking stupid."

We abandoned the van in a red-bricked archway, and ran
across Vauxhall Bridge Road, Danny still shouting, turning
circles in the traffic. I caught him by his hood and dragged
him forward. Above us, helicopters were bending across the
Westminster sky. I could hear chanting in the distance.

I had missed days like this.

We walked down John Islip Street spread out in twos,
reducing our chances of being arrested. Leggit pulled out
an Amplex packet and passed round small blue pills, uneven
spheres, to everyone except Danny. He wouldn't say what
they were, just that they were new, from Holland and weren't
designed to freshen your breath. I swallowed mine in one,
too late to notice Leggit sliding his into a back pocket.

Parliament Square was surging with demonstrators by the
time we arrived – police and TV crews scanning the huge
crowd nervously. Ranks of stamping horses were breathing
heavily on the pavements, half lost in their own steam. It
was a moment I used to savour, the uneasy hiatus: a time
to reflect, to inhale the primitive air.

"Head for the scaffolding," Leggit urged. He was suddenly
at my shoulder, sharp focused, too close. "We wasn't even
meant to reach the square. What a beautiful cock-up."

I looked towards the middle of the crowd. A group of

edgy riot police standing three deep were guarding wooden hoardings. A London Underground poster apologised for any inconvenience. Leggit was right. It was cock-up. Behind those hoardings were clamps, poles, rocks. The march should have been diverted.

We steamed into the front of the crowd, shoving protesters out the way. "Fuck off home, lentilhead," Leggit shouted at a woman who looked like Katrina. I tried to say something to her but I couldn't.

I was sinking.

My arms felt heavy, leaden. The tarmac tugged at my feet like treacle, making it difficult to walk. I looked ahead, trying to focus on Leggit's khaki-cream back, now no more than a smudge. Where was Danny? Blood sluiced noisily through my ears. I felt so tired. The sky was no longer clear. Clouds, ink-black and twisted, were pressing down on me, buckling my forehead. A helicopter hovered, so low I thought it would somersault my severed limbs through the air. The weight of my body was no longer bearable. I had to lie down, flatten myself against the earth, sink towards its core until I could fall no further . . .

Lying prostrate in the middle of a demonstration was not good form, I realised that. It was physically dangerous, but worse, much worse, was the possibility that someone might have mistaken me for a D-bar protester. The sort who held hands, organised die-ins, and locked themselves to railings. The thought hurt me more than my bruised ribs. I wasn't sure if I had been walked on, run over by horses, or privately kicked. Jean Paul had probably been unable to resist a quick toe jab, and the police! What a joke. I would have been carcassed if they had recognised me. Instead I was lying conscious in a cell, glad to be a slaphead.

"Hello?" I called out into the silence. My mouth was parched, in need of a drink. Given my condition and circumstances, I didn't feel too bad. I almost felt high. What sort of gear were those pills? The thought of not seeing Leggit for a while appealed. Where was he in my hour of need? And I hadn't liked the way he had talked of Annalese.

My cell was on a small, dimly lit corridor, at the far end of which was a door. A faint light seeped through a crack at the bottom and there were two people talking on the other side. The cell was pitch black, but I could just make out the shape of a bucket in the corner. It was hard to tell whether the other cells, three, maybe four, were occupied.

"Anybody home?"

"Can't you shut it?" a voice said in the darkness.

I wondered what time it was. The voices grew louder. Whoever it was, they were arguing. Then the door opened, throwing a tidy box of light across the floor of my cell. I covered my eyes, but I could see two people approaching. The profile of one was unmistakable.

"Don't say a word," Walter said, holding up his hand. "I'm not sure I could bear the sound of your voice right now."

The duty officer unlocked the barred door and walked away, not looking at either of us. "Come back John Major, all is forgiven," he muttered.

"He's had a bad day," Walter explained. "We all have." He stood at the entrance and directed me out of the cell.

Once outside – we were somewhere near Victoria – Walter took me by the arm and moved quickly through the cold night air towards his Daimler. There was no driver and I settled myself in the passenger seat. Walter was in no mood to be trifled with; reclining in the back might not be taken the right way.

"Okay kid, I'm not going to lose my temper," he said, slamming his door shut. "But what in God's name did you think you were doing out there?"

"I believe in dockers' rights, that's all."

"Bullshit. You don't believe in anything."

Walter tried to fasten his seat belt, drawing it slowly from its spool, but the buckle kept stopping a foot short. Either it was jammed or the designers had had someone slimmer in mind. He tossed it back over his shoulder and started the car, looking at me briefly. The silence made me edgy as we drove off towards the river.

"Kill the Bill, Kill the Bill," I chanted quietly.

Walter threw me a worried glance. "Are you drunk?"

"Just committed." I felt drunk, though. "Can we stop for a drink? Water."

We were passing over Vauxhall Bridge. On our left the Security Services building was lit up like the Great Pyramid, its warm, sandy colours fooling no one. I wanted to ask him about the tunnel, but thought better of it.

"Does the name Martin Denton mean anything to you?" he asked, braking late at the lights. He didn't notice me flinch. "Yes or no?"

"No."

"Let me tell you something, arsehole. He was working for MI5, a joint operation with Special Branch. This morning he was found dead, in a South London parking lot."

Walter was driving fast, badly, sliding across lanes under a barrage of hooters. A race between him and Jean Paul would be interesting.

"Second point. Does the name Lenny Fisher, 'Leggit' to his friends, ring any bells in your minute, hollow skull?"

"I've heard of him."

"Heard of him! Jesus, Dutchie. He's just been charged with Denton's murder."

I began to feel heavy again, exhausted.

"What's that got to do with me?"

"Someone saw you in the pub."

"So what?"

"So what?" Walter was beside himself, breathless. He

looked at me, then ahead again, just in time to swerve past an old man stepping on to a pedestrian crossing.

"Why wasn't I charged?" I asked, tempted to take him to boiling point.

"Because I said you were working for the Security Services, that's goddam why. And because for some unknown reason, you chose not to kick the shit out of Martin. It was all filmed by the way."

"He wasn't a policemen, then."

"Does it matter?"

"Sometimes."

"He used to be in the police. We've employed smarter guys, too. But he had a family, two kids and a wife who loved him."

I ignored him, and wondered why MI5 was mixing it with Leggit.

"You're scared, all of you," I began, "scared of losing your jobs. I can see the front page now: 'MI5 given P42s'."

"What?"

"You must dread that." I was rambling, lost in establishment initials, still high on whatever it was Leggit had given me.

"Listen to me, Dutchie. You don't seem to understand. This entire project is in jeopardy. Your face was on the evening news. You're walking into the City Monday morning a marked man. Are you committed to this or not? I need to know."

"Do I have a choice?"

He didn't reply. I remembered the crimes Walter had listed the previous night. He could add murder to the list now. Why did he need to blackmail people to work for him?

"Can I ask you something?" I said. "Has anyone gone before me, to the City?"

"You would have been the first."

"And the best you've got?"

"Please, don't use the word 'best'. It seems truly inappropriate right now. Do you know who you rang when the police gave you your one call? Do you?"

"No."

I couldn't remember being arrested, let alone calling anyone.

"You dialled a goddamn hooker. Can you believe that?"

I couldn't, but then remembered the calling cards I had taken from the phonebox. I had to smile. Christ, I must have been out to breakfast, lunch and dinner.

We sat in silence for a while, driving through the night towards Clapham.

"It wasn't a good crack today," I said finally, as we neared the house. "If it makes you feel any better."

"Oh, so that's okay then," he said, his temper refuelled. "Do you know how many policemen were injured out there? Forty-eight. Ten of them badly."

"And I missed it all."

"You're a disgrace to your country, and to your father."

The car turned into the driveway. Charlotte's light was on upstairs. Walter turned off the engine and saw me looking up at her window.

"You'd better watch your butt. She's not happy, I warn you."

"I think I'll kip in the car," I said, feeling the side of the seat for the reclining button.

"Don't push it, Dutchie," he said, leaning across and opening my door.

CHAPTER 12

I crept up the stairs, treading silently on the sides of each step, much as I had done that morning. It had been a long day. Walter appeared to be sleeping on someone else's sofa tonight. After making sure I had gone in, he had driven off. Perhaps he was going to sleep in the car.

At the top of the landing I stopped and listened. My door was diagonally opposite, Charlotte's was to the left. She had left it slightly ajar and I could hear a television inside. Had she heard me come in? She must have seen the car. Tiptoeing, I turned left, almost falling against an Aubrey Beardsley print. A man was standing hand on hips, displaying his telescopic member to a posse of harlots. Who chose these pictures? Walter?

I closed the bedroom door behind me, relieved, and then felt short-changed. I had been steeling myself for a torrent of rage from teacher, but she hadn't reacted. I got undressed, moving around the room with less care, knocking a wire coathanger to the cupboard floor where it settled with a rattle. I coughed without restraint, spat in the basin, hesitated a moment before closing off the cold water tap. The pipes juddered somewhere above me. I wanted to get it over with tonight.

But Charlotte didn't stir. I lay there in bed, the light off, trying to sleep. Could I hear her television? I listened. Nothing but the distant hum of traffic. Clapham was a confused place. A beautiful stretch of grass and trees, carved up by a latticework of roads. I had been here once before, I remembered now, to see Archaos, the French circus troupe. A woman with bare breasts had walked around on stilts, chased by men with chainsaws.

I got out of bed and went to the door, opening it slightly. Charlotte's light was still on. I went back to bed, sat on the edge, looked out of the window, went to the basin. Wincing, I removed the rings from my ear and nose, and lined them up neatly on the glass shelf beneath the mirror. Then I put on the dressing gown hanging behind the door and stepped across the landing.

"It's me, Dutchie," I said, knocking on her door impatiently. "Are you awake?"

There was no response. I pushed the door open and walked in. The room was bigger than mine, with a double rather than single bed. Charlotte was sitting at the end of it, her back to the door. She was watching the television, shoulders hunched, one hand propping up her chin. She didn't turn around. A small light was on beside the neatly made bed. The room was cold, white, and smelt of apple soap.

I stood there, wrongfooted by the stillness, and wondered whether I should back quietly out of the room, try again in the morning, pretend I had never come in.

"Anything good on?" I asked hopefully, watching the black and white screen. It was a trilby movie of some sort. Did spies watch spy films? I took a few steps further into the middle of the room. Charlotte was wearing jeans and a thick, fisherman's jumper which concealed her neck. With effort she turned her head as I moved even closer. Her pallor shocked me. She had been crying and her eyes looked scratched.

"Close the door, sit down," she said, sighing imperceptibly. I paused for a moment, then went over to the door, pressed it until it clicked, not knowing what I felt. I almost wanted to laugh. Was she so upset that I had played truant? I looked around, checking that there wasn't anything else in the room to sit down on, and then perched awkwardly on a fragile dining room chair.

"Had a good day out, then?" she said, lighting a cigarette and moving around to face me. The bed creaked. "Out with the boys." I needed a cigarette too but she didn't offer me one. She was hard to predict, held more cards.

"It's been a while," I said.

"Lost your touch?"

"Popped the wrong pill."

She inhaled, looked away from me. She was more attractive in profile, subtler. I watched as she put the cigarette to her mouth again; her faintly painted lips were pursed, seersuckered, and left rippled imprints on the stem.

"I had a lot of enthusiasm for this project, it interested me," she began. She wasn't speaking naturally. The words sounded prepared, her gaze was elsewhere.

"Me too."

She ignored me. I leant forward and helped myself to one of her cigarettes. She didn't offer to light it.

"There was a real chance for Walter, for you, for us all to do something substantial, worthwhile. That's quite rare in my job."

"I'm sure," I said. I didn't want to be confrontational; I just wanted to move beyond this childish charade.

"That's not possible now," she said.

"Why not? Walter's kosher about it."

"Martin Denton was a good friend. We spent a lot of time together, working."

I got up and walked to the window, tightening my dressing gown as I went. So that was it. I breathed heavily, let my shoulders drop, and heard the sound of Martin's moan. I resented being made to feel bad about the death of a copper. Okay, he wasn't one anymore, but he had been once. That was good enough for me.

"He knew the risks, didn't he?" I said, still looking out into darkness.

"I just don't think I can work with you. I'm sorry. It's not possible. I'll talk to Walter in the morning."

I turned around.

"He tried to squeeze out of a window that was too small for him. He cut himself up." My voice was surprisingly urgent. For the first time, I sensed the project was in danger. "Look, I won't be seeing them again. He would have died anyway."

She sat silently for a few moments and then spoke. "Would you be prepared to testify against Leggit?"

"Testify?"

"The evidence is only circumstantial."

"No, I wouldn't."

"It would be in camera, anonymous."

"I haven't seen Leggit for over a year, I am not involved with him any more. I don't even like the geezer that much. But I can't grass him up, not for a . . ."

" . . . for a what?"

We were so far apart. Perhaps it was better I worked with someone else.

"For a fucking copper. I'm going to bed. What time do we start?"

Charlotte said nothing. I went to the door, stood there for a few moments wondering whether to say anything else, then left. In bed I stared at the ceiling, following the cornicing around and around. In one corner there was a gap, no more than a few inches, but my mind soon plugged it. The room was glowing from the street lamp outside and I didn't feel like sleeping. Instead I thought of Annalese. I feared the image of her in the morgue would come to dominate all others, but the stitched face was fading and I saw her supine on the beach, sitting at the table on the barge reading to Leafe, in bed with me now. It was three in the morning and we had been out with her friends in Penzance. I had been given a cool reception. We were both lying there, each conscious of the other, thinking back separately over the uneasy evening.

"You're a good person, underneath," she said. "Not everyone can see it, that's all."

"That's not why you stay with me."

"No."

"What is it, then?"

"I think I can change you."

"Can you?"

"I have to believe I can."

"And if you can't?"

There was a pause. We had slipped into one of those quiet conversations where different rules applied: whatever we said could not be used again in any future rows.

"Then I don't deserve anyone better."

"You want me to change?"

She paused again. "No. Not really." Rolling over towards me, she linked a leg over mine. "That's the problem. I think I would be bored by someone kind, someone who bought me flowers every day and said they loved me. Flattered, but bored."

"I feel like buying you flowers, sometimes."

"But you never do. You just say 'I nearly bought you some flowers today'."

She pushed some hair out of my eyes. "What stops you going with someone else?" she asked. I never gave her an answer, never said that I loved her. The old rules had returned. Instead, I just let the rhythm of my lungs lull her to sleep.

CHAPTER 13

The next morning I rose early. I felt sharp, optimistic, unlike the day, dawning stillborn outside. A mist hung over the common, diluting the colours of the cars parked along the road. A boy was see-sawing up West Side on his bicycle, weighed down by an orange shoulder sack. I thought of the Thames, its different light and rhythms, and wished I was on the barge.

I rummaged around in the cupboard and found a blue and white stripey shirt. It was far too big for me but I put it on and went downstairs (no tie – it was the weekend after all). *The Sunday Times* and *The Mail on Sunday* were smudged across the hall doormat, photos of the march covering the front pages. I looked for myself, spotted Leggit but couldn't see my own shaved head. In the old days, we used to go back to The George for Sunday lunch, cut out our photos and stick them behind the bar.

There was no mention of a death in a South London pub. Perhaps Walter was lying.

I made Charlotte a mug of coffee and knocked on her door. It was seven-thirty and I wanted to impress, make amends. Silence. I went in, expecting to find her asleep. The room was empty, no evidence at all that anyone had been there. The bed was made up, unslept in, and her bags had gone.

Downstairs I walked around restlessly, frustrated. I checked the sitting room in case anyone was on the sofa, but I was alone. She would come back, I was sure of it. Annalese and I used to walk out on each other regularly. I wandered through to the kitchen. This was going to be my home, where I would return from the tube station every night, Monday to Friday. I wanted to get on, find out about tomorrow, where I was going to work, what I was expected to do. It felt surprisingly exposed for a safe house, large bow windows looking straight out on to the street. I imagined Leggit trying to sell the place: "Safe as houses, safe houses are." I knew they would beat him badly and he would resist, which would only make matters worse.

Charlotte finally turned up at twelve o'clock, hostile and unforgiving, weighed down with three Tesco bags of shopping.

"You've not been arrested then?" she asked, walking into the kitchen and putting the bags on the beech sideboard. I was at the table, reading. She went over to the sink window and opened it. I had smoked the best part of a packet.

"It's been a quiet morning," I said, not looking up. "Trashed the neighbour's Audi, torched the corner shop."

She glanced at me briefly and began to unpack the bags: freshly squeezed orange juice, Ecover washing-up liquid, Basmati rice, red pesto, courgettes, beans, onions, tofu, no meat as far as I could see. Perhaps we had a future together, after all.

"*A Fool and His Money* by Martin Baker," I quoted, reading from the cover of the book I was holding. "*High Finance, Low Living – Understanding Financial Markets and Those Who Work in Them.*"

She wasn't playing ball. I sat there, looking at her shoulders, broad as a swimmer's. Without care she would be fat, but her limbs were toned, athletic. Somehow it seemed appropriate that the first and only time we had touched was when she had locked my neck in a stranglehold. Much less ambiguous than a handshake.

"You still on for it, then?" I asked, stubbing another cigarette into the ashtray.

"Unfortunately."

"It could be fun, living together. Our first home, and in Clapham, too."

She said nothing. A plastic bottle of toasted sesame oil toppled out of one of the bags and fell to the floor. She picked it up wearily, too tired to curse. I noticed her eyes were moist.

"What made you come back, then?" I asked, more softly.

"I was given little option."

"Blackmailed you as well?"

"Not exactly. There was no one else."

"I'm very keen. Up at seven. Even brought you coffee."

She still wished I wasn't there, so I got up and went into the sitting room. Walter had bought some CDs, recommended listening, he said, for foreign exchange dealers. I dropped a disc into the tray, watched it slide inside and turned the volume up. I then stood in the doorway, waiting for her reaction.

"Bruce Springsteen's greatest hits," I said, raising my voice above the music. "One of my favourites, apparently. Crap, isn't it?"

"You'll disturb the neighbours," she said, still not looking up.

I switched it off and returned to the door, resting my hand halfway up the frame.

"Fancy a sherry?" I asked. She continued to ignore me. "Perhaps a quick snifter at the Pitcher and Piano?"

Finally she snapped, smacking a tin of tuna on the sideboard. She turned and looked at me with contempt, standing there in my ill-fitting shirt. "I've just come from seeing Martin's wife," she said coldly. "His widow."

"How is she?" I asked casually. I was going to ride this one, stay above it.

"Distraught. Confused."

She shouldn't have married a copper, I thought, but I managed to restrain myself.

"I've also read the Business section of *The Sunday Times*, found out how much dosh everyone is making."

She wasn't impressed. I snatched up the papers and went through to the sitting room, littering the floor with loose adverts as I went. I didn't know why I bothered. (I hadn't bothered, in fact. I had only read the Business section's headlines, and discovered Sport on the back, where there was a report about crowd trouble at the Millwall game.)

I stared out of the sitting room window on to the common, and watched two women jogging together, trying to work off the previous night. They were barely running, stuck in the mist. I warmed my legs on the radiator and looked at the dresser beside me. Sure enough, there was a sherry decanter, hidden behind some bottles of red wine. I picked it up and held it to the light. The liquid was dark and old, but still clear. I removed the top, sniffed, and took a sickly swig. No wonder she had refused. I heard her climbing the stairs, move around in her room, turn on the TV. Every small creak in the ceiling was annoying. Our beautiful relationship wasn't going to last.

It was late in the afternoon and we were driving across Tower Bridge. Our car wasn't new, but it ran well. A fading red Golf GTI with a sun-roof and central locking doors. Charlotte changed down into second gear, braked. There was a police roadblock ahead. Six months earlier the red and white barriers had been dismantled completely. Now they were back, just in time for Christmas, looking festive.

"Don't say anything," she said, drawing up alongside a policeman. Head hanging in the window, he peered at me, then at the back seat, where there was a 1992 Collins *Road Atlas of Great Britain*, a red envelope folder and the pink middle section of an *Evening Standard*. Charlotte had her purse on her lap and was removing what looked like a library pass.

"I'll need to see the boot," the officer said. Charlotte held the pass close to the policeman's face, confident as a hypnotist. "I'll still need to take a look. Sorry, orders."

He stepped away to let her open the door. "Bloody busybody," she muttered under her breath.

"You weren't insulting a police officer, I hope," I said.

She got out without looking at me and opened the boot. I adjusted the rear mirror and watched. The policeman nodded in my direction, talking, taking time. After two minutes, she climbed back into the car.

"What was all that about?" I asked.

"Have a guess."

"Me?" I said innocently.

"What was it like when you had some hair?"

"Worse."

We drove through the blockade, passed the humourless officers. I put a foot on the dashboard, flicked down the sunguard and looked in the mirror.

"I was beginning to quite fancy myself."

"You look like a convict."

Fenchurch Street was empty, deserted, not how I remembered it at all. There was nowhere to hide. I could see plenty of side streets, narrow and darkened by tall buildings, but where did they lead? Dead ends were trouble. I felt cornered, surrounded. I wondered how I had avoided arrest when we'd stopped the City. (The police had vanned over four hundred of us that day.)

"That's your office," Charlotte said, pulling over in Grace-church Street. "When you get off the tube, turn right and walk down Lombard Street, just over there. Your office is on the corner."

"Is that it?" I said, disappointed. "It looks like a boring bank."

"It is."

"Do we get out? Go in?"

"You haven't got a pass. Everyone has passes."

"So what do I do tomorrow?"

"It's all been taken care of. Just turn up at reception. Someone will be there to meet you." She glanced across at me, worried. "I'm sure I don't need to say this, Dutchie. But you can't tell anyone what this is about. You know that?"

"Mum's the word," I said, a finger at my lips.

We parked in an NCP and wandered the deserted roads, up Lombard street, down Cornhill and Leadenhall. I said little, let teacher do all the talking. She showed me the Bank of England, which I had seen before, and the LIFFE building, which I hadn't. Pret A Manger, she said, would become a part of my life. The City liked sandwiches. The shops were all closed and the police presence was considerable. I behaved myself. Whenever we were stopped I kept my eyes averted, but probably looked more shifty than ever.

We paused for lunch, Charlotte suggesting a hotel near Tower Bridge. She used to go there with her parents, she said, which seemed an odd reason to be returning with me. We walked via the car to pick up the red folder from the back seat.

"What's that anyway?" I said.

"I was hoping you would ask." Her face melted into a smile for the first time that day. She tucked the folder under her arm and turned to me. "This is your life, Dutchie."

I sniffed and walked towards the exit shaft. Boring bitch.

The bar at The Thistle Hotel was surprisingly dark for a room with a large expanse of plate glass along one side. Perhaps it was the mahogany furniture, or the crimson carpets. Still, the view was good: Tower Bridge was just outside, stocky, half-buried, a dark sky fermenting behind it. We were early for Sunday lunch and had the run of the place. The waitress, however, insisted on directing us to a small table by the window, next to the only other customers, a Japanese couple. They smiled nervously. The mother called to their child, who was looking at a model of a nineteenth-century schooner in a glass cabinet near the stairs.

Charlotte was in polite mode, pushing a plastic basket of bread in my direction. My life lay on the table between us. She had done well today, given the circumstances, I had to concede that. But then so had I. Both of us wished we were elsewhere.

"Are you happy with the name Douglas?" she began.

"It's what my old man called me when I was ignoring him."

"But you will turn around if somebody says it?"

"Depends who it is," I said, grinning.

"You ought to know this by tomorrow," she said crisply, trying to restore order. She took a single sheet out of the folder and gave it to me. I got the impression she lived in fear of being taken in. "It's all the important dates in your life," she said. "A CV if you like."

I took it casually but was intrigued. The list bore little resemblance to the one I had written at the service station: 1982–1985, attended Sherborne. That was the same. From then on it was pure fantasy, nightmare: 1986–1988, a crammer in Oxford; 1989, travelling around Europe; 1991–3, Trinity College, Cambridge; 1994–97, Audit Commission; January 1998 joined Jensen Klein Abrahall.

"There's a list here of what O and A levels you passed, but no one's going to ask."

"I did alright in my O Levels."

"I know. We've kept them the same."

"Physics. That was my favourite."

"Mine too."

I looked at her, smiling, making an effort. She must have been headgirl.

"Our Physics teacher, he was crap, a joke," I went on. "He let me wander around on top of the benches at the back, blowing things up, starting little fires."

"You were expelled, weren't you?"

"I chose to leave."

"Why?"

"They wouldn't let me mix my own drugs."

"Seems reasonable enough. Where did you go?"

"All over the place. Bath, Bristol, Hackney."

"And Cambridge? You mentioned you had been there once."

"Yeah. I went to a college ball."

"Really? Which one?" Her eyes lit up.

"I've no idea. There were lots of bastards poncing about in bow-ties."

"You didn't enjoy it then."

"Oh no, I had a great time. Ruined everyone's evening."

She fell quiet, fingering a piece of bread.

"I didn't look in your room. There should have been some clothes."

"This shirt, a couple of ties."

"And you've bought a suit."

I nodded.

"You'll need more. Shirts, socks. It's important you wear a different tie every day."

"You're joking, aren't you?"

"We'll go shopping after lunch."

"Where?"

"Anywhere. Does it matter?"

"You're very maternal."

"I've got my instructions. It's nothing else."

"I won't fuck up."

She glanced at the Japanese couple and smiled.

"I'm sure you won't, Douglas." Her face was full of doubt though, her eyes compressing fractionally inwards.

"Dutchie."

"You were close, you and Annalese, weren't you?"

I said nothing.

"Finding her killers is not going to bring her back, you know that?"

"Keep the advice, thanks."

"It won't."

"But it'll make me feel better, won't it?"

I stuck my feet out into the room and looked at my ridiculous shoes. Policeman's shoes. The man in the suit shop had conned me.

"Is that why you are doing this, for her?" she asked. "Or are you doing it for yourself?"

"Queen and country. Let's go."

"But we haven't finished."

"Bollocks to that. Come on."

We drove to Marble Arch, avoiding Oxford Street at my request. She felt bad for not remembering and I savoured her guilt. Resolutely, Marks and Spencer had kept its flagship store open on Sundays, despite the bombing campaign. Security was tight and people were queuing down the street. I seemed to be frisked longer than most. Charlotte was searched too, her library card cutting no ice with the stocky women in their brown shirts and peaked caps.

"Take this and find yourself some suit shirts, ties, whatever you need," she said, handing me a basket. "I recommend you choose things which don't need ironing. I'm certainly not going to do it for you."

The last time I had been to Marks and Spencer was with my mum.

"Can't I come with you?" I asked, pleading.

"I've got to buy a few things. I'll meet you back here. Twenty minutes?"

With that she was gone, lost in the dense crowd. I looked around, felt my back pocket. I still had money left over from my suit purchase, but it seemed a pity to use it.

Upstairs in the menswear department I chose the most offensive striped shirts I could find: pink and white, green with pyjama-blue stripes and white collars. The ties were not much better. I went for patterned Italian silk, hand-painted English, anything so long as it looked expensive and clashed. Once my basket was full, brimming with patterned socks and boxer shorts, I went upstairs to the lingerie department to have a scoot around. I watched a couple of young Arab women, faces covered, holding up some designer briefs. Then I spotted Charlotte behind them.

"It's alright, I'll stick with boxer shorts," I said. I had approached unnoticed, and was standing at her shoulder.

"God, you gave me a fright," she said, putting down a three pack of high-legs and moving on.

"Aren't you going to buy them?" I asked, looking at the packet.

"You must be joking. They're thirty quid."

"Go on, treat yourself."

"I see you've done alright. Let's pay and get out of here. It's so crowded."

As she walked towards the cashier, I hung back. I had already worked out that the only camera in the department was trained on the over-stretched cashier desks. The nearest security guard was picking his spots in bathroom access-ories. In one deft movement I placed the packet up my jumper, in between my ribcage and upper elbow, and walked after Charlotte.

She paid for my basketload and for some tights, a cream blouse and some woollen leggings, using a card which she held out limply.

"What's that? Another library pass?" I whispered.

"It's my M&S account card."

"No spooky discounts, then?"

"No."

"You know Stella Rimington's now on the board of Marks and Spencer," I said. "Funny thing, that."

"Why? She was very good at running a large department."

"Oh come on. That's not why she got the job. Remember that fuzzy photo? The only picture the newspapers had of her? She was carrying an M&S plastic bag. Talk about coincidence. They've been employing her for years."

Outside in Orchard Street I didn't offer to carry Charlotte's bags as we made our way to the car. There were still people queuing and it had begun to drizzle. It must have been like this during the war – wondering whether you would get blown up before you reached the front of the bread queue or on the way home. As we walked back along the line of people, I looked at them with their Burberry coats, two-tone golfing umbrellas, sensible shoes (I could talk) and Liberty shawls. Douglas would soon be queuing with them.

"It's not worth it, it's a rip off," I said, addressing the line of people. "They've just had to double their prices. Five minutes ago. Honest."

Charlotte turned, saw what I was doing and walked on. I caught up with her. The rain was getting heavier.

"I got you a present," I said.

"You have? For me?"

"Slow down a minute, will you."

She stopped reluctantly. I had both hands behind my back. I could feel the rain running off my head in little rivulets, gathering under my chin, dropping.

"For being such a nice mum."

I held out the packet of knickers. She glanced at them,

then at me. She looked better in the rain, her head seemed smaller.

"Dutchie, you shouldn't have," she said softly, her voice thickening with suspicion. "They were incredibly expensive."

"I know."

Then she paused. "How did you pay for them?"

"I didn't. I nicked them."

"Oh for Christ's sake," she said, glancing anxiously back at the shop and then around her. "You've got to take them back, immediately."

She held them out in front of her, as if they were contaminated.

"They're yours. Nothing to do with me," I said, raising my hands in mock protest.

"What are you trying to prove, Dutchie?"

"I'm not trying to prove anything. I thought you liked them."

"We can't take them. We just can't."

"What do you suggest then? Walk back in there and say, 'I'm terribly sorry, but I seem to have these expensive knickers in my bag.' Get real."

I started to walk on.

"Fuck you, Dutchie, fuck you," she said quietly, and followed.

CHAPTER 14

Charlotte calmed down on the drive home. I concluded she was pleased with the knickers, excited even. She ran through what the foreign exchange dealers at Jensen Klein Abrahall did all day, starting with the basic principle of futures. As far as I could see, it was one big scam, much as I suspected, a job creation scheme designed to make the rich even richer. Originally, it seemed, they were a worthy invention designed to help some poor coffee farmer in Nicaragua sleep peacefully at night. A manufacturer would guarantee to buy his beans in one month's time at a fixed price, regardless of what the real market value might be. If the market price had dropped in a month, the farmer had done well; if it had risen, he could have got a better price. On balance, peace of mind made it a risk worth taking.

Then along come the City boys who decide to make punts on whether the price will rise or fall. For a fraction of the real price of beans, they can buy the right to purchase coffee on a fixed date in the future. They don't actually have to stump up the readies, they just make or lose money, depending on whether the market value falls or rises in relation to the fixed price they bet on. According to Charlotte, ninety-nine per cent of all futures contracts were between fellow dealers rather than farmers. To confuse things further, a large amount of arse-covering went on, hedging of bets, just in case the market didn't move in the direction they had predicted. All of which created an unstable market and mayhem for the farmers. Sod them.

As far as my new job was concerned, I would be working

on the foreign exchange floor, dealing in Deutsche Mark, franc, lira, dollar and sterling. The scam was just the same as coffee beans, with an even greater emphasis on quick profits. It was essential to make sure that when the music stopped at close of business, you weren't down on your deals. Assuming the global market was a hermetically sealed world, someone, somewhere, lost out each day. So what was new?

Back at the house, we kept to ourselves. I staked a claim to the sitting room, while she made a chocolate cake in the kitchen. (She said it was her sister's birthday.) I shut the door behind me, switched on the television and sunk into a sofa. Eddie Murphy in *Trading Places*. I flicked channels, checked there wasn't anything else. I hadn't watched TV for years. On Channel 4, a documentary of some sort, silhouette interviews, distorted number plates. John "Plummy voice" Tyndall, chairman of the British National Party, being asked whether he denounced violence. "I don't condone it," he said.

"Scum," I murmured. The man's voice was unreal. I had once given the BNP a good beating outside a pub in Glasgow. Along with two thousand other anti-Nazis I buried them with bricks and bottles as they left. I watched the documentary, hoping the event would be celebrated, but I couldn't concentrate. My mind was racing. I was nervous. It would be just like the other times, I told myself – Henley Regatta, the college ball – only I would be pretending to be a toff for a bit longer. Several weeks longer. Months even.

I looked around and noticed a photo on the bookshelf. It hadn't been there before. I got up and went to look at it, feeling sick as I approached. It was a photo of me and Charlotte sitting on a restaurant balcony. There were palm trees and the sea behind us was an exotic blue. We were toasting the self-timer with cocktails, grinning. I picked up the frame and looked closer. It was fabricated, a trick, and

I searched for the seam around my neck. I had never been wherever it was, worn clothes like that (turquoise Bermuda shorts, plum-coloured polo shirt), or sat in a restaurant with Charlotte. But there was no seam. It was a professional job; Walter had spared no expense. I wanted to smash the glass and rip out the photo, but I resisted. I had to look credible. Besides, Charlotte was wearing a bikini, barely covering her breasts. She had a good body, there was no point denying it.

I scrutinised the photo again. I needed a fix.

I went over to the phone. Charlotte had gone upstairs. I picked up the receiver and was about to dial when I heard a voice, a rich man talking quietly.

"We'll be together soon," the voice said. "You mustn't let him get to you."

"I know, I know." It was Charlotte. "But he scares me."

"He's a thug. One of those rent-a-mob types. You won't have to be with him for long."

"I know. I know all that. There's just something about him . . ."

" . . . what?"

"He could have turned out so differently. I've never seen that in someone before. The randomness of it. One moment he's nearly killing someone, the next he's all sweetness and light."

"And intelligent. And middle class. I know. So you said. Shame he's so misguided. Look, don't spend too much time there. Just keep an eye on him, a debrief once a week."

"Walter needs more, wants me to appear with him, socially."

"Well, whatever it takes. But be careful."

"I will. I'm sorry. I'm just upset."

"We all are."

"I'll see you when you get back."

"You'll be alright?"

"Yes. Thanks."

"Bye, then."

"Bye."

I tried to time my click with Charlotte's. I stood there for a moment. She was moving around upstairs. Was he a lover? Why did I care? "Nearly killing a man." Martin was alive. She was playing games with me, spying games. No. She just meant I had been there in the car park and had nearly kicked him.

Perhaps she had meant me to pick up the phone and listen?

I went out into the hall. "I'm getting some fags," I called out. "Need anything?"

"I'm alright. Thanks."

Outside in the street the night was crisp, clean. A freezing wind was rifling through the trees, searching for leaves to steal. It was approaching ten o'clock. I walked along the pavement towards the phonebox, idly trying to imagine what scenes were unfolding behind the row of cosy curtains. He was a stockbroker, a small firm, family connections; she worked for an estate agent's. Just back from a weekend with friends in Somerset, they were having their normal discussion on whether to move to the country. He was cleaning his mountain bike. She was ironing his shirts (despite an agreement to share). They were both drinking gin, television on, not really watching, pleasantly surprised by Tyndall's upper-class tones. No, around here someone else would do the ironing; they would underpay a cleaning lady from Streatham, or leave it for the Swedish nanny. (He was giving her one, of course, and had recently agreed a pay rise for the pleasure.)

The phonebox was occupied. I walked on to the tube station, felt its warm currents rising up the escalator shaft, and found another phone on Balham High Road. The Pitcher and Piano was throwing its light on to the uneven paving stones in front of me. I could hear noise, laughing, the idle rich at rest.

"Leroy?" I said, watching the pence disappear. Leroy was only on a mobile.

"Who is this talking please?"

"Leroy. It's Dutchie." Silence. "You remember. Dutchie."

"Dutchie, my man. How you doing?" The man spoke slowly, lilting. He was stoned.

"I'm in Clapham. Anything happening? I need something special."

"Ain't seen you around lately. Clapham. Don't go forgetting your friends now."

"I'm in a hurry."

"Hey, everybody's in a hurry." Everyone except Leroy. "North or South?"

"South. I'm by the tube."

"Get yourself down into Balham, turn left up Bedford Hill. The pink house, half way up on the right. Three knocks on the side door and breathe my name."

I found the house, had to buy more than I intended and was back in my room within half an hour. Charlie wasn't my usual, I couldn't afford it, but it seemed appropriate. I wiped the heavily varnished surface of the chest of drawers. It was blistered at the edges and I snagged the wool of my jumper sleeve. Then I paused. Something was wrong. I couldn't pretend any longer. I never felt guilty about anything; it was a promise I had once made to myself. But Martin's death – he was only a copper, filth – was biting like acid at the edges of my consciousness. I filled both nostrils. Everything became clear when I was high. I knew where I was going. Priorities changed.

Of course Annalese wouldn't come back (Charlotte could be so stupid) but she would be free, I would be free, when her killers were dead.

CHAPTER 15

"Haven't you forgotten something?" Charlotte asked quietly.

"Have I?" She raised her eyebrows, pursed her lips. "Are you serious?"

"'Fraid so."

I leant forward, put a hand on her shoulder and kissed her mouth. She turned and went, leaving me standing on Threadneedle Street, blinking in the cold sunlight. Crowds of people were streaming past, knocking into me. I moved to the edge of the pavement, close to a reassuring stone wall, and let them wash by me like a rip tide.

Given it was the first time I had bought a ticket in years, the tube journey had been remarkably unrelaxing. It was a different crowd from the late-night crew I was used to on the Northern Line, different rules, too. I refrained from smoking. At Kennington a lady stood next to me, waving a shoulder bag under my nose. It was open, I could see a purse, and her back was turned. Somehow I resisted. I even checked myself from stepping up close behind someone to get through the barriers. A stressful journey.

It was a quarter to seven and I had fifteen minutes to make my way to the office. At this rate I was going to be early. Tucking my copy of *The Financial Times* under one arm, I crossed Cornhill to Lombard Street. I was wearing a blue and green striped shirt with white collar, a red and yellow hand-painted tie, my suit and a heavy charcoal over-coat. If Leggit could have seen me now.

I spotted my office from a distance, a dull grey office block. Now I knew how to find it, I cut down St Swithin's

Street in search of coffee. At Charlie's Place, next to Cannon Street station, I read through my biography one more time. I stood at the side bar with my briefcase between my legs. It was a black coffin of a case with a combination lock and my initials, D.R., printed in gold on the side. On closer examination, I noticed there had once been a crown. Someone had removed it and doctored the E.R. to fit my name. They were a crafty lot at MI5, skint too.

Walter had dropped it around the night before, checking to see if I was all set.

"Remember kid, you're a big fan of rugby football," he had said. "If anyone offers you tickets for the Grand Slam, take them."

"Why?"

"Why? Because I can never get tickets. That's why."

He had gone on to talk about Samantha West, and told me to take my time. I wasn't to ask too many questions, too soon. There would be clues in the most ordinary of places. My contribution, he said, was to find out if she had used work to stay in touch with the other terrorists. He had also given me some more money – £100 in cash – and said that it was to last me until my first pay cheque. A bank account had been set up for me, together with a Visa card (someone must have had a word about my credit rating), details of which would be arriving in the post shortly. Walter was serious. I liked that.

Outside the cafe window the young were walking to work, some with college scarfs around their necks, others with folded umbrellas, pumping the ground as if they were walking sticks. I knocked back the rest of my coffee and walked across the road. Two women in Pret A Manger were arranging baguettes. I looked through the window, read some labels, and walked on to the office. Breathing deeply I pushed against JKA's circular doors and entered the foyer.

"Yes sir, can I help?"

A security guard sitting behind the desk was smiling up at me. On the wall behind him Jensen Klein Abrahall was written in big silver letters. To my left there was a rotating chrome bar, like a turnstile, behind which was a small reception area with a low leather sofa. A tall houseplant, potted and wilting, stood next to a wooden table which was covered with magazines, *The Economist*, *The Spectator*, *Financial Adviser*.

"I'm starting work here today," I said evenly, winding in the slack of my old voice.

"And your name, sir?"

Why was the man so cheerful? It wasn't even seven o'clock.

"Mr Reason."

"First name?"

I paused. "Douglas."

"And which department, sir?"

"Foreign exchange, the dealing room."

The man was silent as he looked down a clipboard and consulted another book. I was suspicious of men in uniform, on principle, but I trawled up a genial smile from somewhere.

"Nice morning."

"Yes, sir. Beautiful."

Why did he keep calling me sir? Stand up for your rights, mate, ungovern yourself.

"Take this," he said, giving me a plastic clip pass with my name on it. "Up to the third floor – the lift's on the left – and ask for Dan Willmot. He's expecting you."

"Third floor."

"And welcome to Jensen Klein Abrahall, sir."

Dan Willmot was waiting for me at the top of the stairs, hanging out an immense hand which seemed to envelop my lower arm when he took it.

"I'm Dan. Come on in."

He pressed a series of numbers on a touch pad by the side of the door. I watched as his flattened finger appeared to squash more than one key at a time. His nails were badly bitten. We walked into the dealing room, Dan turning his head slightly towards me. I was a pace behind, dwarfed. Everything about Dan was big: hands, ears, nose, feet. He wasn't wearing any shoes, just black socks, his big toes stretching the cotton.

"You get in alright, then?" he asked.

"Yeah, fine."

"We normally start at six-thirty."

"I was told seven."

"It's no problem today. Not much happening. But when it's busy . . ."

" . . . I'll be here at six-thirty."

I could crawl with the lowest when I needed to.

"This is where it all happens then," he said. His voice was rough at the edges, unpolished, not what I had expected. "That's your desk, over there, by the German flag. We thought we'd start you at the deep end. Deutche Marks."

I looked out across the low-ceilinged room. Telephones were pulsing, voices talked urgently on intercoms. It was smaller than I had expected, more cramped. The lights were dim and there were no outside windows, just vanilla walls. The carpet was cheap blue and tiled. Tired remains of Christmas streamers hung limply from the ceiling corners. Rows of desks were shaped into a large rectangle around the edges of the room, with another block in the middle. Along the back of the desks were banks of TV screens set in wooden casing. The glass was grey, dense with numbers. Different flags, the size of executive toys, were dotted about the place: Japan, France, Great Britain, the European Community. There were fifteen, maybe twenty people, jackets off. An air of controlled vibrance.

"Good call, Kev," someone murmured sarcastically.

"32s almost the same as 4s," someone else shouted.

"What spread have you got in two's?"

"Anyone need any dollars?"

"We're a little bit full on CSFP. I only checked them yesterday. Five or six million. There's a whole bunch of new guys around there."

"Two's", that meant in two months' time, I thought.

"Douglas, this is Pete," Dan said. "He'll be showing you how to piss away our profit."

"Tugger," someone called out as Pete stood up and shook my hand.

"Shut up Toxo," Dan said, not turning around. "He got shagged last night. Make yourself comfortable. Want a coffee, cereal?"

"Coffee, thanks. Black."

"Pete will get it. Won't you Pete, yes?"

I sat down behind Dan and watched Pete go over to the coffee machine. Each dealer, it seemed, had four screens. The end one was divided up into little boxes. I glanced casually down the line of dealers. Two down from me "Toxo" touched the glass with the end of his phone and started talking. There was a plastic bowl on Pete's desk full of soggy cornflakes. A crumpled rucksack lay on the floor by his chair.

Dan ran his chair back, stretched out and interlocked his hands behind his head. The dominant ridge of his nose, now facing the ceiling, was in keeping with his sinewy face, taut with vertical muscles.

"Is that an *FT*?" he asked. I handed my copy to him. He sat upright, looked at the inside page. "Crap, isn't it? No tits." He halved the paper and tossed it back on to my desk. "Watch he doesn't charge you."

Pete was coming back with my coffee, its heat buckling the flimsy cup.

"So, are they paying you?" Pete asked.

"Always on about money," Dan said.

"And you aren't of course."

"Just earn some, yes?"

Toxo came up and joined us, his hand on the back of Pete's chair. He was short, about my size, with an oval face.

"Has Pete told you yet, about his first sexual encounter?" he asked.

"Back to work, Toxo," Dan said.

"He was in bed. It was dark, he was frightened. He was alone."

Pete had a squashed face and his cheeks were slightly puffed, as if he was permanently about to exhale some air. His forehead was sheer, tight, brought to a halt by coarse black eyebrows that started gathering somewhere around his temples.

"Here comes Doris," Dan whispered, turning to his screens.

A woman in a long purple dress walked across to join the gathering. At first glance, I thought the room was staffed entirely by men. I looked around again and counted two other women.

"We had a very large input error yesterday," she began.

"Rose, this is Douglas," Pete said.

"Nice to meet you, Douglas." I shook her warm hand. She smiled and turned to Pete. "Slight problem with your noughts. Concentrate on them today please, there's a sweetie."

"Some chance. Tugger's in the khazi," Toxo said.

"Really?" She was about to go, but leant forward on the top of the screens, youthfully. "Take me through it."

"I had my first ever snakebite," Pete began.

"Sounds vicious," she said.

"Tugger!" someone called.

"Red Rock in one hand, Rolling Rock in the other. That was six o'clock."

"And what happened then?" she asked.

"All I can remember is tearing a nan bread in half, sticking one piece in each ear and singing Dumbo."

"Then he danced around the restaurant with his testicles in a spoon full of burning Sambuca," Dan added.

"Did I?"

"A teaspoon or serving spoon?" Rose asked.

"Serving spoon, please."

"I'm glad I didn't see this," she said, lying.

"His jacket and tie caught fire," Toxo added.

"How did you get home?"

"No idea. I woke up this morning and realised I only had one suit."

"And you were wearing it," Toxo said.

"What about you, Toxo?" Rose asked.

"Raging bull," Dan said.

"I jacked out early."

"Jacked off early," Dan added. "Who with?"

"I don't know her name."

"Right hole?"

"Wrong woman," Pete said.

"Last time he got so pissed he shagged his sister," Dan added, for my benefit. "Up the fudgeshop and he didn't even notice."

And so it went on throughout the morning, all for my benefit, it seemed. No one appeared to do any buying or selling, except Toxo, who placed a £200 bet with Pete that he would bed the same woman again before Friday. Apparently the week before had been hectic, following a hike in interest rates by the Fed, but today was quiet. They were showing off, of course, but I could live with that. I wasn't being challenged, no one was questioning my story.

The morning came and went. Kenny, who dealt in Yen, was busy, but his day was nearly over. He had been in since three this morning. Rose came over and chatted, asked a few harmless questions. She behaved like a mother to her boys, none of whom looked over thirty. Pete showed me around the four screens (the end one was a touch screen telephone, connecting me instantly with dealers around the world), explained about PIBOR three-month futures and OTC swaps. He was helpful, but his breath stank of lager and spices and his leg kept bouncing up and down under the table as he talked. He hadn't been shagged for a very long time.

"Who sat here before?" I asked him, rolling back my chair. I put one foot on the edge of my desk and then took it off again. I had waited until midday before asking the question and it failed to sound casual.

"There?" I sensed the room go quiet for a moment, miss a beat. "Samantha."

I pressed my back teeth together and thought of the photo.

"Where is she now?" I asked breezily.

"God knows. She was here one day and gone the next. The last time we all saw her she was going out to buy everyone sandwiches. We thought she'd been run over."

"But she hadn't?"

"No. Phoned in at the end of the week. Said it was family trouble. Nothing personal, not with us anyway."

"Phoned?"

"Yeah. Or did she write to the boss? They had something going. I can't remember to be honest. She never came out with any of us."

"Except on Fridays," Charlie said, smiling slackly. He walked on past us, hands in pockets.

"Chuckster gave her one," Pete said, nodding at him.

Charlie – I could barely bring myself to call him Chuckster

– was how I had imagined everyone would be: a tosser. In fact he was the only one of his kind on the floor. He wore a multi-coloured waistcoat and rearranged his hair a lot. According to Pete, he didn't have to work, but he got bored doing nothing at the family home. A good man despite his wealth, that seemed to be the consensus. And he had bedded Samantha. Somehow we would have to become friends.

"Pastrami on Walnut, Tugger?" Toxo asked.

"I've done that," Pete replied. "O.d.'ed badly."

"Seven weeks wasn't it?"

"Too many. I feel a Ham on Mediterranean coming on."

"Mayonnaise?"

"Then again, there's always Hot Tuna Melt."

"If Birley's looks good I'll get a Melt. Otherwise Ham. Douglas?"

"Yeah, Feta on Marbled. Thanks."

"One Feta."

I had done my homework. A Berlin Whirlitzer was tempting, but I didn't want to show off.

I watched Pete shovel a spoonful of cornflakes down his mouth and return to work, scribbling some numbers on a notepad. He was ugly, unlaid, the butt of office jokes, but he was quick around his screens, mentally dextrous, a "rocket scientist" according to Dan. Everyone sung his praises whenever he was out of earshot: he knew more about the Deutsche Mark than the Bundesbank. After he had finished the deal he was on, I asked him what he had just done.

"300 Deutsche Marks. I've just agreed to buy them in one month's time from BZW."

I sniffed. I had been expecting larger amounts.

"Not that much, is it? 300 Deutsche Marks."

Pete looked at me, searching my face.

"300 million Deutsche Marks," he said earnestly.

I sniffed again. "Relatively speaking I mean." I remembered Charlotte's words on the phone the previous night –

"He's not stupid either" – and was grateful she hadn't heard me.

Just before lunch arrived, Pete inadvertently gave me my first lead about Samantha. It wasn't much but the day suddenly had a reason. He was explaining Reuters Dealing 2000, the e-mail system which dealers use to send messages to each other.

"You see here," he said, pointing at the second screen from the left. "Kredietbank are offering Deutsche Marks. Red March – that's March next year. They've sent that message to the JKA dealing room, and I've picked it up. It's a pretty unexciting rate so I type in 'NO TKS CIAO'."

"Could they send a message directly to you?" I asked.

"They use a general prefix for the bank, JKAB. Anyone in this room could take it. But as it's Deutsche Marks I'm the only one who's interested. So there's no need for it to be addressed directly to me."

"But if they wanted to?"

"They could, I suppose. Technically it's possible. You would have to set up your own prefix."

I looked at my own screens; they were still unintelligible. According to Walter, dormant terrorist units seldom knew who the other team members were. They never met until the day they were activated, opting to communicate cryptically. Walter had mentioned some ways they could stay in touch. Reuters 2000 was a possibility. It was a difficult subject to raise without arousing suspicion, but I needed to know what deals Samantha had made on the morning she left. Charlotte had said the City was paranoid about malpractice and kept tape recordings and printouts of everything. Was there a record of all these matey business transactions?

"I was thinking, Pete," I asked, failing to sound casual. "Is there something I can take home tonight, a transcript of conversations like the one you just had with Kredietbank?"

"A transcript?"

"Yeah, to familiarise myself with the jargon. It's all a bit foreign at the moment."

"Sure, sure. Not much has happened today. We could get a print-off from last Thursday. Bloody mayhem it was."

"I'd appreciate it."

"No problem. It's a good idea. Debbie dear," he called, stretching his fists into the air and yawning. Behind him was a partitioned-off room where three secretaries were typing.

"Yes Pete?"

"Dear Debbie, could you give my friend here a print-out of Thursday's transactions? A copy."

Debbie came over. She was compact, high-heeled.

"Just Deutsche Marks?" she asked.

"Yes," I said.

"That shouldn't be a problem. Do you want it now?"

"Thanks."

I watched Debbie totter back to her office. She removed a ticker-taped print-out from a filing cabinet and went over to the photocopier in the middle of the room. I needed to talk to her.

"Coffee?" I asked Pete.

"Just had one, thanks." And I had just got it for him. Cursing, I got up and walked towards the coffee machine, stopping at the photocopier.

"Thanks," I said, standing a little too close to Debbie.

"New here are you?" she asked.

"Yeah." I lowered my voice. "Is it possible to get print-outs from further back?"

"How far do you want to go?" She asked, enjoying the innuendo.

"Three weeks," I replied coldly.

"When do you want them by?"

"Tonight."

She looked at me for a moment, taken aback by my sudden bluntness.

"Research," I continued, letting my face dissolve into a smile. "I'm very keen."

"You're sitting by Pete aren't you?" she said, moving the conversation on. I nodded imperceptibly. "I'll bring them over."

It was a longshot, but judging from the first morning, dealers spent all day typing messages to each other. "Nothing there, bye for now." "Sorry, another time. Ciao." Samantha might just have received an unusual message.

"Douglas, line three. It's your girlfriend."

Toxo was holding his phone receiver in the air, looking down the row of desks, grinning. For a second I froze.

"How do I work this?" I asked, staring at the phone screen.

Pete was on the phone himself. He leant across and touched a box on the glass saying "line three", cupping his own phone under his chin.

"Douglas, is that you?"

"Charlotte," I said stiffly, trying to regain my composure. "How are you?"

"Don't sound so formal. I'm your girlfriend, remember? We had great sex last night. I was just ringing to see if you are alright."

"Everything's fine. Thanks."

"Will you be back for supper?"

"What? I'm not sure what's happening yet."

"Ring me. You should go out if you can. Have a few drinks."

"I won't be late."

I hung up. It was all too surreal. Way beyond. My old man would be ringing up next with tickets to the opera.

At five o'clock the office went across the road to The Frog and Radiator. We each drank five pints of beer in an hour. Everyone, that is, except Chuckster who had gone to the gym in the basement to tone his stomach muscles. I tried to buy my round but I wasn't allowed. I didn't complain (I was running out of money) and sat in the middle of a velvet banquette, penned in by Dan and Pete. Dan was pissing me off.

"Come on Douglas, what's the deal?" he asked.

"What do you mean?" I said, sensing trouble.

"I mean, we've never had anyone on work experience before."

"It's just the boss, trying to get something for nothing," Pete said.

"It doesn't add up," Dan said. "No offence, but I asked for another dealer."

"Give him a break, he's only just arrived," Pete said.

I drank heavily from my glass.

"The boss is a friend of the family, yes?" Dan continued. "Perhaps you're from the Fraud Squad. I don't mind if your dad's chairman of the Bank of England. I just need to know."

I struggled to gauge how serious the conversation was becoming.

"Why put me on Deutsche Marks if you think I'm shit?" I said.

"I never said you were no good."

"Because I'll fuck up quicker and you can get someone else?"

Dan returned my stare and then looked away. I had to keep control.

"Ignore him," Pete said quietly to me. "Whose shout is it?"

"Pete," Dan asked. "How much would we have to pay Debbie to suck your dick?"

I needed a break, and squeezed out to the Gents. The

urinals were all occupied and I went into one of the cubicles. There was a window above me and I thought of Martin. I came back out, washed my face in a basin, and returned to the bar. There was a seat next to Toxo. I could relate to him, he was an outsider. There was something desperate in his manner, the false camaraderie. Maybe it was because he was the only black guy on the dealing floor. Like Pete, he took a lot of ribbing. Some of it induced fragile, token smiles, like my own. The blacks I knew would consider working in the City on a par with joining the police. Coconut stuff.

"Dan, he's the boss, right?" I asked him.

"Yeah, he's in charge of the floor. Briggs is the big boss. He wasn't in today."

"You like Dan?"

"He's a good man. Don't tell him I said that. No, he's alright, works us hard."

"He's an arsehole."

"He's always like that to begin with."

"Where's he from?"

"From? Does that matter?"

I didn't answer, hoping the silence would coax out more information.

"He used to work on the LIFFE exchange, in the Sterling pit. You know, the guys in bright jackets, doing all the funny hand signals. Then he moved up here."

"Most of these guys, they've been to university?" I asked.

"Maybe half. It varies. Dan left school at sixteen and became a runner in the pit. Pete read pure Maths at Cambridge."

"You been here long?"

"Me? A couple of years."

"And you like it?"

"Yeah, it's a good laugh."

"Despite the hassle."

"Hassle?" He looked thrown.

"Gyp. Aggro."

"Where you coming from, man?" he asked laughing, letting some steam out of the conversation.

"You get a lot of lip."

"I give as good as I get. The markets were quiet today."

"Hey Toxo!" Kev shouted across the table. He was sitting next to Debbie. "How many two p's was it? She doesn't believe me."

"Forty-three."

"Forty-three?" I asked.

"It's nothing. Crazy man." Toxo was laughing.

"He once put forty-three two pence pieces up his fore-skin," Pete said, sliding past. "Forty fucking three! They wrote about him in *The Lancet*."

At six o'clock, I made my excuses and left. Clearly the manager had taken me on under the guise of work experi-ence. It was a good story. It kept my options open, allowed me to leave the firm without suspicion.

I meandered across the street, wondering whether Chuck-ster was still downstairs in the basement fine-tuning his pectorals. Then I saw him, coming out of the office. He went to the boot of a black Porsche, parked on the other side of the street. Opening it, he pulled out a pot plant, snapped the lid shut and went back through the revolving doors. I watched, surprised. I was too drunk to talk. There was no rush, I told myself. But I knew there was. This guy had been with Samantha, poked one of the people who had killed Annalese.

"Chuckster," I bayed, waving my arm in the air. I prayed no one I knew would ever hear me. Chuckster was coming back out of the building.

"Douglas. Been across the road with the lads?"

"Yeah. They like their drink."

"Dear chap, it's only Monday."

"You trading in plants, then?"

"Oh that. No, I've been meaning to bring one in for ages. We've got dozens of the damn things at home. The one in reception seems so sad, don't you think?"

"Can't say I noticed."

"You see, that's my point entirely. Nobody even notices them anymore. Can I give you a lift somewhere?"

I looked at the black Porsche, its fat bitumen wheels. In the eighties, I had danced on the roofs of a dozen of them. They still had an aggressive opulence, the dual exhausts, the smugness of the low curves.

"Which way you heading?" I asked, hoping the answer was north.

"Across the river. Battersea any good?"

"Near enough."

I climbed in and sat rigidly in the moulded seat, barely believing what I was doing. I didn't say anything as Chuckster twisted and turned down to the Thames. Twice I was asked if everything was okay. The heating was adjusted, the angle of the seat was changed in three dimensions, the balance of the CD player was altered in favour of the rear speakers.

Then I began to relax as we accelerated down the Embankment, the lights on Chelsea Bridge burning like crossed stars. Prodigy was coming at me from four sides (Walter's choice of music had been way off target). I was enjoying myself, I had to admit it. The power of the engine was invigorating, pressing me against the seat, cosseting me from the outside world.

The company could have been better, though. Chuckster was from another planet, untroubled, languid in his arm movements, most comfortable in life leaning gently backwards. I didn't have to worry about talking. Conversation flowed freely: the lights in Regent Street ("so sweet"), the increase in river traffic ("so obviously right, somehow"), the charm of London's parks ("so European, so un us"), all interspersed with unprying questions. "Had I seen the lights?" "Did I like parks?" and so on. But he never mentioned work or brought up anything remotely uncomfortable. Once I tried to get on to the subject of the bombing campaign, but the conversation was steered gently in the opposite direction – the inordinate amount of maintenance involved in vintage cars (a friend of his had his Bentley damaged in the Baltic Exchange blast). Undeterred, I tried again.

"I think I was at school with Samantha West," I began, trying not to slur my words. "The name sounds very familiar."

"Now there's someone I can't fathom. It's not true by the way. I didn't 'have her' as Toxo probably said. What a preposterous fellow he is. Lovely but quite ridiculous. I just took her out for a drink. Felt sorry for the old girl."

"Why?"

"She didn't seem awfully good at making friends."

"Were you surprised when she left?"

"Yes and no. She wasn't happy at the firm, that was patently obvious. But the manner of her departure, now that did surprise me. Nobody leaves at lunch-time on a Wednesday. Particularly that Wednesday. We were about to be given our bonus. And she knew that."

"Maybe she didn't need the money."

"Could be, could be. But I've never heard of a dealer turning down a bonus. It had been a good quarter, too."

Chuckster never disagreed with anything either. The only contretemps of the whole journey took place while we were waiting at the lights to turn left over Albert Bridge. A young kid in a baseball hat cleaned his front and back windows. I waited to see what would happen, whether Chuckster would pay him. He didn't. Instead he smiled politely as the child went about his business and then pulled slowly away when the lights changed. "Peasant," he muttered quietly.

The car nosed into Clapham West Side. Chuckster had immediately offered to drop me off at the house when he heard how close I lived.

"Here we are dear chap. And your wife waiting in the window. The pleasures of domestic life."

I glanced across at the house. Charlotte was at the kitchen sink, looking out. She gave a little wave when she saw me.

"She's not my wife."

"Good man," he said, leaning across and closing my door. "Your secret's safe with me."

"See you tomorrow." At least it would impress the neighbours.

CHAPTER 16

"Jesus fuck. That man's unreal. He has no idea how the rest of this country is living. Unless people take the fight to him, why should he? He drives from Battersea to the office and back again in his pissing Porsche without a care in the world."

"Do you want a drink? Sherry?" Charlotte paused, barely suppressing a giggle. I ignored her. "Gin and Tonic?" she said, one hand over her mouth. "Special Brew?"

We were standing in the kitchen. I had taken my jacket and tie off and was in the process of releasing my shoes, hopping about on one foot as I fiddled with the laces.

"I don't even blame the bastard," I said, almost falling over. "It's not his fault he's so fucking ignorant. He's lived all his life in another solar system."

Charlotte went to the fridge, pulled out a can of Special Brew, and handed it to me. She then sat down at the table and poured herself a glass of white wine from an open bottle.

"So, how did the rest of the day go? Did you make any money?"

"No. I didn't. I hope they are paying me for this."

"Would you take their money if they were?"

"No I'd stick it up Chuckster's arse so he knows what it's like to be buggered."

"The Porsche was a nice touch. There can't be too many of those left in the City."

"They should all be melted down. It even had a fax machine in the back for fucksake."

"Have a shower, unwind. You've had a tiring day at the office."

"Ha fucking ha. I'll tell you another thing. Samantha West had something going with the chairman."

"What?" Her face tightened.

"Apparently she and him were close."

"Who told you?"

"Tugger, Chuckster, Johnny Biggles, who cares? One of them did."

"Are you sure?"

"If you don't believe anything I say, we are wasting our time."

I walked towards the door, undoing the clip on my trousers. I had to get shot of my clothes.

"Okay. You're sure," she said, watching me go.

Upstairs in my room I cut a couple of lines. I was more tired than I realised, more drunk too. I tried to think things through, but I was feeling increasingly paranoid. If Samantha West was close to the chairman, she was just being careful, taking out clever insurance. It was a risk, but her cover was less likely to be blown if she was sleeping with the man who employed her. Was it just coincidence, then, that this particular chairman was also friendly with MI5? She never realised how close she was to the enemy. Or perhaps MI5 knew her real identity and made sure she was killed. In which case what was I doing poncing about in the City? It was all part of a plot to rescue me, bring a fallen citizen back into the family fold.

"Do you want me to iron your shirt?" Charlotte asked through the closed door.

"It's still in its wrapper."

"Remember to take the pins out."

"Yes, mummy," I said and gave her the finger.

A few minutes later, I walked unsteadily down the stairs

with the inch-thick pile of print-out Debbie had given me. Charlotte had started cooking in the kitchen.

"I presume you like fish?" she said.

"If I have to."

I sat down at the table and searched energetically through the reams of paper, as if I was letting out rope. I was going to crack the City, suss its systems and then shaft it. The print was small. I closed my eyes, swallowed.

"What's that?" she asked.

"It's a record of all the conversations between JKA dealers. They flog money to each other on a thing called Reuters 2000."

I was slurring my words and could feel her gaze linger on me.

"I know the system."

"I thought it would be interesting," I said, pausing, "to know what Samantha West was saying to people before she let off her bomb."

"How far back does it go?"

"Three weeks. She might have used Reuters to talk. Providing they're all dealers. Which we don't know for sure, of course."

"Walter's pretty certain."

Pretty certain? What weren't they telling me? Samantha and the chairman: that wasn't right. I stopped sifting through the print-out and looked up at Charlotte. Her back was turned. She had switched on a food mixer, and I watched some carrots spin and dissolve, one piece bobbing, avoiding the chop. Quietly, I stood up and walked towards her. I tried to stand still but I was swaying. As I rocked forward I grabbed her around the waist, pinning her arms.

"Somebody's lying," I said, bending her back against my leg.

"Dutchie, get off. You're hurting me."

I was squeezing with all my strength, much tighter than I realised.

"Walter – how much does he know?" I shouted.

"He's told you everything. Let me go, please, you're hurting."

"So why was Samantha West pally-pally with the chairman?"

"I don't know."

"You said he is a friend of MI5. What's he doing then, fucking a bloody bomber?"

"He didn't know. It was just chance."

"Am I being set up?"

"No. Please."

I let her go, tossing her away from me, and stood there, wavering. She went to the sink, poured herself a glass of water and walked towards the door.

"That's not the way this is going to work, Dutchie. You're drunk. Been out with the boys. That's fine. But don't ever touch me again."

She left the kitchen and went upstairs. Annalese was right. Chemicals made me feel hunted.

I poured some water as well, drank four glasses quickly, and sat down at the table. I was just being paranoid. Picking up the print-out again I found the day of the bombing, December 22nd, a Monday. Some of the messages were signed PM, others SW. Pete Marshall, Samantha West. Dealings with Citibank, Credit Agricole, BZW. It meant nothing to me. I would have to ask Pete if there was anything strange about them.

Charlotte came back into the kitchen a few minutes later and went to the stove. On her way out, she dropped a bowl of carrot soup down on the table and took hers to the sitting room where she was watching television. We were obviously eating separately. The soup smelt good. There was a fish pie in the oven, she said. I didn't feel guilty. It was a score which needed to be settled, a return handshake. After I had drunk the soup I went through to the sitting room. Charlotte was sitting on the floor, one arm on the seat of the sofa. She didn't look up.

"I've found the day," I said, sitting on the other end of the sofa and holding out a single sheet of print-out. She looked at me and then back at the television.

"Anything interesting?" she asked.

"You tell me. It's all bollocks."

"You're not worried about going in tomorrow, are you Dutchie?"

Her sudden concern surprised me. "Why? Should I be?"

"No. But if anything ever bothers you, talk to me about it first. You'll make mistakes if you're nervous. Let me see that."

I passed her the sheet of paper which she looked at for a while.

"Where do you go during the day?" I asked, with as much charm as I could muster.

"You don't expect me to answer that, do you?"

"Just wondered. Somewhere in the City. It's got to be. Unless you get on the tube and come back here again."

"It's a small PR firm. Awful place."

"Don't go in then."

"I have to be credible too."

"Why?"

"In case we go out."

"Out? Will we have to?"

"If you're asked."

"None of the blokes in the office are involved in this. They're wankers but they're not terrorists."

"Maybe not. But you can't afford to arouse suspicion. People talk. The City's a small place."

"What do you think?" I asked, nodding at the print-out in her hand.

"Ask someone about Kiruna Kredit. Casually, though. I haven't heard of them before. They were offering Swedish kronas against pesetas. That's a nightmare transaction. No one in their right minds would even say no thanks."

"No one except Samantha."

CHAPTER 17

There was more activity the next morning. The ceiling seemed lower, the intercoms more urgent. Dealers were standing up, calling across the room. Pete acknowledged me with a barely raised a hand. He was talking on the phone, leg still bouncing. (No one had offered Debbie enough.) I sat down and logged on. My instructions remained the same as yesterday: watch unless the chairman said otherwise.

I poured myself some cereal, read Dan's copy of *The Sun*, and waited for Pete to calm down. Over by the coffee machine I looked closer at a pinboard covered with holiday snaps: Dave and Toxo posing in sunglasses on a ski-slope, Pete wiped out, suspended upside down in some red fencing. I looked harder, searching for Samantha, and spotted her in turquoise at the back of the group. She had been thorough. Would I have to go skiing?

"Douglas? Simon Briggs."

I turned round to see the chairman. He looked younger than expected, tanned with short, sun-bleached hair, and was standing too close to me. He shook my hand. "Do you want to come through?" he asked. His breath was minty, his teeth too perfect. He also had a faint Afrikaans accent which hardened the occasional consonant.

Briggs's office was at the far end of the dealing room, near the Yen. It wasn't spacious; a chair either side of an oak desk and a row of screens along one wall. A Nike sports bag was by the door, the towelled handle of a squash racket sticking out of one end. His desk was clear except for a

Union Jack, smaller than the ones outside, and a photograph of a blonde woman.

"Have a seat. How are you enjoying yourself?" he asked with absurd enthusiasm, closing the door.

"There's a lot to take in," I said, sitting down.

"Of course there is. It must all seem very mysterious." He moved round to his side of the desk and settled back in his chair, looking at me as if we were old friends. "MI5 and I go back a long way," he said, switching the subject suddenly, enjoying the conspiracy. "I was only too pleased to help again."

What did he mean by "again"?

"Any idea who's behind them? The bombs?"

I didn't reply. I was impatient to leave.

"I'm sorry. I shouldn't have asked. Pete will take care of you."

"He's already shown me around."

Briggs stood up energetically and walked over to the window, where he fingered a hole in the blind.

"Pete's a good operator," he said, squinting out through the gap he had now made. He had his back to me. "Watch what he buys and then look for a similar deal elsewhere. Hedge carefully and you'll be okay."

"I was planning on just watching."

"Why?" he said, turning. "Get your gloves off. Enjoy yourself. You might as well. I don't suppose you will be with us for ever."

"As long as it takes," I said, watching him sit down again. He had thick, white nails, scalloped and well nourished.

"Quite. There's one other thing." His confidence had suddenly given way to awkwardness. He put one finger in his mouth and began to rub a gum, staring at the floor. "I gather you've been asking around about Samantha West. I'd rather you didn't."

"I was just curious."

"I know, fine. It's not good for morale, that's all, when someone leaves the firm. Bit of a shower. They start asking me for more money."

He pulled a broad, fluoride grin, trying to make light of it. How much did he know?

"Nothing happened to her, did it?" I asked, conscious that I shouldn't.

"Not at all. Family trouble." He paused and sat back again, adopting his former, more chummy tone. "I always wanted to be a spy, you know, but they wouldn't have me. Wrong university. Wrong handshake," he added, laughing. I had to get out of there. The man's zest was overbearing.

"Pete's waiting for me," I said, looking at my watch. "The RPI's out at 9.30."

"Of course. Money calls."

He went to the door and held it open for me.

"Any problems, you know where I am. Go well."

I vowed to be back, with a machete. I walked past him, feeling his light fingers on my shoulder. *Only too pleased to help again.* The company had assisted MI5 in the past, that's all. Walter had described him as a friend of the service.

Or did it mean that I wasn't the first to be doing this? If so, what had happened to the others? *The terrorists will kill you if they suspect anything.*

The rest of the morning was frustrating. I wanted to ring Charlotte but I couldn't risk talking to her about anything. There was little opportunity to ask anyone about the printout. Pete was on a roll and had lost interest in me. Everyone else was locked into their own screen dialogues. No one was calling on Swedish krona or pesetas. It was all Deutsche Mark, dollar, lira. The RPI came and went, causing a brief flurry of activity. I watched the bank initials flash up on the screen, the jokey messages between Pete and faceless people in Geneva, Paris, Frankfurt. Did they know how ugly he was?

"Pete, catch," Dan said.

Pete swivelled on his chair just in time to catch a bunch of keys sailing through the air.

"Take a look at the new phones, yes?" Dan said. "They've just installed them down at the back-up."

"Today?"

"Please. Briggs says it's important. Enterprise House, near the Arena. Should be exactly the same system as this one."

Dan walked away.

"What's that all about?" I asked.

"Oh, nothing. A pain in the arse. Why can't he go?" Pete glanced at Dan, who was fixing a coffee.

"Go where?"

"Docklands. We've got a contingency dealing room there."

"What for?"

"All the big firms have them these days. In case we get bombed."

"What, you mean if this place blows, we all move down to Docklands?"

"In one. It's identical to here, only more cramped, if that's possible."

At twelve I offered to get in the sandwiches and took everyone's orders. I wondered whether I should ask for money. Nobody was offering. I had given Pete a couple of quid yesterday. These people were tight, that's why they were rich. What did I expect, charity workers?

Pret A Manger was packed and I took my place in the queue. As I drew closer to the till I reached for the wad of notes folded neatly in my back pocket. It was empty. I sniffed and peeled off the queue towards the coolers at the back of the shop. I didn't have a bank account yet and the money was on my chest of drawers at the house. I could see it clearly. Either I was going to leave the baguettes in a neat pile on the shelf or I had to walk out of the shop with them under my arm. I couldn't return to the office without them. They would think I was mad. A dealer with no money?

I looked at the shop entrance. It was narrow, near the till, and jammed with people squeezing past each other. I could try breezing out but it wasn't ideal. There were two women on the tills, maybe a hidden camera somewhere. Calmly I rejoined the queue and waited my turn.

When there were only three people left between me and the counter I looked out of the window for someone to pass, someone with a bag. Where was the street life in this place? A woman in her thirties, plastic bag in each hand, walked into frame. Perfect.

"Excuse me," I said suddenly. "That lady's just left without paying."

"Which one?" a cashier asked. Heads turned and there were murmurs.

"Her, with the bags," I shouted. "I saw her filling them with rolls a second ago, just now."

Both women moved to the door. I followed them, aware of the commotion brewing nicely behind me.

"Disgusting," someone said.

I turned to join in the chorus. "And it's us who have to pay in the long run."

"Where did she go?" the cashier asked.

"There, just crossing the road," I said, pointing down the street. "With the bags."

The cashier walked, then started to run awkwardly after her, wobbling on her clogs. "Hello? Excuse me!" she called.

The other woman stood on the doorstep, hands on hips, watching her colleague.

"Can someone kindly serve those of us who choose to pay for our sandwiches?" a man said from inside the shop.

The lady went back in. I took one look at the other cashier, now talking to the woman with the bags, and stepped out of the shop in the other direction.

It wasn't the most relaxing lunch-break and I had a problem on my hands next time around. I couldn't go back to Pret A Manger. Would anyone notice if I ordered from elsewhere? These people were connoisseurs. They would notice.

Dropping Toxo's Spicy Chicken in front of him, I hung around, leaning against the edge of his desk. Pete was across the other side of the floor.

"Do you know a bank called Kiruna Kredit?" I asked, tucking into my Icelandic prawns.

"Never sold me anything," Toxo said. "Why?"

"They called on Swedish kronas against pesetas. Made 32/28 in three months."

"Crazy, man. It's probably some part-time outfit in Dubai, somewhere like that. They come on occasionally, time wasters. Don't touch them. Dan, have you . . ."

" . . . Why do they call you Toxo?" I said, interrupting him. "Why?"

"Just wondered," I said, smiling.

Dan overheard the conversation and came over. "Because he arrives in the morning still intoxicated, that's why. Toxo Thompson. A very toxic individual."

Toxo smiled proudly and turned to his screens. At least he had a nickname, a bit of character. I suddenly wanted to take him into my confidence, explain what I was doing, why I was asking questions. There was no need to pretend with him, he would understand.

Instead I went back to my desk to watch the PIBOR futures rise and fall all afternoon.

When I got home that night Charlotte was out. She had been back and gone again. No note, just her work coat draped over a kitchen chair. I felt exhausted. If something had happened in the afternoon I might have been less tired, but nothing happened and that was even worse. Pete shadowed me through a small deal, but I was made to hedge it, which irked me. Then it annoyed me that I was irked. I hadn't made a killing, but so what? I had to remind myself what I was doing.

Remember the coffee farmers.

I found the money where I had left it and took my suit off, treading on the trousers as I left them. I briefly contemplated some coke but decided against it. Until I had the measure of my new routine, I would keep the nose clean. I owed it to Annalese.

Downstairs I wandered around listlessly, flicked through the TV channels, read a Blockbuster Video catalogue, went back into the kitchen, thumped the wall. What was I doing, working in the City? A Tops Pizza menu had been pinned to the side of the dresser, left thoughtfully by Walter. I ordered a Four Seasons, then rang back, cancelled it, had a row. I hadn't heard anything from Walter. Charlotte was my only contact, the only evidence that my fake life was real. Walter said he would drop by at the end of the week. I was looking forward to reporting back, letting him know that I could shovel this capitalism shit, that my old life was one of choice, an informed decision. "We need to talk," I scribbled on a scrap of paper, and was asleep by the time Charlotte returned.

Sleepy-eyed, Charlotte stood by the sink, looking out over the black common, shivering in the cold. It was ten to six in the morning and I was surprised to find her making coffee.

"I got your note," she said.

"Yeah, listen. I saw Simon Briggs yesterday, the chairman. He's a friend of MI5, right?"

"A very old friend."

"So that's why he says to me, 'I'm only too pleased to help *again*'."

"Is that what you've got me up for?" she asked, turning.

"Yeah."

She sighed and took two mugs over to the coffee pot. "He's helped in the past. That's all he meant."

"You see, I thought he might have meant that I wasn't the first person to go after the bombers. That others had tried and failed. Which means someone is lying to me."

"No, He didn't mean that. I've told you. No one is lying. You're the first."

The rest of the day passed uneventfully. The quiet markets allowed me to blend in seamlessly as a spectator. I wasn't going to risk dealing again. I might get hooked. Charlotte had put my mind at rest, but an unfocused doubt still lingered. Walter hadn't told me everything, I was sure of that.

After work I dipped seven pints, the same as everyone else, and just resisted headbutting Chuckster. He was too easy-going, too affable. On Thursday I went to the pub again, only it was eight pints this time. Friday, they said, was drinking day.

The remorseless schedule was taking its toll, physically and financially. Being skint was the only real threat to my cover. Rounds were expensive – £18 a shout – and bets were constantly being placed in the office – £500 that Manchester United would beat Newcastle on Saturday, £50 on the Dallas Cowboys winning the NFL Super Bowl. I had £40 left in my pocket and explained I wasn't a gambling man, but it was untypical, eye-catching. Dealers gambled.

Homelife was no more eventful. I accepted that Charlotte could have been worse. In the mornings we went through the charade of kissing each other goodbye; in the evenings, we talked briefly about any developments at work, but kept our distance. She was more wary of me when I was drunk. We didn't share any more joints and she kept out of the bathroom when I was having a bath. The anonymous routine suited us both. If we discussed anything other than work we would argue, maybe even fight, we both knew that.

I tried a few times to ring Annalese's mum, but without success. I wasn't sure I could cope anyway. Leafe would be missing Annalese. At least my life had a purpose of sorts. One night I had a nightmare about Matt, Katrina's old boyfriend. When I woke up I couldn't remember much, but he had been talking about Annalese again, making wild accusations. Katrina had kept shouting that it wasn't true – "she would never do a thing like that" – but I didn't know what either of them were talking about.

On Saturday morning, at the end of my second week at work, I slept until noon. Occasionally I broke the surface, peered out at the magnitude of my hangover, and slid under again. I had lost count of how many pints I had drunk. When I finally stirred from my room for some breakfast, Charlotte kept an eye on me, more so than usual. She called out my name when I climbed back upstairs, checking to see if I was still in the house and she came with me when I went out for some air. She apologised, said it was orders, and linked her arm through mine as we walked across the common to the shops. She smiled a lot and told me not to look so glum. People might be watching. Walter was satisfied with how things were going, she said. He wouldn't be visiting. Officially he was giving me two months to come up with something; unofficially, he had expected results in two weeks.

If things continued in the way they were going, a part of me wouldn't mind if it took two years. Samantha West and the other bombers had chosen well when they settled on the City for their day jobs. I had worked out what I was supposed to be doing, which was a mistake. I was beginning to savour the mayhem. I liked trying to bust the complex systems designed to hold us in check. I was warming to the anarchy of it all.

CHAPTER 18

"It's no different from a bingo hall," Charlotte said, stepping out of the taxi.

"You don't have to wear a jacket and tie for bingo."

I followed her on to the pavement. She nodded at me to pay the driver. I looked at her for a moment – why couldn't she pay him? – and then turned to the cabbie. We had to keep up appearances. I had taken black cabs before, but this was the first time I had paid for one.

I wasn't happy. It was approaching midnight and, unlike me, Edgware Road was showing few signs of tiredness. The shops were still open and people were buying their groceries, even getting their hair cut. The entire dealing room, in its wisdom, had decided to meet up at a West End casino, just in case there wasn't enough adrenalin coursing through our bodies already. I couldn't get out of it. Toxo had taken the trouble to sign me and Charlotte up as members on Friday (thereby complying with the casino's twenty-four-hour membership rule).

Charlotte was genuinely looking forward to it and had dressed up for the occasion: pearl choker, ankle length evening dress (black and split), fur collared coat, heels. I was in my only suit. I had wanted to wear a discreet earstud but she had forbidden me. She liked it, she said, which surprised me, but the casino management might not.

We found the casino easily enough. It was the building with the string of white limos outside. The doormen, two chiselled blocks of granite, searched me more thoroughly than the others in the short queue. Charlotte stood patiently, smiling as I held my arms out. I sweated trouble like garlic.

"What the fuck are we doing here?" I said after they had finished, making sure they were still in earshot. I strode up some stairs under a huge chandelier and on into the main gambling hall. Charlotte followed me, catching up with a trot.

"We're here because dealers like gambling," she said quietly. "We'll do more harm than good if you start behaving like a child."

I stopped, turned towards her, checked myself. The cavalry had arrived. Chuckster was coming towards us, cigarette in hand.

"Douglas, splendid to see you," he said. "I didn't think you were coming."

He shook my hand, beamed at Charlotte, then looked back at me. I turned away, gazing out across the roulette wheels.

"I'm Charlotte," she said, looking briefly at me and greeting Chuckster.

"Charlie. The lads in the office all call me Chuckster," he said, glancing at me again. I was still ignoring him. "Have you spent your entrance chip?"

"We've only just arrived," Charlotte said.

"Follow me, follow me. I'm feeling so incredibly lucky tonight. Anything could happen."

Charlotte tugged my sleeve. "Come on. Try to be human."

I followed on behind them, dropping back a few yards. Chuckster was wearing a dinner jacket, wing collar and scarlet bow-tie. His waistcoat looked Indian, woven from gold and silver thread. The entire hall had an air of unrestrained opulence. The carpets were deep piled, blood-red, the low slung chandeliers throwing clandestine light on the gamblers below. There were four roulette wheels towards the front of the hall, one of which was crowded with punters,

Arabs and Chinese. The others were empty and staffed by young croupiers – short red skirts, diaphanous white blouses – spinning the wheels listlessly, chatting amongst themselves.

In the shadowy distance six kidney-shaped blackjack tables stood waiting like banquet stalls, cards fanned across the blue beige. There were two more tables in the centre of the room, one of them crowded, the other with a man playing on his own, shoulders hunched in deep concentration. Along the side of the hall another game was in progress, a bald croupier flicking cards over with a flat wooden palette. Ten, maybe twelve people were playing.

Chuckster signed Charlotte in at the reception desk, and beckoned me to join them. I left them to it, watching as they moved over to one of the empty roulette tables, where they sat down and spread a few chips. Charlotte was smiling, enjoying herself. I was drawn by a large crowd around the main roulette wheel. After signing in, I went over to stand at the back of the group, jostling to see what was happening. An immaculately dressed Arab pushed me to one side. The atmosphere was tense: money mixed with muscle. I moved around to the rope which cordoned off the wheel, and had a better view down the full length of the table.

At the far end a man in his sixties with wind-tunnelled grey hair was smoking a cigar. The people around him studied every move he made. On his right a stunning woman in crimson whispered something in his ear, then checked numbers off a list with a pencil in front of her. She looked like his moll, a third of his age. The man half-heartedly waved a hand in the air. A croupier dropped a chip into the tip box. "Thank you sir," the staff all chimed, obsequiously. As the wheel span again, silent, oiled, the man began to build a small house on thirty-six, yellow rectangular chips with 10,000 written on them. I had heard about high-rollers but never seen one before. I had never been near a casino, except to break the windows of one in Birmingham a few years back. (Once or twice I had watched a game of poker at The George, in a back room after hours, but never played it.)

Two along from the old man I spotted Pete, hemmed in on all sides by Chinese. Pete was concentrating hard, writing something down, playing the rocket scientist. He looked hassled. Across the table Dan was drawing on a cigarette. Sat next to him, presumably, was his woman, talking intimately in one ear. She looked older than him, more sophisticated, even taller. Dan watched the wheel as she talked, caught my eye through the smoke, and stared past me. I had a problem with Dan.

"Won yourself a fortune?" It was Toxo, grinning at my shoulder.

"Not yet." We both watched the ball stop on eight. I glanced at the old man. He was unmoved as the croupier bulldozed his house.

"That man at the end, how much has he just lost?" I asked.

"Forty-five."

"Grand?"

"He made sixty the go before. Hey Douglas, that your woman over there?" He nodded in the direction of Charlotte, who was listening attentively to Chuckster.

"Charlotte, yes. Have I introduced you?"

"Not yet. Far be it from me man, but Chuckster moves. He knows how to turn on the charm."

"I noticed."

"You rowed or something?"

"No." I thought about the situation for a moment. I was being asked to feel jealous because a woman called Charlotte was being chatted up by a dickhead in a dinner jacket. Reluctantly I found it in myself to say something, to react.

"She likes casinos more than me."

"She's fit. I would get him off your screen."

"Yeah. Listen, you're right. I'm bushed tonight. Thanks."

I put my hand on Toxo's shoulder in appreciation and walked away from the roulette wheel. I wandered around the two central blackjack tables. The man sitting on his own looked like a Colombian gangster. Half his face was hidden by mopped black hair, the other half obscured by pillars of yellow chips. I looked closer. Each chip had "50" on it, running through the pillars like a stick of rock. The man was winning serious money. A senior member of staff looked on unimpressed, arms folded. Another punter, an American who was standing with his legs firmly apart, kept talking, offering advice, commenting, as if he knew better than the gangster. Clearly he didn't.

"Give the guy a Rembrandt," he said to the croupier. Everyone ignored him. "I tell you," he continued in a drawl, turning to me, "when that paint hits the felt, and the bank busts, man, it's the best feeling in the world."

I moved away in case I hit him. Charlotte and Chuckster looked quite a couple, I had to admit. Her in pearls, him in his techni-coloured dreamcoat. It was hard to believe but he now appeared to be smoking through a slender silver cigarette holder, waving it around as he talked. I wanted to go home, but I couldn't. It was time to reclaim my woman.

Approaching the couple from behind, I came up fast and put my arm on Charlotte's shoulder. In the same moment as she turned I planted a wet kiss on her lips and somehow spoke with tender intimacy.

"How's it going, darling?"

It was worth it just for the expressions on both their faces. I couldn't tell who was the more surprised. Charlotte, the professional, regained her composure quicker and put her hand gently on mine.

"Coming to join us?" she asked.

"Thought I might. Just had to get a feel for the place first, smell the money, check it was clean."

"Quite right, quite right," Chuckster said, moving his leg imperceptibly away from Charlotte's. He didn't know where to look.

"So, what do I do with this?" I said, holding up the chip I had been given on arrival.

"Put it on a number dear chap and pray to your god," Chuckster said, exhaling smoke with a toss of his head.

"Charlotte, when's your birthday?" I asked, regretting the words instantly.

"It would have been nice if he could remember, wouldn't it?" she said, turning to Chuckster, covering for me with a smile.

"Happens to the best of us," Chuckster said.

I thought fast.

"Eight it is, then," I said, leaning across the table and placing my bet. At least I could remember Annalese's birthday. We watched the ball bounce and clatter against the spin of the wheel, give up the fight, come to rest. Eight it was.

"Good call," Chuckster said enthusiastically. He seemed genuinely pleased.

"Beginner's luck," I said, watching with surprise as the croupier pushed a stack of chips my way.

"Fortune favours the brave," Charlotte whispered in my ear.

I tried not to think about what I was doing. I was still coming to terms with the ease with which the old man had just lost forty-five big ones. Charlotte was ordering my chips for me, making them into neat, equal piles.

"Do you play polo, Douglas?" Chuckster suddenly asked.

I laughed but somehow made it sound like a cough. Charlotte was in trouble, too.

"Can't say I do, Chuckster."

"You see, I was wondering whether you and your lovely lady friend here would like to come along and watch a game. Next weekend perhaps. If the weather's bad, why not come up anyway."

I couldn't think of anything to say. Fortunately Charlotte stepped in, ending the stunned silence.

"That's a lovely idea, very sweet," she said, pausing. Come on, I thought, but . . . "But Dutchie's allergic to horses. Something in the mane."

"Really? Who's Dutchie?" Chuckster asked, confused.

"Douglas, I mean Douglas," she said quickly.

"It's the same with cats. I just start sneezing and can't stop," I said.

"Oh dear. You poor fellow. Charlotte, why don't you come up first and Douglas could follow later, once the all clear bell has sounded and they're safely back in stables. Good idea?"

He was a persistent bugger, was Chuckster. Charlotte valiantly made excuses for the next few weekends while I won again, this time with my own birthday. In an act of recklessness, I had put ten chips on twelve and had pocketed £350. Next go I put it all on red, trying to rid myself of my capitalist gains, and duly doubled my money with another twelve. It was getting embarrassing. Toxo came and joined us, along with Pete, who was looking forlorn and broke.

"Hey, my main man," Toxo said, putting an arm on my shoulder. "You're breaking the bank."

"What you should do now is put half of it on red again," Pete said earnestly. "If it's black, stay with red and put it all on. Keep doubling if you lose. It's the only way."

"So speaks a man who's just lost four grand. Ignore him. He's full of systems, full of shit. Sorry," Toxo added politely, for Charlotte's benefit.

I was enjoying myself too much to listen to Pete and his systems. My own method was entirely random, inspired by ignorance, infallible. Chuckster left me to it. Charlotte put her hand conspicuously high up on my warm thigh, watching, encouraging, telling me I was doing just fine.

At 1 a.m. voices were raised at the far end of the hall. I looked up to see the doormen escorting the man who had been playing blackjack on his own. He was being walked to the door, silently, offering no resistance.

"What's all that about?" I asked Pete, who was still trying to fathom my system.

"I was watching him earlier. He might have been counting cards."

"Cheating?"

"Technically it's not. He's just trying to predict which cards are still in the shoe."

"So where's the problem?"

"Casinos don't like it. Card-counters can wipe out a week's profit in one sitting."

I watched as the man calmly put on his coat and left. I wished I had talked to him.

By 2 a.m. I had made £6,000. Charlotte had to pull me away to the taxi. It could have been more, of course, but I had lost £2,000 in a single, reckless bet just after 1 a.m. I had enjoyed myself, particularly after Pete explained that casinos, in the generous spirit of free market capitalism, always ensured that the odds were stacked firmly against the punter. How could they lose? And yet here I was making a small fortune. That made me feel better. Casino as enemy. I could live with that.

As we got into our taxi, however, the door held open for us by yet another man in a uniform calling me sir, the buzz faded. Behind our taxi a black executive Volvo estate pulled up. A man in a dinner jacket and white silk scarf stepped out, and walked into the casino. More idle rich.

"You were right. Stick to bingo," Charlotte teased. We

were sitting at opposite ends of the wide cab seat. Hostilities had been resumed.

"Six thousand pounds," she continued. "My, that should stoke the fires of the revolution for a while."

"Shut it. Alright? You've made your point."

She sat silently for a few seconds, but she was unable to resist continuing.

"Chuckster's a nice man, isn't he? A real sweetie."

I put my head against the cold metal of the cab, feigning sleep. I didn't have much of a case. I knew that, she knew that. If I had lost £6,000, that would have been an act of obscene opulence. But I had won it. Walked in with nothing, come out wads up. Beaten the system, just like the card-counter, only I hadn't been thrown out.

What would Annalese have said? I could hear her now, untroubled, practical. "Just don't get mugged."

CHAPTER 19

On Thursday morning, after three days of dealing, something else happened which troubled my proletarian roots. Just before ten-thirty, I walked out of the office for a quick break and returned to find the dealing room in an advanced state of panic. Even Debbie, usually insensate, was agitated. Pete looked up briefly.

"The Bundesbank's cut its Lombard rate by half a per cent," he said.

I stared at him, bewildered. The news was delivered with an urgency usually reserved for declarations of war. *Are they invading too*? I settled down in front of my screens. Pete was lost in his own world. If only he understood women the way he did numbers he would be getting laid every lunch-time. Lying on top of his rucksack was a paperback, *The Newtonian Casino – How Algorithmns Can Break the Bank*. Sometimes it was best just to accept defeat. I had counted my winnings three times yesterday, in my room, away from Charlotte.

Pete broke into my thoughts, told me to call up Bank Austria, find out what they were bidding in six years. Two frantic minutes later, I was staring at the screen, exhausted.

"That's what I call a home run," Pete said, standing over me. "If you were on commission . . ."

" . . . Am I?" I asked, despising my own greed.

"Welcome to the club," an Afrikaans voice said behind me.

Briggs's hands were on my shoulders again. I spun around

instinctively, checked myself. The chairman winked and walked over to sterling.

£50,000 profit in approximately 120 seconds. Slower than the spin of the wheel but more addictive in its mayhem.

Confused, even richer, I waited for more instructions, but Pete was less forthcoming. It was his commission I was now taking. I was on my own. If that's the way he wanted to play it . . .

Credit Suisse was flashing up 58 offer in four years. Pete was talking on the phone, taking another message. It sounded alright, nothing too extreme.

"Toxo, how are we in fours?" I asked.

"So so. We could do with some more. What are they offering?"

"58."

"Check with Pete."

Pete's whole body was now turned away from me, shielding his screens, safeguarding his knowledge.

I bought them. I don't know why and I didn't like the enthusiasm of the seller's response.

"What the fuck?" Pete said, looking at me, then his screen.

"I just bought some four years."

"I know. Why?"

"You were on the phone," I replied, distracted.

"Buying fours. We're over, well over. Shit. What were you doing?"

I wasn't listening. I hadn't been for the past couple of seconds, not since Reuters had flashed up a new pitch from Kiruna Kredit: "SEK/ESP 3 M SWP32/28."

"There's your bank again, Douglas," Toxo called out. "Crazy deal, man. They must be nuts."

I stared at the screen. Pete had seen it too but had taken a call on line six. He waved his hand in my direction, shaking his head. "Ignore them," he said tersely, his hand over the receiver.

Without hesitating I typed in "NOT FOR ME TKS BIFN."
Pete looked at me, puzzled, but was drawn into his telephone conversation again. I looked at my watch – 10.35 a.m.
– and wrote it down. Even I knew that kronas against
pesetas was not your regulation deal.

Things calmed down around 1 p.m. I was back to spectating,
on Briggs's advice, so I took a different gamble and offered
to buy in the sandwiches. I needed to get to a phonebox as
much as anything, to talk to Charlotte and tell her what had
happened. She had given me a number in case of emergency.
Kiruna showing up on my screen constituted something, I
just wasn't sure what.

I walked down Lombard then Prince's Street, careful not
to swing too close to Pret A Manger, and thought about
Charlotte. What did she do all day? It sounded so boring,
pretending to be in public relations. The whole PR business
was a pretence, wasn't it? Perhaps she had wanted to be
the dealer – she would be a lot better in the office than I
was, less awkward around men, better on the phone – and
then decided it was too dangerous. Charlotte prodded risks
first, turned them in her hand, dropped them if there was a
hint of unpredictability.

I stepped off the pavement to cross over to Charlie's
Place, but I got no further than the kerbstone. The ground
shuddered. I knew immediately what it was. The bang followed quickly, more of a thud in my chest than a crack.
Close, maybe five streets away. I looked over towards Moorgate and saw oily smoke billowing from an office block. My
stomach tightened as I thought of Annalese halved in the
street, the store manager, the silence. Then I heard the plate
windows, incessant as a waterfall. I turned to the wall,
pushed against it with one hand and vomited.

Inhaling air hard and repeatedly, I forced myself to walk
down the street in the direction of the blast. The traffic had

slowed. Drivers were pulling over, winding down windows. One car, a Fiesta, three-point-turned and drove off in the opposite direction, the driver pale with shock. I could hear distant sirens growing louder, shouting, screams, the calling cards of panic.

I kept myself walking against the flow of running people. As I turned into Moorgate, I saw enough to know that I could go no further: an office block shredded and smoking, all its windows gone, curtains hanging out like dead men's tongues. A fire was catching in the reception area. People were running in most directions, some were lying still in the street, tossed like acrobats out of their building. One man was stumbling, head in hands, jacket ripped, lost.

Jostled and knocked, I walked quickly back down Prince's Street. I had to get to a phone, tell Charlotte there had been a bomb, that I'd replied to Kiruna. Had I triggered the explosion? The thought lodged itself just behind my forehead, pressing outwards, trying to search out some guilt. Kiruna had nothing to do with the bombings; it was just a small operation in the Middle East. It was reasonable for it to deal solely on days like today, when there was easy money to be made.

I found a phonebox in Cornhill, and waited while a man told a loved one that he loved them even more. He kept the door open for me, and gave an unfocused look.

"You alright?" I asked.

"I'm alive," he said, pausing at his own profundity.

Charlotte was engaged. I tried three times in quick succession, then slammed my fist on the flat shelf next to the phone. I sensed people gathering outside. I didn't want to turn around because I knew I would have to let them in. Again I tried and again she was engaged. I started talking anyway, ignoring prim instructions to replace the handset.

"These people behind me think I'm talking to someone. Let me introduce myself. You killed my woman. If you hadn't done that, I might not have made a few grand this morning. Thank you. These people might not be queuing now. You're dead. D'you hear me? I know your game."

I tried Charlotte again and got through.

"There's been another bomb."

"I know. Where are you?"

"I'm in a phonebox."

"Are you alright?"

"I think so."

"Big?"

"There's not much left of Moorgate."

"Be at the house as soon as you can. Walter's meeting us there at two."

"What do I say to . . ."

The phone went dead.

CHAPTER 20

Walter and Charlotte were in the sitting room when I arrived, watching the news on television. The low table in front of them was littered with sandwich wrappings, some glasses and a bottle of red wine. One of the sandwich packets was unopen, presumably left for me. I couldn't even look at it. No one said anything as I sat down on the sofa next to Walter. He smelt of alcohol. I watched the footage, scanning the background as a reporter spoke live from the scene. Eighteen people dead.

My journey back had been quick but stressful. Twice I thought I was going to be sick. Since the Oxford Street bomb I had felt little or none of the trauma the hospital had prepared me for. My brain had processed the shock in manageable soundbites. But now the scenes were repeating themselves uncut, loop-taped.

We sat in silence listening to a statement by a nameless man from MI5. The bombers, he said laconically, were near to being found.

"I need some good news," Walter said, turning to me. "That guy's lying." Walter was wearing a light grey suit and had taken off the jacket and slackened his tie. He seemed tired, older.

"I made fifty grand for JKA this morning," I began. "And a few for myself."

They both looked at me silently. What were they worried about? I had been the one they had nearly blown up. Twice.

"Not many people walk away from two bombs you know," I said.

"Dutchie, we're running out of time," Charlotte said. "All of us."

I looked at her and then pulled out a sheet of paper from my jacket pocket.

"This is a print-out from December 22nd, the day Samantha West blew herself up in Oxford Street. At 11 a.m., she was contacted by an unknown outfit called Kiruna Kredit, who offered her Swedish kronas against pesetas. She said 'Not for me thanks, bye for now', the way we wankers do in the City. Two hours later a bomb went off. One week earlier, 15th December, 1 p.m., Kiruna also made contact with her. Again she turned them down. Same message: 'Not for me thanks, bye for now.' Three hours later a bomb went off. Those are the only two times Kiruna has attempted to deal with JKA in the last month. Except today. At 10.35, they offered Swedish kronas against pesetas, same deal, 32/ 28 over three months."

"What did you do?" Charlotte asked.

"I typed 'Not for me thanks. Bye for now'. The way you do."

"You should have ignored it."

"But I didn't."

"Why not?"

"I wanted to see what happened. Two and a half hours later a bomb went off."

"And killed eighteen people."

"Dutchie," Walter said, speaking slowly. "Are you sure this bank has never contacted JKA on any other days?"

"I've only gone back a month."

"Was there anything exceptional about the markets today?"

"The Germans cut their Lombard this morning," Charlotte said, before I could answer. "Half an hour early. There was a lot of activity across all currencies."

"What about the other dates?" Walter continued, still looking at me.

"I've checked them," I lied. "The markets were quiet."

"We need to stick some more on these guys. They might just be opportunists. Have they been offering around Swedish kronas to everybody?" Walter asked.

"I don't know," I said.

"To find out we'd have to go through the records of every bank in the City," Charlotte added.

Walter pulled out a handkerchief and dabbed his brow. He then leant forward, poured himself a glass of wine and half-heartedly offered the bottle to us. Neither of us moved and he sat back.

"Okay, let's take this one stage at a time," he began. "It's a big assumption, but supposing Dutchie is right and Kiruna is coordinating the bombers, talking to them on Reuters 2000. They could be doing that from anywhere in the world. We need to make contact with the guys on the ground."

"But we don't know who else is receiving the messages," Charlotte said, lighting a cigarette. There was a pause in the conversation as we watched her shake her hair and exhale.

"Why don't we send a message ourselves," I said, sitting forward. I suddenly had an image of Dan calling to Pete, the keys arcing across the room. Charlotte and Walter turned to me, recognising I might be on to something, but not sure exactly what. I wasn't certain myself. "We set up on our own," I continued. "Get into Reuters. Sign ourselves on as Kiruna Kredit."

"And how do you propose we do that?" Walter asked, losing interest again.

"JKA has got a contingency dealing room. They all have."

"And?" he said, still not convinced.

"It's obvious, isn't it?" I was losing patience with him. He hadn't come up with any solutions himself. "We could deal from there."

Charlotte looked at Walter, who dimpled his chin and looked away. "It might work," she said. "If we could get into the system."

"Next week," I continued, "we contact every bank in the City, offering them Swedish kronas against pesetas. Just like they did today. Same rate. See who bites. Someone did."

"Hey, hold up," Walter said. "We might not have the budget for this, even if it's a good rate."

"It's only money," I said. "Anyway, we wouldn't have to buy or sell anything. We'd just send out the messages."

"But what would we be saying to them?" Charlotte asked. "What exactly does bidding or not bidding kronas against pesetas mean?"

She looked at Walter again, who was lost in thought, tugging at the loose flesh of his throat.

"You're the experts," I said. "As a novice I'd say it means if you buy the deal, it's your turn with the gun-powder. If you say not for me thanks, it's somebody else's go."

"There is one problem with that," Charlotte said. "On the day Samantha West turned it down, she blew herself up."

"I know," I replied. "I'm just guessing. I'm not a spy."

"What happens if it means something else, if we activate them in some way?" Charlotte asked.

"Another bomb goes off," I said. "It's a risk we take."

"It won't," Walter said, sitting back. "Dutchie's right. Kiruna is delegating, nothing more. The guy who buys the kronas is picking up the Semtex, the one who says no thanks goes along as back up. Something like that. It's up to them what they do with it." Walter got up, and stretched in front of the window. He was wearing a thin belt which drew his trousers together too tightly at the back, creating extravagant, ungainly pleats. "I feel stronger already," he said, turning to face me. "You've done well, Dutchie."

There was a pause. I wasn't sure I had followed the last leap, but Walter's manner had changed dramatically.

Charlotte smiled across at me, letting her eyes linger. I turned to the TV and thought of Annalese as the weatherman pointed to Cornwall and warned of storms.

Charlotte saw Walter out into the street, presumably to speak to him in private. He also needed some help with walking. He had drunk a whole bottle of red wine on his own as we chatted. I wasn't certain it had been consumed in celebration. It was a small lead, we were only starting. But it seemed as if some weight had been taken off his shoulders. He looked vindicated.

While they were outside I rang the office again. Earlier I had explained to Dan that lunch wouldn't be arriving because I had been caught up in the blast. It was nothing serious, I said, but I had gone for a check-up. I spoke to Debbie this time, said that I was still shaken and would be in tomorrow. Just as I was about to hang up she dropped her voice.

"The boss was asking questions this afternoon," she said. "He wanted to know why you needed a print-out."

"What did you tell him?" I asked casually.

"I said you were familiarising yourself with the incomprehensible world that is foreign exchange dealing," she said awkwardly. I could never tell when Debbie was winding me up.

"I am."

"I know. Don't come in until you're feeling better."

CHAPTER 21

"He seemed chuffed enough," I said, as Charlotte came back down the hall. I was sitting at the kitchen table, lighting a cigarette.

"He doesn't usually drink like that," Charlotte said.

"Oh come on, the guy's a pisshead."

"Not at lunch-time."

She sat down opposite me. It was a while since we had been at the table together, alone.

"You're not going back in are you?" she said, taking one of my cigarettes. "You look dreadful. May I?"

I nodded. "I've just rung the office. I'm alright."

"You've done well."

"Will he give it a crack?"

"It looks like it. Next week perhaps." She paused. "Were you frightened, when it happened again?"

"It brought back things I was trying to forget."

"You'll never forget them. No one does."

"All those bankers, dead in the road." I began to laugh drily. "I almost felt sorry for them, can you believe that?"

"Christ Dutchie, it's a natural enough feeling," she said, sitting back, exhaling.

"If they had died in the revolution I would have been dancing in the street."

She paused for a moment, looking at me with a faint grin. "Do you really believe in all that?"

"In all what?" I countered.

"That there will one day be this great uprising of the people?"

"Yeah. So does the State. They wouldn't be risking coppers like Martin if they didn't."

"No one believes in the revolution anymore. Communism's dead."

"Please, spare us the insults," I said, pushing my chair back, trying to get some distance between us. "It's got nothing to do with Communism. I'm not a Communist."

"You don't really believe in anything, do you? A bit of copper bashing now and then, to keep the testosterone levels down. That's all it is."

"I would never turn down the opportunity to smack old Bill. That's quite true. But it's got nothing to do with testosterone. It's because they represent everything I hate about the wankers who run this country, that's why. The workers are entitled to fight back."

"And that includes killing people."

"They'd kill us, given the chance."

"Us. Who's us, for Godsake?"

"The oppressed. The working classes."

"You're not working class. You're not even middle class. How can you possibly say us?"

Charlotte got up from the table and went over to the Aga, where she opened one of the lids and put the kettle on. She was seething, her actions swifter than was necessary.

"If I see a black man given a beating," I continued, putting one foot on the edge of the table. "I have to be black do I, before I can cross the street and help him?"

"You're more likely to be beating him up."

"You have no idea, do you? Not a fucking clue. I'm not a racist. My old man's a racist. The couple who live next door to us are racists. You are, for all I know. I bet you cheered when Mandela was set free, when he became President. I didn't, not because I liked De Klerk, but because I knew that in Soweto they would still have to fight to be heard."

"I never realised you cared so much."

"Don't patronise me."

I sat in silence for a while, looking out of the window. Normally our conversations ended with one of us walking out, shouting, but we both stayed where we were. Following on so soon from the bomb and the talk with Walter, this confrontation felt different, drained of any real hostility. There were suddenly limits, an underlying awareness of the need to cooperate with one another. Charlotte had turned, and was leaning with her back against the Aga rail, tidying a tea-towel hanging over it.

"Did Annalese believe in the revolution?" she asked quietly.

"In her way."

"You argued a lot?"

"Would it make you feel better if I said we did?"

"It doesn't bother me. I'm just being nosy."

"She believed in lots of things."

"But not the revolution."

"What do you believe in? Stella for President? I'd sooner vote for Norman Tebbit. Anything for a quiet life."

"One day I hope you'll understand."

"I don't think you realise how patronising you are."

"When this is all over I'll explain. I promise."

"Explain what?"

Charlotte paused for a moment, looking at the floor. Not for the first time, I sensed that I wasn't being told everything, that information was being concealed from me.

"Explain what?" I repeated.

"We all have to make decisions," she began, lifting her eyes towards me. "Annalese had that right taken away from her. She was left with no choice. It's important you hold on to that."

I spent the afternoon in bed, drifting in and out of troubled sleep. Explosions ricochetted across my dreams. Dusting myself down in the shop I would walk to the door and be thrown back across the floor by another rush of air. Each time I tried to leave I was thwarted. Once I made it out on to the pavement and held a conversation about the revolution with the top half of Annalese. She lay there, just a torso, propping herself up on her elbows and talking calmly about peaceful protest.

Charlotte brought me tea and sat on the end of my bed for a while. I was glad I didn't have any sisters. If I had, they would be like her and I would hate them. Naive middle-class women who couldn't understand why some people chose not to come home at Christmas.

"You were calling out," she said, touching my leg lightly.

My reluctance to confide in her was fading. I sat up a little, pulling a pillow awkwardly behind my head, and sipped some tea.

"What was I saying?"

"Something about Annalese."

I paused, gave in. She could be anyone, it didn't matter. I needed to talk.

"The bomb blew her legs away."

"I know."

"Her best bit." I tried in vain to laugh.

"Do you feel guilty?"

"It didn't have to happen. We could have been somewhere else. I thought it was Christmas."

"Have you tried writing to her? It can help. Putting thoughts down on paper. Saying things you didn't say."

I thought about our conversation in the night, never saying I loved her, and stared up at the ceiling.

"You know, sometimes I can't even see her face."

"Do you have any photos?"

"I did. They were on the barge."

"The barge is safe. I could get them for you."

"That's not the point. I was with her for a year. You would

have thought that somewhere in my head I might have stored a few images. But all I get when I think of her is a lump in the street covered by a grey nylon anorak. I can see the manager's face all right. Fuck him. I'd only known him for a minute. That's odd, isn't it? Maybe I didn't love her."

"I don't think it's odd at all."

"The only reason I'm not dead is because I was poncing around in a shop for tall people. Tell me the logic in that. She needed some shoes, so she went to Pied à Terre. A sensible enough thing to do and she was blown to pieces."

She said nothing, sitting there upright at the end of my bed, cupping her hands around a mug of tea. She let me rest, talk some more.

"She never wanted to come to London anyway. I shouted louder, said Cornwall was boring. It's all that remains of her now. I'll move there when I've found them, live in a teepee, make an effort with her crustie friends."

"Start a quieter revolution," she added, smiling.

"I want them dead. It's the only thing I am sure about."

"I understand . . ."

" . . . but. Leave it."

"I was going to say I know how you feel."

"I doubt it."

I turned away to the wall, regretted confiding. We were silent for a while and I slid towards sleep. Then I became aware of her voice, slow and soft.

"In Belfast once, a gunman came into a pub where we were all drinking. He shot two officers in the face, killing one of them. We were very close. I watched him die in the hospital. Two days later I was in the queue at Sainsbury's, not far from the Falls Road. The person in front of me was the gunman."

"How do you know?" I said quietly, filling the pause. I was still facing the wall, my eyes now open.

"We knew who the players were, who they had killed.

Proving it in court was another matter. There was never enough evidence."

"You should have taken him out yourself," I said, turning over and propping myself up on the pillow.

"I nearly did, in the car park. I carried a gun in my handbag."

"But you didn't."

"I had a career to think about."

"Then you don't know how I feel." I fell back and sighed. "I would have shot him, fuck the career."

She got up, drew the curtains, and left me to sleep. "Think of me when you find them," she said, and closed the door.

CHAPTER 22

As excuses went I decided that being caught in a bomb blast was hard to beat. For once I had breakfast in the daylight. Charlotte told me to tread carefully, not to trust Briggs, the chairman. Walter had been on the phone the night before, when I was asleep, expressing concern. Charlotte said he was just being over-cautious, but there was a question-mark over Briggs's relationship with Samantha West. It had been an indiscretion, nothing more – Briggs had no idea who he was sleeping with – but Walter was nervous.

The tube journey passed quickly. I sensed I wouldn't be a commuter for much longer. Things were coming together. I might even have a chat with Chuckster today, talk about peasants. I leaned against the revolving door and nodded to the security guard. A new face.

"Mr Reason?"

"Yes?"

"A package for you. Could you sign here please?"

The man was polite, but no sirs. It was meant to be company policy. I had checked with Debbie. As I took the pen, I saw the lift door open to my left. I looked up. Three men came out and approached the security barrier. The guard nodded at them. Without pausing, I dropped the pen and moved quickly towards the door, not quite running. Another man was coming in from the street. Behind me I heard the rustle of raincoats. Suddenly the man in front of me tried to grab my lapels. I raised myself on to my toes and headbutted him in the nose, cracking it like a walnut. Pushing him to one side, I ran out into the street. Yet another man was getting out of a Mondeo, parked outside the entrance.

I turned right, sprinted down Lombard Street, almost losing my balance as I span into Birchin Lane, and ran. Heart thumping, I searched for cover, dreading dead ends. Feet were clattering behind me, getting closer. Passing the Stock Exchange, I went down Throgmorton Street, spotted Bank tube entrance and half jumped my way down the stairs. The ticket foyer was crowded, but not enough. I ran up to a barrier, smacked my hands down on the grey boxes and leapt over. I hadn't done it for a while and my foot caught, sending me flying. Picking myself up I sprinted down an escalator, saw a train and dived into it as the doors were closing.

Wheezing like an asthmatic, I forced air into my lungs, leant forward, and held on to the chrome bar for strength. The carriage was full and a murmur rose and fell. All eyes were on me but no one said anything. I stayed on the train until the end of the line, Edgware, by which time there was no one left in the carriage who had seen me arrive. I got out, walked slowly to the escalators and let them carry me to the surface. Only then did I realise I was in Zone 4. I didn't care anymore. Walking up to a man in a uniform, I made my excuses, expecting a £10 fine. He waved me through.

"I don't know who they were," I said. "They knew who I was."

"How many? Charlotte asked. "Four did you say?"

"Six, if the security guard was in on it."

"Where are you now?"

"Edgware Station."

"Get away from there. They'll be checking every station on the Northern Line."

"Who's 'they' for fucksake?"

"I can't tell you now."

"I need to know."

"I think they were from MI5."

"What?"

I swallowed hard, gripping the receiver tightly.

"I said I would explain to you. I can't now."

"Wait a minute, I'm not going anywhere," I said, looking around the tube foyer. A lorry thundered past the entrance, rattling a loose manhole. I put a finger to one ear. "Let me get this straight. You just said to me that those men were MI5. Is that right?"

"Dutchie."

"Answer me."

"Yes, that's what I said."

"Then who the fuck are you?"

"Keep your voice down. It's not safe to talk on the phone."

I thought about slamming the receiver down. I looked about me despairingly. Someone had come up to use the phone.

"Dutchie, there's a pub called The Duke of Wellington, up near the Watford bypass, about a quarter of an hour's walk from you. I'll meet you there at eleven. Lose yourself, Dutchie. Please."

She hung up. I stood holding the receiver, facing the foyer. It suddenly felt a dangerous place to be standing. I put the receiver down calmly and walked out into the sunlight. I resisted running; I didn't know where to run. I thought about hailing a cab, then wondered who might be driving it. I had to calm down, not be paranoid. Where was I going? I looked at a man selling flowers. Could I trust him? Buster Edwards used to sell flowers. I asked him where the pub was and the man obliged with simple directions, said it was near St Mary's Hospital. It wouldn't be open yet, he added. I must have sounded like an alcoholic. My legs started running, I couldn't help myself, and they didn't stop at the pub. On

I went, up the hill, knowing I could find my way back by
eleven.

Charlotte walked into the main bar ten minutes late. There
were two old men by a fruit machine, otherwise the place
was empty. I was sitting in the corner behind the door, next
to the cigarette machine. I had already drunk one pint of
Export and was halfway through my second.

Charlotte sat down on a squat, cushioned stool, looked
around her again, then turned to me.

"I'm sorry about this, Dutchie," she said.

I sat in silence, taking in her appearance. She was wearing
jeans and a pullover. By her feet she had placed a small
canvas hold-all.

"We've got to go. I'm worried about Walter."

"What about me?" I said loudly. "Tell me what's going on."
She looked around anxiously.

"We can't talk here. Come on. I've got the car outside."

I finished my pint while she waited at the door. The car
was around the corner on a double yellow line. A stout
female traffic warden was walking towards us.

"Get in the back," Charlotte said, opening the driver's
door.

"You're parked on a double yellow line," the warden
began flatly. She was standing next to the front passenger
door, her feet set apart. Charlotte ignored her, got into the
car, started the engine and drove off. I looked behind us,
and saw the warden writing down the number plate.

"That might have been a mistake," I said.

"Silly cow. I was leaving."

I smiled. She was coming round.

"So what's going on?" I asked, sitting back in the seat.
The beer was relaxing me.

"Like I said, they were probably MI5."

"I thought you would say that. Who do you work for then?"

"When I was in Northern Ireland, I worked for MI5. But I don't anymore, not directly. I work for Walter."

"And who does Walter work for?"

"He's employed by the government. His brief is to keep an eye on MI5. He's an ombudsman, a watchdog. It was one of the first appointments New Labour made. They are suspicious of the Security Services, always have been, ever since Five tried to destabilise Wilson."

"So why was Walter interested in the bombing campaign?"

"He thought that someone in MI5 knew who was behind the explosions and wasn't saying anything. Maybe they were even supplying them with semtex."

"You're shitting me," I said. "Tell me you're making this up."

"You've got to understand, Dutchie," she said, glancing in her rear mirror. "Up until recently, MI5 were expecting the chop. Forty per cent of their budget was spent on Irish terrorism, but what for? The ceasefire was holding. So they turned to organised crime, drug busting. They had no choice. Nobody wanted to, particularly the older ones. It was demeaning. Special Branch territory. Police work. They hated it."

"Are you saying that MI5 were letting off these bombs themselves?"

"No, not directly. They're too clever for that."

"They got someone else to do their dirty work. Sounds about right."

"This was only Walter's theory, remember. He had no evidence to back it up, nothing to show to the Home Secretary. But then you come along with your little discovery and it all begins to fit together."

"I can't believe no one else noticed."

"No one else was looking. That's the point."

I sat forward, propping my elbows on the front seats.

"Whose hand is actually on the detonator, then?"

"People who think Gerry Adams is selling out. Hardliners. MI5 knows who they are. If Walter's right, Five arranged for them to come over to the mainland, fixed them up with jobs."

"In the City. People like Briggs, the chairman."

"Yes."

"Why use someone like him?"

"MI5 blackmailed Briggs years ago. He's no trouble, a soft touch, helps whenever anyone asks."

"How did they blackmail him?"

"Caught him in bed with a horse, a Greek boy, I don't know. Someone his wife wouldn't have approved of."

"A black woman?"

"Perhaps. Somebody in MI5 must have approached him and explained that Samantha West needed a job. He obliges. He has no choice."

"And then he sleeps with her."

"If you say so."

"Likes the idea of shagging a spy."

"But she wasn't. She was a terrorist. He had no idea."

"Then along comes Walter, says he's also from MI5, and asks for me to be given a job."

"He obliges again. He has no choice."

"Which is why he tells me how nice it is to help *again*."

"Exactly. Then when this bank, Kiruna Kredit, which must be operated in some way by MI5, suddenly receives your answer from JKA, they pay Briggs a visit. Ask him what's going on. Rough him up a bit. He assumes they must already know but he tells them about his other visit from MI5, from Walter . . ."

" . . . and tells them about me."

" . . . and you. MI5 realise they have a problem. The ombudsman is on to them."

"So they turn up at the office with a reception committee."

"They will go after Walter as well."

"And you." She nodded, turning to me. Her face was close to mine and I could smell perfume on her neck. "But he's the government's official ombudsman," I continued. "They can't touch him. They can kill me. I don't exist. I'm expendable. As everyone keeps telling me."

"Walter doesn't exist either. Officially. Nor do I. Our existence would be an admission by the government that they didn't trust the Security Services. There's already a parliamentary select committee to look after them. Why have an ombudsman as well?"

"What did I tell you?" I said, sitting back. "The state's fucked."

"I'm more worried about Walter."

"Where are we going?"

"His aunt's. Neasden."

"Neasden? What's she doing living there?"

"No idea. He stays with her occasionally."

"And we're living in his house?"

"There was no budget for Walter's little whims."

"So you used me. Cheap and expendable."

"I went back to Clapham after you called. The house had already been searched, turned over. I've grabbed a few things. We can't stay there."

"So where are we going to live?"

"I was wondering about your barge."

"You saw it last."

"It's just down the river, nearer Woolwich. They'll be looking everywhere. Sit back and keep your head away from the windows."

Events were beginning to make more sense. There was little comfort in what Charlotte had said. I felt exposed. Walter no longer represented resources. He was on the outside, a loner, and so was Charlotte. We all were now. But the discovery that MI5 had helped to kill Annalese, so obvious somehow, chimed with my revenge. In an instant the bomber's death had become my fate. Nothing else seemed to matter anymore. Terrorism was part of the state. It was official. I felt vindicated. I should have known.

We drove fast through driving rain down to the North Circular. At Neasden we turned off and pulled into a car park in front of the IKEA superstore. Apparently, Walter's aunt lived in a road off Drury Way, which we had just turned down. It seemed an increasingly unlikely place for a single old woman to live. I sat quietly in the back as Charlotte studied an A to Z, watching her fingers trace across the map. She started to bite a nail. It would be strange returning to the barge, and with someone else. She was right, though; it was the perfect bolt hole. We could slide along the river at night, stay moving.

"It should be just at the end there, Lovett Way. It's in that estate," she said, looking up.

"Shall we walk?"

"No. You don't understand what we're up against, Dutchie. They could be here already."

She took the car out of the car park and down into the red-bricked estate. I couldn't picture Walter coming here at night, let alone his aunt. The flats looked rough; there was graffiti on the walls, Tesco trolleys abandoned in alleyways, a burnt-out car in front of a row of rusted lock-ups. It was still raining and the tarmac was shiny. We slowed to a walking pace, following the road around a corner.

"Number twenty-three," she said.

"In there, that's nineteen."

She stopped the car and we got out. Charlotte checked around her. Her nervousness was making me feel edgy, unarmed. We walked across the uneven paving stones down a walkway. Either side of us walls rose five blocks up. We passed under a stairwell, puddled and smelling of urine.

"Twenty-three's up there," I said.

I went first, treading quietly. I didn't know why. If anyone was here they would have seen us already. We went up three flights and walked along a balcony to twenty-three.

"I don't like this. There's only one way out," Charlotte said, looking over the edge at the car below.

"Shall I knock?" I asked.

"We don't want to frighten her," she said.

"You knock then," I said, then looked closer at the door's dented metal edge. "Someone's tried to force their way in." I walked up to number twenty-four, and then on to twenty-five. "Nothing unusual," I said, coming back. "Someone's had a go at the whole block."

She knocked and froze as the door opened fractionally. I looked at her, pushed it open further and walked in. We stood in a tiny hallway, damp and musty. There was an old tweed overcoat hanging on a hook, and two fur hats. She nodded at the coat. It was Walter's.

"Hello? Anybody home?" Charlotte called.

There was no answer.

"Stay at the door, I'll go in," she said.

"No, you stay here," I said. She looked at me for a moment, then gave the faintest nod.

I turned into the cramped kitchen. There was an ancient gas hob, and a hot water heater above a stained white plastic bowl in the sink. Beneath my feet the lino floor was sticky, unswept. An empty bottle of wine stood by a pedal bin, which was spilling over with potato peel. A half-eaten tin of tuna was on the sideboard, bothered by a fly.

I turned around and went down the corridor, drawn towards the end door, open, ajar. On my left was a small sitting room. Briefly I looked in. A copy of *The Daily Mail* lay across a brown sofa, half-covered by a tartan rug. The

TV in the corner was an old black and white with a Sputnik aerial on top, next to a photo of Walter looking much slimmer. I left and moved towards the open door at the end of the corridor. My mouth had gone dry. The carpet was yellow and black-patterned. Sixties, maybe earlier. I pushed the door open and swallowed hard, trying to reverse a sudden tightening in my stomach.

The room was pale, light filtering through filigree net curtains, throwing delicate patterns across the bed. Apart from a wooden chair, it was the only piece of furniture in the room. Sitting upright in it, half covered by a sheet, was a teenager, smooth-chested, barely adolescent. His face was all wrong for his age, too grey, cheeks pallid and withdrawn like an old man's. The eyes were closed and his forehead stained by a red mark, no bigger than a Smartie. Sprawled across him, half fallen out of the wooden chair, was Walter. His wound was not so neat. A corner of his head had been chipped away, shot from the back more than once, leaving a crenellated edge. His mouth was twisted as it lay pressed against the boy's lap, the sheet drenched in lumpy blood.

I walked quickly down the corridor, pressing my tongue hard against the back of my top front teeth. Charlotte was waiting outside, keeping an eye on our car. She turned as I came out of the door.

"Quick. In the car," I said, marrying the door gently to its frame.

We shuffled down the stairs in tandem. "What was it?" she asked breathlessly.

"Just drive. To Woolwich. They got there first."

CHAPTER 23

"I need to know what you saw," Charlotte said, accelerating into the outside lane.

"Are we being followed?"

She glanced anxiously at me, then in the rear mirror.

"Dutchie, was his aunt there?"

"Not exactly."

"What do you mean?"

"There was a young bloke lying in his bed, a teenager, ill-looking. Walter was sitting next to him. Someone had shot them both." I was trying to say the words impassively, but it was difficult. "He didn't even have time to turn around."

I noticed Charlotte's knuckles tighten around the steering wheel. Her eyes were moistening at the edges, making the limpid whites look even clearer. The scene in the bedroom had been shocking; its stillness transfixing. But by the bottom of the stairs I had shoved the images to the back of my mind, storing them untidily. Now, as I heard Charlotte sniff, I saw the rough edges of the wound, the gap between his brain and the skullbone, the awkwardness of his position. Clumsy in death, too. I had never disliked Walter, never liked him much either; being American gave him a certain neutrality. There was nothing to kick against. Sometimes he spoke like my father, usually when he was drunk, but most often he was unjudgmental, liberal even. I didn't understand him.

"Would Walter have turned me over if I hadn't cooperated?" I asked.

"Yes. He didn't want to. He liked you. You were a source

of fascination to him. But he knew he couldn't keep you out of trouble for ever."

"You're not telling me he really altered my file?"

"He doctored it almost every week. There was a lot of data. Someone didn't like you."

I fell silent.

"He didn't have to blackmail me," I said after a while. "If he had told me at the start, right, this is what I think, MI5 killed Annalese, I would have played ball."

"Would you?"

"Fuck yes. Instead he lied to me. Wanted to make me think I was working for the State rather than against it. Like it was a challenge for him. Another slice of social correction for Dutchie."

"He needed to know how serious you were."

I looked out of the window, away from Charlotte.

"The smile on his face when I turned up in a suit. You should have seen it. His face nearly split."

There was an awkward silence.

"Will you miss him?" she asked.

I didn't know. I hadn't seen him for seven years, then all of a sudden I was living in his house, arguing, fighting with him. I thought of him asleep on the sofa, snoring, half on the floor. There was something tragic about him moving out of his own house, living in a damp flat with a teenage lover.

"He was an obese bastard, wasn't he?" I said, countering my own emotions.

"Christ, Dutchie."

"He never used to be that fat."

She looked across at me. I could feel my Adam's apple rise, disappear, and push out lower down. She stared ahead again.

"He believed in what he was doing," she said. "MI5 had too much power. He didn't think that was healthy."

"They still have. We're going to die, aren't we?"

She didn't answer, concentrating instead on joining the motorway. The rain had picked up. Diesel spray from lorries was testing the wipers, smearing the windscreen with flat islands of colour. We had decided to head out to the M25, go the long way round, and approach the barge from the east rather than cross the centre of London.

"Our only hope is if we can get enough evidence," she said. "Then we can contact Downing Street directly."

"Downing Street?" I laughed. It represented such different things for both of us. "You have such faith, don't you? It amazes me. What do you think the government will do? They've probably all been photographed porking horses too. I might as well get out now. Walk down the middle of the motorway. I'll have a longer life."

"What do you suggest, then?"

"We've got no option. We should find out who the other bombers are and then kill them. What happens after that doesn't really matter, does it?"

"It might not to you."

Neither of us had changed since we'd met each other. We hadn't conceded an inch. I wouldn't have had it any other way, but it suddenly struck me as sad.

"Okay, we'll compromise," she said, glancing nervously in the rear mirror again. I turned around to look. There was a blue Astra sitting close behind us. Charlotte moved over to the inside lane to let it pass. It slowed, drifted across too.

"We'll compromise," she continued, drawing strength from repeating the words. "Let's try to find out who the other bombers are. If we do, I'll go to Number Ten and you can do what you like. It won't affect the evidence against MI5 if the bombers are dead or alive. Do you know where JKA's back-up dealing room is?"

"Isle of Dogs. Near the Docklands Arena."

"Too central."

"It's near the barge."

"We'll just have to risk it," she said, sitting more upright in her seat. "We've got company."

I turned around again. The Astra was still there, further back now. I could just make out two figures through the spray.

"What do we do now?" I asked.

"Sit tight."

I wondered what she was going to do. A turn-off was approaching. The Astra was thirty yards behind us and we were going sixty miles an hour, in the inside lane. The hard shoulder, its smooth surface scraped away, had been coned off, and the lanes were narrower than normal. There wasn't much traffic around. In the distance a juggernaut was driving in the middle lane, a row of white pea lights lining the roof of the cab like a Christmas porch.

"Face the front," she said and a moment later she was standing on the brake, throwing us both forward. We skidded, beginning to veer towards the cones. The front left wheel clipped several. I could feel the rubber buckling underneath, smacking the underside of the car. As we slowed, Charlotte pulled down on the steering wheel sharply, taking the car over another cone and on to the rough hard shoulder. I turned to see the blue Astra, also braking hard, skid to a halt in the middle lane where it had swerved to avoid our car. In the same moment, the juggernaut, horn blasting, ploughed into the back of it, shunting the car forty yards along the road. The noise of twisting metal was deafening. Meanwhile, Charlotte now had our car facing in the opposite direction to the flow of traffic. Without hesitating, she accelerated down the bumpy track and turned right up the slip road.

We both sat there in silence, breathing hard as we approached the roundabout.

"Have you done that before?" I asked, trying to piece together exactly what had happened. She didn't answer. At the roundabout we turned right over the bridge, crossing the motorway. I looked out at the accident below us. The juggernaut was jack-knifed across two lanes and another car, a Mini perhaps, had hit the back of it. The Astra had turned over and was lying on its side. Four or five people were standing around, two were lying on the tarmac. Cars had started to queue back, one or two slowly passing the accident in the outside lane. Charlotte's gaze was still fixed on the road in front of us.

"I don't want to know," she said, taking the car back down the slip road and rejoining the motorway, clockwise this time.

We found the barge close to the Thames Barrier, moored on the south side. It had taken us two hours to get to South-East London, coming off the motorway at several junctions, using smaller roads, returning to the motorway again. On balance we had decided it was worth the risk of staying with the car until we got close to the barge. I knew a lock-up in Charlton where we could leave it. The lock-up belonged to Leggit and I figured he wouldn't be using it for a while. It was a short walk from there to the river and we moved swiftly along the tow path, past the cement works, through the refinery, and on until we found the barge.

I felt strange as it came into sight. It was good to see it again – it looked much smaller than I remembered, dark and subdued against the water – but I expected to see Annalese in a window. And then I saw her, smiling out from under her tangled hair. My heart skipped a beat. It was the newspaper photo I had stuck above our bed.

Charlotte stood on the quayside, keeping a respectful distance as I forced the cabin door open, splitting the wood on the sliding roof hatch. Inside it was cold and airless and smelt faintly of sandalwood. I looked at her bus pass photo on the table, and heard emotions echoing distantly. Then, from further inside, I heard something else, a weak cry, barely more than a scratch in a throat. Nervously I went through into the bathroom, knowing what I would find.

Emaciated and wobbling, Lamorna tried to stand when I stroked her, but she fell over. She was on the floor, below the sink. I leant down and picked her up, worried I might squeeze the last breath of life out of her tiny lungs. I put the plug in the sink and managed to pump out a few dark drops of water, then lowered her gently into it. She drank slowly, her tongue feebly flicking the surface.

I looked around. On the tiny chrome-fenced shelf below the mirror, there was a mascara stick, Annalese's toothbrush, a pair of earrings, some lipstick. Evidence she had lived. I picked up the toothbrush, smelt it, then rubbed it slowly on my gums. I could hear Charlotte stepping on board. I caught myself in the mirror, still wearing my ridiculous Italian tie and striped shirt.

"It's charming, Dutchie," Charlotte was saying next door. I walked through into the bedroom. Unlike me she had to bend her head, and she was stooping awkwardly.

"Did she make this?" she asked, rolling a beaded necklace through her fingers. It was still snaked across the rim of the mirror, where I had replaced it.

"Yeah."

"It's beautiful. Where are the stones from?"

"Cornwall. Treen beach."

I felt strange, ill at ease. She was looking at the newspaper photo of Annalese.

"Do you want coffee? Black?" I asked.

"Thanks. We should have brought some food."

I went to the sink, then remembered there was not enough water. The last drops were being lapped up next door. I didn't want Charlotte to discover Lamorna. It would be too emotional, represent too many other things. We shouldn't have come back. The barge was better left how it was, undisturbed, a tomb.

"We're out of water," I said. "Did anyone follow us here, you reckon?"

"I don't think so." She paused for a moment, rubbing the tops of her arms for warmth. "Are you frightened, Dutchie?"

I lit the camping stove, leant down and touched a cigarette to the flame.

"Have you done that before? On the motorway?" I asked, ignoring her question.

"No."

"You just assumed they would veer right, because the hard shoulder was coned off . . ."

" . . . please."

"They were only coppers. No one else looked hurt. Not badly anyway. You pulled a great stunt."

I knew my tone would upset her, remind us of our differences. I needed to remind myself.

"I'll get some food," she said. "Any preferences?"

I let her leave in silence. A few seconds later I stuck my head out of the forward hatch.

"Cat food," I called after her. She turned and looked at me, dropped her head and walked on.

Yes, I was frightened, sitting on the edge of the bed with Lamorna. Not counting my time with Annalese, I had spent most of my adult life tilting against the conspiracy between politicians, police, the Security Services, the establishment. Never once had I thought it could circle me completely. There would always be gaps, pockets of foolish decency, politicians who had opposed the poll tax, for example, liberals like Walter. But I had chosen to ignore them. The system taken as a whole was geared against the have-nots, that's what mattered.

Now there weren't even any woolly do-gooders left.

Walter was dead. It was finally me against the state and I was scared, shit scared. Charlotte was my only ally, but she was really one of them. They would only shoot her. What would they do to me?

Annalese would never have let me be sucked into this showdown. She knew you couldn't win. I was just beginning to see it her way when she died. If you can't beat the system, live outside it. But it was too late for that now. They would keep looking until they found me. I had to fight. It was what I was best at.

"How long had she been shut in?" Charlotte asked, cradling Lamorna in her arms. "Poor little lamb."

"A couple of weeks."

"She's so small."

I was cooking a version of soy bean masala, standing at the small hob in my old clothes, and drinking my way through a four-pack. Charlotte had bought it, an obvious gesture. We were both making an effort, trying to be friendly, warm even.

"How did Walter move the barge, anyway?" I asked.

"He's got friends." She was sitting at the table, emptying a bottle of Rioja.

"He once worked for the CIA, right?"

"A long time ago. When the Americans wanted to know what MI5 was up to. Just like the government today. That's why they employed him. He was used to spying on spies."

"As a child I was never allowed to ask him what he did."

"Was he a good godfather?"

"Crap. Used to give me children's books from the 1920s. *When We were Five* for my fourteenth birthday. Can you believe it? I told him I preferred cash. He stopped giving me presents after that."

"He always wanted children, he told me once."

"He told me his wife was run over by a lorry."

She went quiet. The story seemed even more pathetic now.

"I was thinking," she said. "We're exposed here and I'm sure it's illegal. Walter must have bribed someone. Perhaps we should head back up river, where you used to be."

"Greenwich? They'll be waiting."

"We'll be nearer the dealing room. No one knew you were there," she said.

"Walter did."

"I know. It was in your file."

I looked up at her. "And he removed it?"

"They thought you were still in Cornwall."

CHAPTER 24

We slipped our moorings and passed through the beaten panels of the Barrier towards the North Greenwich peninsula. I was glad to have company. London no longer represented opportunities. The water was murkier than usual, rippling in the weak stern light. Strands of steam were rising off Canary Wharf, lit by its glowing pyramid. I could never seem to escape from the building. It looked indomitable, coiled, threatening to press higher into the sky if required. At night, we used to count the number of occupied floors. Like a church appeal, the rising layers of light charted the recovery of Docklands. We cheered whenever a floor was extinguished. On the other bank a flame from the refinery licked the darkness like a blow-torch. Annalese used to call it a candle.

The wharf was quiet when we arrived. Most of the boats were sealed up for the winter. I watched Charlotte standing on the bow, stretching ashore with a rope. She was practical, dextrous. Before MI5, she said, she had done a short service commission in the army. Her father had disapproved of her new job as an ombudsman. He was in the Navy, had a good war in the Gulf. In his book it was bad enough keeping an eye on the Security Services, even worse doing it on behalf of a Labour Government. I suppose she was like Walter, decent enough in her way, naturally misguided.

"I'm going to have a word with the foreman," I said, jumping on to the jetty. We had tied up next to the dilapidated cruiser, on the other side from our original berth.

"Don't be too hard on him," she said.

I wasn't going to be hard on him, I just wanted an explanation, for the record.

A light was on in the Portakabin at the back of the wharf, by the gate leading to the tow path. I cupped my hand against the glass and saw Victor inside, sitting back in his chair watching a small black and white TV.

"Dutchie, I didn't recognise you," he said, as I walked into the office. The man's voice was almost unbroken, comically high. "The hair, it's all gone."

"My barge disappeared, too," I said, turning off the TV.

Victor might have been a confident man once, but something traumatic had happened, like an injection of oestrogen, or an industrial accident. He was physically huge, his body built like a lagged boiler, but he spoke nervously and had never harmed anyone. The wharf owners employed him as a visual deterrant, hoping that intruders would split before he had a chance to open his piccolo mouth. I had called his bluff once, never been troubled since.

"Honestly, Dutchie, I had no choice, the man, he was very pushy. He said it wouldn't be harmed. I'm sorry, Dutchie, you know I am."

"Did he pay you?"

"No. A small amount. He asked me to go away for the day. It was nothing. Twenty pounds. I've spent it, Dutchie. He said the boat would be safe."

"It's outside. We're staying here a few days."

"Good, good. A few days? You can't stay overnight. They've been checking."

I looked at him, then went to the window and peered out. The barge was out of sight, hidden from the tow path.

"Who's been checking?"

"Port of London. You need a licence now. Too many people are sleeping on the river. It's me who gets the trouble, Dutchie. They take it out on me."

"Let me know if anyone comes asking questions."

"Yes, of course. Anything you say. You don't want the twenty pounds back then. Because I've spent it, you see. Took the wife out."

"If anyone asks, I'm not here. Understand?"

I walked over to the door.

"Yes. Where will you be?"

I stopped without turning around and waited a few seconds.

"I've got you, Dutchie. It suits you, the shaved head. Shan't say a word to no one."

We drank some more before we slept, laughed about my first deal, the trip to the casino. Then we talked about Walter and fell silent. Our intimacy, however contrived, was unsettling. At least in Clapham there had been some space. Here we couldn't eat apart, sleep apart. The barge was pressing us together, mentally, physically.

"It must be strange for you, being back on the boat again," she said. The wine had given her neck a faint rash.

"Where are you going to sleep?" I asked.

"In the bed, I hope."

I kept eating, not looking up at her.

"Unless you're hiding a kingsize Habitat sofabed somewhere. Is it a problem?" She started to laugh. "We can sleep head to toe if you'd prefer. Providing you wash your feet."

I remained quiet, pushing my food around.

"They might be more chatty," she added.

"It's where we slept together. The last time I held her, before she died."

"I'm sorry," she said, her voice becoming serious. "Silly. I was forgetting." She got up, sliding out of the narrow table. Standing with her back to the sink, she looked briefly either side of her.

"There's not really anywhere else," she said. "I think we should both stay on the barge."

I finished my food in silence, then went out into the cockpit for a smoke.

I tried to imagine what Annalese would say if she could see me now, if she emerged out of the darkness and saw me alone. We would sit and talk. I would ask her how the market had been; she would extract from me gently what I hadn't done during the day, suggest evening classes in pottery, ride my anger, run her fingers through my hair, knead the back of my neck, kiss my forehead, sing to me, hold my head against her breasts, love me. Then she would hear Charlotte moving around below and I would have to explain.

We had once talked about death, in the bathroom. I was having a shower and Annalese was cleaning her teeth.

"If I die before you," she had said, "you'd better not sit around feeling sorry for yourself all day. You'll find someone else, won't you, get on with your life?"

"Would it matter if you knew them?" I had asked, knowing that we each prided ourselves on never being jealous. We had water in those days and I leant forward, feeling the jet beat against the back of my neck.

"Whoever you like, love." There was a pause. "Was there anyone in particular?"

"No." Another pause. "How would you feel if it was someone like Mia, or Katrina?"

I knew it was cruel. She didn't say anything, then I heard Leafe running through the barge into the bathroom.

"Either one would look after you," she continued. "I'd rather it was one of them than some dozy old tart from Hackney. Leafe wants to compare willies."

Charlotte was already in bed when I went back inside. She was reading one of Annalese's books about ley lines in Greenwich. She had repositioned the lamp on the small bedside shelf and was holding the book above her, casting moving shadows.

"That's my side," I said. She lowered the book, lighting up the room. "I always sleep by the window."

"Okay," she said. Looking at me, she crabbed awkwardly across the bed, then turned back to her book. It was harder now to read, and she moved it about, trying to find the best light, altering the dimensions of the room. It was so easy to re-establish the right tone with her, keep everything how it should be.

In the tiny bathroom I cleaned my teeth, noticing she had left her toothbrush on the side of the basin. I put my own back in the mug with Annalese's. In a small cupboard on the shelf I found a round wicker jewellery box. Annalese had lots of boxes, but this one contained current favourites. I rummaged around, found a small gold stud and slid it through my left ear. I looked at it in the mirror and then I noticed Annalese's mascara on the shelf. It had been moved.

"Have you used this?" I asked, standing in the doorway, holding the mascara up like court evidence.

"No, Dutchie. Why would I put mascara on before going to bed?"

"Don't even think about it."

I went back into the bathroom and wondered what to wear in bed. Usually I slept naked, even in winter. It looked like she was wearing a T-shirt. I settled on the same, and my boxer shorts. I rolled half an inch of toothpaste into my mouth, spread it behind my upper lip with my tongue and walked into the bedroom.

"Did you know that the old Bishop of Stepney tried to open a chapel at the top of Canary Wharf?" she asked.

I was concentrating on not touching her legs as I slid into bed. She didn't look up, kept reading. The bedding was warm. I had lied about it being my side. It was where Annalese had slept. I was hoping her imprint might still offer some comfort.

"Here's another thing," she continued. "If you extend the south-west angle of the pyramid on top of Canary Wharf to the ground, it falls directly on the Greenwich ley line. Apparently the builders knew this and put a crystal from Cornwall up there, you know, actually in the pyramid, to pacify it."

"Can I turn out the light?" I asked. I knew all about the crystal. Annalese had been incensed when she had first heard about it, vowing one day to return the stone to Cornwall.

Charlotte looked across at me. I had both arms down by my side.

"Dutchie, I'm not going to eat you. Relax. Get some sleep."

She turned the handle on the kerosene lamp. The light lingered, shrunk, popped. I turned away from her, pulling the duvet. She pulled back.

"You know, I think I am going to start my own class war," she said after we had settled down. "Try to make the middle classes less hung up about sex."

Who was saying anything about sex? I kept quiet. Cocky bitch.

"The working class, if such a thing still exists, is so much more relaxed about sex. Don't you think? They just get on with it. Bonk crazy, they are."

We both heard a footfall on the jetty outside.

"What was that?" she whispered.

I didn't know. "Probably Victor going home," I lied.

"Bit late, isn't it?"

We heard another sound, unmistakably someone trying to walk slowly, undetected. I slid out of bed. Holding my breath I moved the curtain a fraction and looked outside. Five feet away I saw someone's legs. Whoever it was, he was standing with his back to the boat. I got a faint whiff of cigarette smoke. I let out some air, then breathed in again.

"Who is it?" Charlotte whispered impatiently.

I signalled calmly with my hand for her to be quiet. I felt anything but calm. The man started walking towards us. He was wearing Hush Puppies, jeans, tartan socks. I let go of the curtain, hardly moving it. The shadow of a man bent down, trying to look in. Suddenly there was a knuckle tap on the glass. I stayed motionless. We both waited, forgetting to breathe. The man was standing upright again, scratching, writing something. Then he moved around to the cockpit and seemed to step on to the boat. It rocked gently as he stepped off again and walked away.

I raised my shoulders, let out a long sigh and sat on the edge of the bed, rubbing the back of my neck. I began to laugh a little with relief.

"Who was it?" Charlotte asked, touching my shoulder.

"More fuckwits in uniform. Haven't they got anything better to do?"

"Dutchie. I'm scared. Please."

"Port of London Authority. That's who it was. No one's meant to sleep here overnight. Can you believe that?"

"Don't start. It's late."

I was still awake two hours later, staring at the ceiling dimly lit by a lamp on the tow path. The orange light reminded me of my room in Clapham. Charlotte was asleep beside me, keeping a respectful distance, her breathing shallow. Perhaps she knew more than I did, or was just braver, but the future looked short and bleak. Tomorrow we would break into the dealing room. I would try to give her time by taking out the alarm, but I was out of touch. We would have to move quickly. Between us we could get the system up and running and log into Reuters. The set-up sounded identical to JKA's main dealing room, an exact copy as Dan had said. It would then be a matter of faking Kiruna's call code and contacting every dealer in London. Someone had to respond. The worry was if the real Kiruna bank was planning another bomb for tomorrow; there had never been more than one in a week.

"Are you awake?" Charlotte asked. I looked across at her. She was lying on her back, eyes closed. "What time is it?"

"Two, maybe later," I said, surprised to hear her voice.

"Dutchie, do you think they died today? In the car?"

"Maybe, maybe not. Someone had to die. You must have killed people in Northern Ireland?"

"No. That was different anyway. It was a war."

"Against terrorists. Those people in the car were as bad as terrorists. They had blood on their hands. Over fifty people."

She was silent for a while. "I don't understand you."

That was a relief, I thought.

"Don't you feel anything, for them, for Martin?"

I managed not to flinch at the name.

"I don't think he died," I announced after a pause, wondering why I had chosen to say the words now. It was a gamble. She had recovered too quickly, hadn't mourned enough. And then there was the overheard telephone conversation.

"What makes you think that?" she asked.

"Nothing in the papers."

"There won't be if we die."

"It was just more blackmail, wasn't it?" She didn't answer. "But no, in answer to your question, I wouldn't have felt anything if he had died."

She turned away. I felt relieved, vindicated.

"If we do die," I said after a long pause, long enough for her to have fallen asleep, "will anyone miss you?" She didn't answer. "Because if there is, ring them tomorrow." I paused again, confident she had gone. "I thought about phoning my old man, but . . ." I let the sentence die away into the night. I was tired.

" . . . but what?" she whispered, barely keeping the conversation alive.

"I thought I should tell him about Walter."

She turned and put an arm across my chest, moved a warm leg closer to mine. "No one else will," I said.

I slept intermittently, troubled by practical thoughts of the next day, whether it was all worth it. Why didn't I just disappear to Cornwall, leave Charlotte to the state? But the desire for revenge kicked back at me, made my legs warm, sweaty. I turned to look at Charlotte. Her arm was still draped across my chest. She was sleeping on her front now, her right leg bent, linked over mine. The contact was comforting. I remembered the strength of her grip when I had lunged at Walter, how strangely reassuring it had felt, how uninhibited. Her confidence intrigued me; it led her into situations which tested her precious middle-class values. Like the accident on the motorway. It had been executed with visceral bravura, skill, and yet it had created nothing but moral dilemmas for her ever since, dilemmas which I enjoyed watching, untroubled by them myself. It was the same prompt that had made her stride into the bathroom. She had to keep going once she was in the room, cough her way through a spliff.

And then those comments about sex. She would be adept, no question, a player. It was a natural extension of her physical prowess, her lithe easiness. But would she wrestle with the consequences?

Slowly I ran my hand along the back of her thigh, watching her face for the slightest reaction. I looked closer at her earlobe, the tiny earring indents, as if the skin had been sucked through from the other side. At one time she had worn four. Somehow I couldn't see Stella approving. I traced the curve under her buttock, taut and full, until I touched her other leg. Moving upwards I encountered material, silk. I tried not to laugh. I thought of her undoing the wrapping, sliding on stolen goods, succumbing. Gently I began to massage both buttocks, letting my fingers slide in between. Imperceptibly I felt her legs part, no more than a fractional readjustment. I slowed, watched her face. Her eyes were closed but she let out the faintest murmur, more of a hum. It could mean anything, stop, go on, untypically ambiguous. A second later, maybe two, she moved her left leg slowly away, as if she was swimming breast stroke in slow motion, and raised her hips. I slid my hand underneath and began to massage her inner thigh, one side, the other, firmly, in between, rubbing against the moistening silk, pressing.

Her thighs stirred to my rhythm. She moved her hand from my chest downwards, first outside my shorts, kneading, then clamp-gripped. She slid across the bed, sat on her knees above me, pulled off her T-shirt, began kissing my stomach. I lay back, wondering what I had unleashed, savouring her imminent guilt. The light on the tow path made her flesh glow, effervesce. She pulled my shorts away. I repsonded, loosening, feeling her hotness again. "We should go shopping more often," she whispered, and drew me slowly into her.

CHAPTER 25

I woke in fits and starts, hounded into the daylight by turbulent dreams. Charlotte was lying peacefully next to me, murmuring only when I disentangled myself from her warm limbs. It was just gone ten. We should have been at the dealing room by now. I stood on the cold lino floor, leant across the bed and circled a hole in the condensation on the window. It was a clear day and I could see Canary Wharf, two-dimensional against the bright blue sky. I glanced down at Charlotte, spread diagonally across the bed. Her arms were cradling the only pillow. There was a patterned patch on her cheekbone, where it had been pressed against the rough mattress. Then I noticed something else, half hidden under her T-shirt. I looked closer, gently pulling up the cotton on her buttock, and saw a small rose etched neatly into her skin. It looked fresh, a recent job.

Outside I walked around on the jetty, filling up the water tank, checking ropes, shaking off the intimacy of the night. I glanced at some anemones on the side of the barge. Annalese had painted them on our first day aboard, to remind her of Cornwall. I thought of her sitting there, patiently watched by Leafe who had paint all over his hands. A part of me had hoped her death would be emancipating, take me back to the heady days before I had met her. But it hadn't. I had tried. Christ, no one could accuse me of not trying. I had marched with the lowest, held my head high in The George. But what had happened? I had ended up feeling bad about a dead copper (who wasn't even dead). And now I had just got myself laid, sweetly as it happened, and I was feeling guilty. Annalese had left me a different person; there was nothing I could do about it.

I came back inside and changed into my suit. Charlotte was sitting on the edge of the bed watching me. She smiled and stretched a hand through her hair. Perhaps she would feel regret later. Somehow I doubted it. I would need her knowledge of computers today, but she was going to be a liability, I could tell. She had too much faith in the State, too many blindspots.

Something else was worrying me, too, a thought that had been chasing its tail, incessantly, through the night. What if Samantha West had been operating entirely on her own that day? If the only person who had killed Annalese was already dead? Where did that leave me? Walter had been sure the bombers worked in twos, one to handle the semtex, the other to be on hand in case anything went wrong. I had to believe that, otherwise I was wasting my time. The thought made me feel sick. Visiting my dad, living in my godfather's house in Clapham, working in the City, sleeping with a woman called Charlotte – these hadn't been public-spirited gestures. They were for Annalese.

"What are you staring at?" I asked, adjusting my tie in the mirror. Charlotte had been scrutinising my face for clues.

"Are you feeling okay?" she asked.

"Yeah."

"Have you got a camera?"

"A camera? Somewhere, why?"

I watched as her reflection felt around under the blankets and retrieved a pair of knickers. Businesslike she threaded her feet through them and stood up. They were a good fit, an inspired choice. Then she removed her T-shirt, picked up her bra from the table and put it on, brazenly. No remorse, not even a hint.

"We might need one today," she said, tucking a breast into its cup.

"What do you want a fucking camera for?"

I walked out to the cockpit, bent down and pulled open the engine hatch, letting it bang noisily against the side. She was winning the game I had started. She had been since the day we met. I looked at my hands. They were covered in grease and I searched for somewhere to wipe them, contemplating my suit trousers. I hated wearing suits.

"I need evidence, Dutchie." She was standing in the cabin door, holding out a cloth. "Here, use this. They won't believe me if I don't have any evidence."

I took the cloth without looking at her, wiped the worst of the grease off, and removed my jacket, placing it carelessly on the seat.

"What are you doing?" she asked, picking up the jacket. I rolled up my sleeves, and put my hand down into the hatch, careful not to touch the sides.

"The camera's in the bottom cupboard, by the bed," I said, stretching down further into the hole and feeling around in the darkness.

"What are you looking for?" she asked again. I could sense her standing closer, peering down over my shoulder.

"You do it your way and I'll do it mine," I said, and carefully lifted out the shotgun.

I walked briskly along the tow path, swinging my heavy briefcase in one hand. It had been a tight squeeze, but I felt insuperably stronger with a gun by my side. Charlotte had also told me to pack a book called *How the City Works*, one of her teaching manuals. She had salvaged it from the house in Clapham when she had gone back there to pick up her belongings.

She was walking along a few yards behind me, occasionally breaking into a trot, telling me to slow down. There was a lot to do. We passed Wimpey Wharf, where a crane was scraping gravel from a boat's bowels. Beyond it an avenue of limp derricks stood forlornly. They hadn't been used for years and it was as if someone had left them there as an example, perched on rotting tripods for all to see, heads bowed in shame.

I slowed up at The Trafalgar Tavern. A barman was just opening for business. I was past him before he had secured the front door to its catch. By the time Charlotte came in I was already sitting at the bar, nodding in her direction. She shook her head. She looked even more nervous than I was. There was a strong smell of beer in the air, a legacy of the previous night. The barman came back from the door, and flicked on a hi-fi stack beneath the till. The music was too loud and he rolled it down before pulling my pint. Charlotte was putting coins into a cigarette machine on the wall. The river behind her was reflecting a diffuse, neutral light through the bow windows, enough to pick out specks of dust swirling in the draught from the door.

"It's the City," I said to the barman, after emptying my pint in one. "Gets to you after a while."

Charlotte told me to relax in the foot tunnel, as I accelerated down the gentle slope to the river bed. According to a commemorative plaque at the entrance, there were over 200,000 enamel tiles lining the walls. Many were stained or missing, the gaps passing by us like punched holes in a computer tape. I used to bag a lot of money here, from people like me, breezing past in their suits and ties. There was a point in the middle of the tunnel where two security cameras had been placed back to back. Directly below them it was possible to sit undetected. A man in the know with a mongrel Alsatian puppy was playing his guitar, moaning gently.

At Island Gardens we waited for a train to Bank. I touched

Charlotte's arm when it arrived and nodded down the platform. Grown men were pretending not to compete for seats
at the glass front of the carriage. It soon became an
unseemly scrum. Charlotte smiled. I was pleased she was
here. We both seemed to note where the blue-uniformed
guard was, and sat as far away as possible, at the back of
the train, facing the wrong way, watching the masts of *The
Cutty Sark* slip into the distance.

The dealing room was somewhere between Mudchute and
Crossharbour. I remembered Dan telling Pete it was called
Enterprise House. We got out at Mudchute, walked down to
ground level and decided to follow the line of the track,
suspended above us on smooth round pillars. Charlotte
looked up nervously. Our train twisted away through the tall
buildings like a toy, its windows flashing in the sunlight on
a tight, grinding corner. I think we both felt it was just a
matter of time before we were arrested.

It took us fifteen minutes to find Enterprise House. Charlotte saw it first, a squat, mirrored block standing on its
own. At the front it looked out across a small, worn playing-
field. A man was standing in the middle of it throwing a ball
for his dog. I pushed half-heartedly against the main
entrance doors. They held firm. The foyer was bare except
for a cheap formica table with a phone on it, next to a copy
of *Yellow Pages*. In the corner there were some pots of paint
and a pile of decorators' stained dust sheets. On the wall
above them a chrome sign indicated that JKA occupied the
ground floor and Morgan Stanley the floor above; presumably they had a contingency dealing room, too.

"Weird isn't, it?" I said. "All these empty buildings. Just
sitting here, waiting for a bomb to go off."

"Are we wasting our time?" Charlotte asked, a little
vaguely. She was shielding her eyes from the sun and looking
out across the playing-field. "Someone's going to see us."

"Not if we're careful," I said, trying to sound bullish. But she was right. The place was exposed. There was a main road running down one side of the field, offices on the other. Our plan suddenly seemed rather desperate. I walked over to the narrow gravel path which bordered the building and followed it around to the back. It was more sheltered there. A large grass bank rose steeply, throwing the bottom half of the building into shadow. We could be seen from a school a hundred yards away, towards the main road, but otherwise we were out of sight.

"I'll break one of these windows," I said, as Charlotte came around the corner. "There's a chance they're not alarmed, but I doubt it. More likely the police will be here in five minutes and take a look around."

"What will that achieve?" she asked.

"They'll have keys."

Charlotte looked at me for a moment. Her day had suddenly stopped being ordinary. The night had briefly halted events, checked our momentum, but we were back now to where we were before, hunted, running.

"I thought you knew all about burglar alarms," she said, leaning against the building's glass corner.

"I was bluffing." I bent down, flicked the catches on my briefcase and pulled out the gun. "Stand back."

Just as I was about to crack the glass with the gun handle, we heard a van draw up at the front.

"What's that?" Charlotte asked.

I put the gun back in the case and moved quickly round the side of the building, careful to avoid the noisy gravel. I reached the front corner just in time to see a man in white overalls disappear through the front doors. Perfect.

"Who was it?" Charlotte whispered at my shoulder.

"A decorator. Hear that?"

We listened to the faint beep of an alarm system waiting

to be disengaged. I turned to Charlotte, grinned and started walking round to the back of the building.

"This is what we do," I began. "I'll go in there in a moment, once he's switched everything off, show him my JKA card and tell him I've come to look at the dealing room screens."

"Don't shoot him, Dutchie."

"I'm not going to shoot anyone. Unless the cops turn up."

"Morning," I said, surprising myself with my cheerfulness. "Looking good." I nodded up at the half-painted ceiling.

"Oh, we're getting there," the decorator said, setting up his step-ladder behind the desk. He seemed harmless enough.

"Come to check the screens," I said, nodding at the JKA door. I didn't want to walk up to it. Presumably it was locked.

"Right. Bloke came down last week to look at the phones."

"Yeah, Pete. He said he left the keys here. Did he leave them with you?"

"With me? No. I've got my own set." The man's cheeks flinched imperceptibly just below his eyes.

"Oh, thank God for that," I said, putting my briefcase down on the ground. "For a moment I thought I'd come all this way for nothing."

The man hesitated a moment. "I'm sorry, I'm not authorised to open this place up. Not for anyone."

"I've got my pass," I said, pulling it out of my pocket. I was trying to make light of the conversation but I could hear my own voice growing tense.

"But no keys," the decorator said.

"No keys." I smiled, holding my empty hands out.

"I'll have to ring security. What's your name?"

The man was already by the phone. I watched him for a

moment. He glanced up at me then started to dial. As he looked down I opened my case and pulled out the gun.

"I suggest you don't do that," I said, cracking the barrels shut and pointing the gun at him. "Put the phone down." The man's face blanched. His grip on the receiver went limp and he dropped it over the side of the table. I walked up to him, grabbed the swinging phone and put it back. Someone was talking on the other end.

"Now unlock the doors, like I said. And nobody will get hurt."

The man fumbled with a bunch of keys, walked across the foyer and unlocked the door, his hand shaking. I glanced out across the playing-field – nobody had seen us – and then pushed him into the room. Another beep was sounding. I looked at a dark box on the wall to our right and nodded towards it. The man opened it up, taking his time.

"Move it," I said. "If the alarm goes I'll shoot you."

The man silenced the system.

The room was small and cramped; a musty smell mixed with new paint. Pale blue light was pouring in from the wall of windows. Unvarnished plywood desks were crammed into every available space, the banks of screens grey and lifeless. The atmosphere was disturbingly still, ghostlike, as if everyone had left in a hurry hundreds of years before. It was cold, too.

"Kneel down in the corner and put your hands behind your back," I said to the man.

I brought out some twine which I had found on the boat and went over to him. He was looking straight ahead, his eyes glazed, in an advanced state of shock. I hadn't even done anything to him yet. I bound his wrists tightly to his ankles, forcing him to lean backwards. He didn't say a word. His skin was cold and clammy. When I had finished, I turned to get Charlotte and met her walking in.

"Is everything alright? she asked. "You didn't come and get me."

"Everything's fine."

Charlotte was looking past me at the decorator kneeling in the corner. I turned around to look at him.

"He's alive, it's alright."

"At least sit him on a chair."

Charlotte was good on the computer, said it was part of her training. Within ten minutes she had called up a display similar to the one I had stared at all day in the office. The other screens were on, too. One, at the far end, was flickering, horizontal bars rippling across the glass. It was an odd sight, the empty seats, the silence. I expected Toxo to walk in at any moment, scratching his balls, talking about his latest encounter.

"Problem," Charlotte said, cutting across my thoughts. "It's not letting me log on as Kiruna."

"Why not?"

"The system's set up automatically for JKA."

She sat back and lit a cigarette.

"So what do we do now?" I asked.

"We need a password."

She hesitated a moment, exhaling smoke, then pulled her chair forward and set to work again. I felt excluded by her tenacity. For the next thirty minutes she attempted to hack into Kiruna Kredit using words she said were common currency in MI5. If she didn't come up with the right one, she said, there was little else we could do. There was also the possibility that the real Kiruna might be logged on and notice that someone else was trying.

I paced the empty space, frustrated, trying to help, throwing out suggestions: "Semtex", "Stella", "Collins". She didn't even bother to type them in. Her patience was even more annoying. She sat placidly, systematically working her way through a mental list of seemingly innocent words. Every five attempts she was barred, and had to re-boot the system, start again. At times her choices seemed alphabetical – "deal", "demon", "dice" – then she would suddenly type in something from her past – "Armagh", "Eniskillen".

"No one tries this many times," I said, walking over to the decorator. He was now sitting in a chair, head bowed forward. I checked the twine, pulling on it aggressively.

"Patience, Dutchie. It's a machine, not a person."

"They're sitting somewhere, watching us, having a good laugh. I know they are."

"Do you have any other ideas?"

I didn't and went outside for a smoke.

"We're in," she said calmly as I came back through the door.

"How?" I asked, walking quickly over to her. I looked at the screen. Sure enough, Kiruna was up and running, ready to deal. "Why didn't you tell me?"

"I just have."

"What was the word?" I asked, walking away, down past the row of flickering screens. Each one was now showing the same display.

"Does it matter?"

I looked across at her. She was like a prim teacher, her back straight.

"Yeah, it does. What was it?"

"You don't need to know. It's irrelevant."

"A State secret, huh? You take the piss you do. Tell me what the fucking word was." I was shouting now and the decorator looked up.

Charlotte studied the ground then lifted her head reluctantly. "Douglas," she said quietly.

I stared at her in disbelief. For a moment I thought she was addressing me. Then I realised. The implications flooded over me, too many to contemplate.

"It's a coincidence, Dutchie. Nothing more. The word changes every day. They often use names of people."

I sat down quietly at a desk two down from her and lit another cigarette. She was right, it was chance, random. Even so, I could have done without it. The name had always felt uncomfortable, as a child, in the City. If it meant everything was a set up, that Walter was implicated in some way, it also meant that Charlotte was involved. But she wasn't. She wouldn't have been sitting here with me if she was. Perhaps it was just one of MI5's sick little jokes.

"Start thinking of banks," she said. "There's a list in the book." She nodded at my briefcase on the ground between us. I opened it and pulled out *How the City Works*. "Look at the list in the back," she said, hesitating, "and pray for a little luck."

We both knew that if we managed to make contact with a terrorist, we might inadvertently set in motion another bomb attack. It was a risk, but more people would be killed in the long run if we didn't try. That's how she explained it. I expressed less concern. We didn't know what the message "NOT FOR ME TKS BIFN" actually meant, if anything, but it seemed logical to assume that it was either a blank refusal by a bomber, or an acceptance to provide back-up. We weren't exactly about to start World War Three.

I stood with my back against the desk, legs crossed, and started calling out company names, like a roll call, students of capitalism. Each time I said a name she typed in the initials, inserting L for London if necessary, then flagged up the message "SEK/ESP 3 M SWP32/28". No one in their right mind would look twice at the call. I tried to imagine them all in their dealing rooms. Perhaps it was a quiet day. At JKA, Dan would be ordering people about, Pete would be crunching numbers, dreaming of Debbie.

"Chuckster, he was a tosser, right?" I said, watching her type.

"He appealed to women more than men. He was easy company, flattering. Nice bum too."

"Credit Lux."

We were getting on better now that I had something to do.

"You weren't jealous were you, Dutchie?" she asked.

I didn't answer. On the screen a message had suddenly appeared. "NOT FOR ME TKS BIFN." We both stared at the words, barely daring to breathe.

"I hope we haven't lit any fuses," she said quietly. "What's the address?"

I fumbled with the book, trying to find the entry. "Canada Square. Canary Wharf," I replied. "Just up the road."

"We're looking for someone with the initials C.M."

I walked away from the screen, tapping the book against my legs, and then turned back, just to check I wasn't imagining it. The message was still there. "C.M." – who could that be?

"First of all we've got to find out their full name," she said, "then, well, it's up to you what we do next." She swivelled around in her chair and looked across at me. "All I need is a picture of him."

"It might not be a man," I said, my thoughts beginning to run ahead of me.

"Okay. Let's assume C.M. is a woman. Fair enough. Are there many female dealers?"

"A few," I said, looking out of the window.

"So where does that leave us?" she asked. We both knew we were on to something, desperately close in fact, but neither of us knew the next move.

"We could ring reception, I suppose," she said. "Say we've found a company diary with the initials C.M. on it."

I looked at her again. That was it. Reception.

"I'll take her some flowers," I said impulsively.

"What?"

"Turn up at reception, say I'm a dealer, fallen for someone with the initials C.M. Sex on the superhighway. It happens all the time."

"And then what?"

"I insist on giving them personally. She comes down, we know who the other bomber is."

I knew at once that I was right, that we had found our next move, but Charlotte was hesitating, playing the long game.

"There might be more than one bomber," she said.

"We're running out of time, Charlotte," I replied, putting the book away and locking the case.

"I still think we should keep calling round the banks."

"What, until someone buys the kronas? We don't know what might happen. We don't know what we might have already set in motion."

I nodded at the screen.

"I didn't think you cared," she said.

I picked up the case and started walking towards the door. I didn't care. I was just in a hurry.

"OK, so you've given her the flowers, then what?" she asked, pushing back her seat and standing up.

"Follow her home. Ask her if she was in Oxford Street on 22nd December."

"And if she wasn't?"

I stopped and turned towards her. "I'll kill her anyway."

I knew the words would shock her. I needed to say them myself. I felt animated by the charge they left in the air. It was down to basics now. Life with Annalese had been too complicated. The state was trying to kill me. I needed to retaliate first. It was as simple as that. Just like the good old days.

Charlotte went over towards the main power switch in the corner, next to the alarm.

"Wait," I said, walking back to where she had been sitting. I put the case down and sat in front of the screen.

"What are you doing?" she asked, still standing in the corner.

"The system thinks we're Kiruna, right?"

"Dutchie."

"This won't take a second. Get me back to JKA, will you?"

"But you said we haven't got time."

"Just do it," I said, knowing my tone would frighten her.

She came over and reluctantly exited from Kiruna, then booted up the system again. JKA's signature came on line.

"Party-time," I said quietly.

I had to do it, reassert myself, show that the last few weeks had been an academic exercise, a means, nothing more. I typed in the following message, feeling sorry for Pete (it was nothing personal): USD/DEM IN 100 USD. I knew I didn't have long. Someone at JKA would block me, but it was a gesture.

"Dutchie," Charlotte said. I ignored her. A reply had appeared on the screen: 1.5320/1.5300. Without hesitating I typed in 1.5320 TKS BYE and stood up, smiling.

"What have you done?" Charlotte asked, intrigued.

"Left them with a little present." Dan would do his nut.

I activated the alarm system and we walked out, leaving the door ajar. It was Charlotte's suggestion. The police would untie the decorator when they came to investigate the alarm.

CHAPTER 26

I stepped off the train at Canary Wharf and walked through the chrome framed doors to the shopping mall at the bottom of the tower. Charlotte dropped back, watching me from the other side of the hall. The wealth of the place took me by surprise, every surface glistening with an expensive sheen. I bought a dozen red carnations from a floral boutique, and stepped on to the escalator. Glancing around to get my bearings, I looked up at the vast slabs of marble rising on every side, opulent, unblemished.

Downstairs I set off across more marble towards the bank of lifts. I was preparing my story for the reception desk up ahead when I heard a familiar voice behind me.

"Douglas."

I froze. I didn't know whether to ignore it and step through the lift doors, now opening, or turn around. I turned to see Dan from JKA coming towards me, his big hand outstretched.

"What are you doing around here?" he asked, smiling.

"Job interview," I replied, glancing at the waiting lift. What did he know? My abrupt exit from JKA's foyer would have been seen by someone. Rumours would have been circulating within minutes.

"Who isn't?" he said. "You probably heard. It's all change at JKA."

"No?"

"Briggs, the boss, he was sacked."

"Sacked? Why?"

"Interfering with a minor. Officially. Unofficially it was his own son. Can you believe that?"

I winced. No, I couldn't believe it. Briggs messed up inadvertently by talking to Walter, the ombudsman, so MI5 had cashed in their collateral. At least it wasn't a horse.

"Which firm, anyway?" Dan asked, looking at the carnations.

"Credit Lux."

"Good outfit. Nice bunch of lads over there. Hope the flowers clinch it," he added, winking.

He patted me on the side of my arm and walked away. I glanced up towards the mall and saw Charlotte leaning over the balcony rail. Breathing a sigh of relief, I nodded to her discreetly and walked on.

The reception desk was thorough but no trouble. Credit Lux was on the thirty-eighth floor, the guard said, before asking me to sign in. The only other person in the lift was a man in a beaten leather jacket with shoulder-length hair which he kept sweeping back. Propped up against the wall next to him was a large thin black case. He had a canvas bag slung over one shoulder and I could see a flash-gun poking out of one of the pockets. I wondered how Charlotte was going to take her photos. A muscle in my left calf began to twitch violently. I pressed my foot down hard into the floor, and lifted my toes, trying to stop the spasm. Dan could have made life a lot worse. Clearly my departure from JKA had raised few suspicions. In fact, it must have seemed a sensible thing to do. JKA was the joke of the City, no place to gain work experience.

The lift opened and I turned right, following signs to reception. A man brushed passed me as I pushed through the swing doors, catching against my flowers with his elbow. I walked on to the desk.

"You shouldn't have bothered," the security guard said, beaming up at me. I wasn't in the mood, and glared back at him. "Yes, sir," he continued, clearing his throat. "What can I do for you?"

I put my briefcase on the floor between my legs and cradled the flowers loosely. "I want to deliver these to a dealer, a friend of mine," I began.

"And the name?"

"I don't know the name. I only know her initials. C.M." I paused for a reaction; the guard duly looked up at me.

"Early stages is it?" he asked.

"Yeah, early stages."

"Shan't breathe a word, but I can't call her down if I don't have a name, can I?"

I could see he was beginning to enjoy himself.

"I don't know it," I said coldly. "We haven't met yet. We've only talked on Reuters, the computer system." I waved the flowers in the direction of his own terminal on the desk. He looked at me for a moment, weighing up the possibilities, wondering whether I had become a security risk. I managed a smile.

"C.M., you say?" he said, not convinced. I watched his bruised thumbnail track down the list of phone extensions, and stop.

"Bad news I'm afraid," he continued, his head still down. He had a small blister on the top of his head. "Depending on which way you fancy it, of course." He looked up at me, unable to resist a grin. "The only C.M. I've got is a man. Carl Meacham."

"That's the one," I replied, too hastily. "It's not what you think. It's for a friend."

"Of course, sir. You've just missed him anyway. He went out barely a minute ago."

I didn't wait to explain any further. It was the man I had passed on the way in, I was sure of it. I left the flowers on the desk, picked up my briefcase, and walked quickly to the lifts, stabbing at the button impatiently. The security guard was already on the phone to someone, looking at me as he talked.

Nobody was in the lift and I had a clear run down. As the doors opened on the ground floor I spotted the man at the top of the escalator, walking towards the station. I looked around for Charlotte but couldn't see her. She must have come up in the lift behind me, ready to take a photo at reception. I couldn't wait for her and ran across the concourse to the train. The man was boarding near the front. I jumped on as the conductor was closing the doors, and sat down near the back.

"That was cutting it fine," Charlotte said from somewhere. I turned around. She was sitting two seats behind me. The train moved off and she came forward.

"The bastard was on his way out as I was going in," I said.

"I know. I was behind you. Different lift."

"How did you know it was him?"

She hesitated and we both looked at the man sitting passively up ahead. His hair was rich and black, well oiled. There was something Hispanic about his complexion. He wasn't tall but he had broad shoulders. The back and sides of his head had been shaved severely. Charlotte still said nothing. I glanced at her. Her skin was paler than usual.

"I've seen him before," she said eventually.

"Where?"

"Standing in a queue."

"At the supermarket?"

She nodded. I looked at the man again, more cautiously this time. He suddenly had pedigree, form. I felt my legs glow. According to Charlotte he had killed a string of British soldiers, not just her friend.

"Did you get any photos?" I asked.

She didn't answer. We sat there in silence. I knew what she was thinking, that she had no excuse now, no career considerations. I wondered how close the friend had been. Would she be able to see it through this time? I doubted it.

"How well did you know him?" I asked casually, looking out of the train window. A luxury yacht was moored alongside a deserted boulevard beneath us. I would have to come back here, the place had changed.

"We were engaged," she said quietly.

"And you did nothing?"

"I came back to England, asked for a transfer."

Her tone was becoming defensive, tetchy, and she signalled for me to be keep my voice down, nodding at the man. He was out of earshot. The train was made up of two carriages linked by a flattened, circular plate, hypnotic in its loud, grinding movements as it followed the curves of the line. There were no more than ten people on board, spread thinly through both carriages.

"Who was that on the phone the other night?" I continued, barely lowering my voice. "The posh git you were talking to."

She looked at me for a moment, genuinely surprised.

"There's nowhere lower for you to sink really, is there?" she said.

"And you've never listened to anyone else's conversation? It's your job, isn't it?"

A lady in the middle of the train, on one of the side seats facing inwards, turned towards us. Again we sat in silence, close, bristling.

"He's someone in the Foreign Office," Charlotte said, after a long pause, so long that I wondered what she was talking about. "We hardly know each other."

"Have you rung him since?"

"He's out of the country. There's nothing he could do anyway."

She dug her elbow into my ribs. The man was on his feet, waiting to get off at Shadwell, the next station. Charlotte was sitting on the outside seat. I motioned for her to get up, but she stayed seated as the train stopped. Then, just as the doors were about to shut, she got up and we stepped briskly on to the platform.

I let her take the lead. She did this for a living, after all, and her earlier disappearing act had been bemusing, impressive even. We followed the man at a safe distance, tracked him down the station's lightweight stairs and under a railway arch. He was walking confidently, not looking around, at least not that I could tell. I found myself tucking in behind Charlotte, nervous, suddenly self-conscious, trying to let my free arm hang naturally.

The man had taken a small road which ran along the side of the old railway line. He wasn't going home. There were arches on the right, some converted into lock-ups, others hollow and overgrown, but no houses. On the left was The British Sailor, and a fenced-off yard stacked up with used tyres. Chained up in one corner was a rottweiler, barking as we passed.

Charlotte stopped outside the pub. It seemed unlikely, she said, that a man in a smart suit would venture far down a dodgy road in the East End. Sure enough he soon stopped, fifty yards ahead of us, in front of a hardware shop. Rolls of garden fencing, tools, and metal dustbins were spilling out of the converted arch on to the pavement. Perhaps he was just a DIY enthusiast, not a bomber at all? For the first time I saw him check in either direction. He moved forward, partially concealed behind a pale blue council van jacked up on the kerb, then he was gone. I hoped Charlotte knew what she was doing.

"We can watch from up there," she said, nodding at an upstairs window. "You stay here until I'm in the window. Mine's a brandy, a large one."

She walked into the pub, leaving me standing in the street. I shifted awkwardly from one foot to the other, glancing up at the window. I would forget how to stand soon. The dog was barking itself hoarse in the yard next door. A man in a vest poked his head out of a window, looked in my direction and disappeared back inside. I felt even more self-conscious, and slid my case backwards and forwards on the pavement with my feet. I then realised the problem. I was nervous, more than I had ever been before. If only we knew what the message meant. On each occasion "NOT FOR ME TKS BIFN" had been typed in, and there had been a bomb. So it was fair to assume there would be one today. Triggered by us. But what role had the woman played? What role was this man going to play? He was clearly picking up something. The best we could hope for was that there was only one bomber and we were following him.

Charlotte tapped the window above and I went inside to the bar.

Upstairs was deserted. Cues lay across a torn pool table in the corner. There was an empty glass food cabinet, and a wooden box on the wall, padlocked and pockmarked with dart holes. We sat at a table in the window, watching, waiting. No one came out of the hardware shop. I considered checking the back, but Charlotte told me to stay. The man had never been caught, she said, because he didn't do unusual things. He wasn't about to climb out of windows or run across backyards, particularly if he was picking up Semtex. Calmly, he would walk the fifty yards back down the road, maybe even stop for a drink.

Charlotte went down to the bar for another herself. I declined. When she came back, her manner had changed. She sat in silence for a while, tearing a beermat into tiny squares and lining them up like tabs of acid.

"Dutchie, there's a chance there will be a bomb this evening. In the middle of the rush hour."

"I know. It would have happened sooner or later."

"If something goes wrong, we've got to live with that."

"Not for very long. You knew the risks." I turned away and looked down the road. "He's taking his time, isn't he?"

"What are you going to do when he appears?" she asked. I glanced at her. Do? She knew very well what I was going to do. I noticed that her glass was already empty. Two doubles in as many minutes.

"He'll probably have twenty pounds of Semtex in his case," she continued. "Are you just going to walk up, and pull your gun on him?"

"No, I'm not. What are you planning to do?" I asked in return.

"Ring the police. Tell them he's got a bomb. They'll defuse it and no one will die tonight."

I drank deeply before speaking. That's all I needed, Charlotte going moral on me.

"That wasn't the deal," I said, wiping my lips with the back of my hand.

"I thought he might have been going home, Dutchie. But we've given him instructions. I can't be responsible for a bomb."

"He killed your man."

"Simon wouldn't want any more bloodshed."

She was beginning to slur her words. I hadn't seen her lose control before. Another day and I would have been intrigued, bought in a few more brandies. But she was threatening to be stupid.

"When you saw him come out of the lift you wanted to kill him," I said. "You put your camera away and got on the train, just like me."

"I know."

"So what happened?"

She leant forward over the table, her head in her hands.

"I left Ireland to get away from all this," she said, rubbing her hands up and down her face, as if she was washing, trying to wake up. "Away from how I felt in the queue, how

I felt just now when I saw him again. You're right, I wanted to kill him but . . . that's what kept the Troubles going for twenty-five years."

I didn't know where to start. We could be here all day if she wanted to talk about the Irish Problem. She'd be quoting Parnell next.

"You don't get it, do you? If you ring the cops now, they might catch him, I doubt it, but if they do they'll let him go again, because a suit will turn up from MI5, take someone aside, explain he's their prisoner."

"But do you have to kill him?" At these words, she looked around, checking the place was still empty.

"You can't leave him to the state, Charlotte. It won't work." I leant forward and swept the bits of beermat gently off the table. "He is the State."

She seemed to believe me, at least for a while. Five minutes later she took pictures as the man passed beneath us carrying a large accountant's case not dissimilar to mine, and together we followed him back on to the train.

He was heading south on to the Isle of Dogs again. I tried to think where he was going. The Greenwich foot tunnel, perhaps. It was busy in rush hour. A well-placed explosive and a lot of commuters would take an early shower. But he got out at Canary Wharf and went into the shopping mall. Charlotte took some photos as he walked past the shop where I had bought the flowers.

"What's he up to?" she asked.

"He's going back to his office," I said, watching the back of his head disappear out of sight on the escalator.

"He can't be. Not with that lot in his case."

"Are you coming?"

The concourse was filling up with people on their way home. Charlotte hesitated, looked through me, at the escalator, the situation we were in. I didn't have time for her delicate conscience and started walking towards the stairs. They were less busy than the escalator. Halfway down, I could see the man pass the bank of lifts servicing the lower floors.

"Dutchie," Charlotte called out. I stopped. I didn't want to hear any more, but I turned briefly. "Good luck," she said.

I found the man standing in front of the lifts which serviced floors thirty-nine to fifty, the top. His own office had been on the thirty-eighth so he wasn't about to blow up his boss. I went and stood close to him, resisting the temptation to stare. The doors opened, disgorging two spreading businessmen.

"I got my secretary to do the proposing," the fatter of them said, chuckling.

"Dictation?"

"God no. I left the words to her. Women know what they want to hear, don't you think?"

"So you did your entire courting by fax?"

We both stood aside, letting them roll past, and stepped into the spacious lift together. We had it to ourselves.

"Thirty-nine please," the man said, turning away. Perhaps I was too ready to hear it, but he spoke with the faintest of Irish lilts. Physically, he was more compact than me, bunched, swarthy. I let my finger hover above thirty-nine, but didn't press it. I touched fifty instead, and stepped forward, blocking the panel from his view. I felt in control, relieved that Charlotte wasn't here to complicate things.

The doors closed and the two of us moved upwards. Everyone was heading home and I didn't expect anyone else to join us. The man stood with his feet placed firmly apart, confident, not afraid to catch my eye. His arms were folded. I glanced at our two cases, fakes both of them. They suddenly seemed as subtle as false moustaches. It would have been interesting to compare notes with him. We had much in common. We had both played the dealer, endured a world we despised for our separate causes. I wondered if he had ever enjoyed it, just for a second or two.

The lift indicator moved towards thirty-nine, beyond it, and I knew the time had come. The man leant forward to look at the panel, noticed and smiled.

"Sorry," he said, "I wanted thirty-nine."

I felt remarkably calm as I squatted down and unclipped the case locks. I wished I could have shot him there in the lift, but that would have still left me with the bomb.

"I know what you wanted," I said, looking up at him. "There's a cracking view at the top."

In what felt like the same action, I pulled out the gun, snapped it shut, and stood up, pointing it at the man's chest. He didn't flinch.

"The top it is," he said.

I looked at him for a moment, standing in front of me, arms still folded, his lips pursed in a wry smile. There was some untrimmed stubble just below his sideboards, where his smooth face met close-cropped hair. His equanimity was disturbing. I could feel the synaptic connections breaking, the reasoning that linked this man – my age, maybe a couple of years older – to the crumpled manager, the silence, the anorak in the street.

"I think you might have made a mistake," he said, looking at my gun. He probably knew his weapons, could tell from the burrs that it was a Black and Decker job. Still, a gun was a gun.

"When the doors open," I said, hearing my own voice, scrutinising it for weaknesses, "you're going to walk out as if nothing's happened. Unfold your arms."

"Perhaps I know you from somewhere?" the man asked, holding his arms up. His accent was becoming stronger.

"Oxford Street, maybe Moorgate. Open the case," I said, more urgently. He cooperated, squatting down just like I had, undoing the straps with slow, steady hands.

"Show me," I barked. It was a formality, but I needed to see what was in the case, just to make sure. If it was empty . . . The man pulled the sides softly apart and held it towards me. Inside were plastic packages, a mass of coloured wire, and what looked like a video timer display. It said: 6:15, 6:14, 6:13.

"As you can see, we haven't got long," the bomber said, his accent finally outed.

Six minutes. The man was a lunatic. I knew in an instant that I would still be in the building when the bomb blew. It was just a question of where.

"Give it to me, closed," I said, banishing a wobble from my voice. I buried my left foot into the floor to steady myself.

The man obliged again. He placed the case in the middle of the lift, looking at the gun all the time. We began to slow. I picked up the case and could barely believe how heavy it was. I knew he was watching me and I held it effortlessly. There must have been more explosives in the lining. I then looked at my own case. I couldn't carry both. If I left mine in the lift, sent it down again, someone would see it and tell security. In the present climate they would evacuate the building in an instant.

Wrong case, right thing to do.

CHAPTER 27

I expected guards as the doors opened on to the fiftieth floor. The place had been reopened as a viewing gallery before the bombings started, but had since closed again. I jabbed the gun into the bomber's back and told him to walk. There was no one about. Offices were still in the process of being built. Step-ladders, paint tins, partitioning panels lay strewn across the open-plan floor. It didn't feel like the top.

"Oi! This floor's closed to the public," a voice said to my left. I spun around to see a security guard walking towards us. He hadn't clocked my gun yet. I kept the bomber between us.

"Don't say a word or I kill you both," I whispered into his ear. I could smell his aftershave, expensive and sweet. The connections were being re-established. The man was a coward. He had only ventured across to mainland Britain because he was being protected.

"Is this the fiftieth?" I asked the guard.

"Forty-ninth. No one's allowed up here."

"Show me the way to the top," I said, standing back, so he could see the gun. The man's face visibly whitened. He was in his fifties and hadn't looked well anyway, his grey hair nicotined at the front. "And give me your radio," I said, waving the gun roughly in his direction. (If I had pointed it directly at him, he might have died of shock there and then.)

He passed it to me, his raw knuckles trembling. I put the case down gently and looked around. Behind us the lift doors were sliding shut, my own case standing solitary inside.

"If no one fucks up, you won't get hurt. What channel's security?" I asked.

"Security?" the guard echoed.

"If there's an emergency?"

"Channel Nine."

I looked at the receiver, pressed nine and the line crackled opened.

"We haven't got long, pal," the bomber said. I jerked the gun into his spine and he stumbled forward.

"Shut it."

"Security," said a distant voice.

There was a transmit button on the side of the unit. I pressed it, looking at the guard in front of me. His arms were hanging loosely by his side, oscillating gently with fear.

"There's a bomb in your lift," I began. "You've got six minutes."

"Five," the bomber said.

I switched off the radio and tossed it across the floor.

"How do we get into the roof?" I asked.

"The roof?" the guard said, barely able to get the words out. I wished he would stop repeating everything I said.

"Yeah. The roof. I know there's a way in."

"Why do you want the roof?"

"Don't ask fucking why. Just take us there."

The guard led us to a small service lift behind the main shaft. I pushed the bomber in first, then flicked the gun at the guard.

"Which button? And don't even think about pressing the alarm," I said, standing by the panel. It was a much smaller lift and we were too close to each other. I hoped the ride wouldn't take long. If I was the bomber I would try jumping me at this point. I leant against the wall, keeping the gun in front of me, waving it restlessly between the two of them.

"The arrow," the guard said weakly.

We rose less smoothly than before, jolting to a halt a few

seconds later. The doors jerked open and daylight poured in. We were surrounded by windows. London stretched out below us, matchboxed, the Thames picked out like a strip of foil by the dying sun. I could see the Barrier to the East, glowing red hot, and beyond it the span of Dartford Bridge, its lights beginning to wink in the dusk. The gallery itself was deserted, left in a hurry. Tables and chairs were clustered around a counter where coffee had once been served.

"You're right about the view," the bomber said. "We've got three minutes."

"Where now?" I asked the guard.

He was beginning to wheeze. He glanced up towards the far corner of the room as he turned around. He didn't have to say anything. I was already looking at a caged ladder, leading to a hatch in the ceiling.

"Move," I said, pushing the bomber towards it. The case was beginning to hamper circulation and I arpeggioed my fingers across the handle, careful not to drop it. I was carrying enough explosives to restyle the skyline.

The guard went first, followed by the bomber. I came up after them, at a safe distance, stepping slowly on the metal rungs. We waited as the guard fumbled with his keys. Then the lid swung open, banging on the floor, and we entered the aquamarine world of the pyramid. I didn't need the gun to get them up there. The luminescent colours gathered us all in like moths. We were entranced, momentarily free, a few seconds from death.

Once inside, I signalled for the bomber to move away from the hatch. The wind outside was deafening, plangent. I looked around, searching for something. The place was a vast chamber, just like a chapel in its focused ambience. We were standing on chilled metallic sheeting. Above us the roofing was opaque, translucent to the West where the sun was melting the blue panelling into shards of orange. In the middle there was a low block of industrial casing. It looked like an air-conditioning unit, and was humming loudly.

Then I saw it, on a small plinth next to the casing, directly below the apex. I backed over, keeping my eyes on the two men. It was a beryline crystal, just like in the book, glistening, holy, about eight inches long and five wide. I picked it up, put it in my jacket pocket, and replaced it gently with the case.

"Two minutes and she'll blow," the bomber said above the noise of the wind.

"Is that really a bomb?" the guard gasped. His voice was barely audible.

"Yeah. It's really a bomb," I said, coming back over to them.

"Can we go, now the spiritual bit's over?" the bomber asked.

"Take off your clothes," I said, ignoring him and pointing at the guard. "Jacket, trousers, hat."

The man looked at me disbelievingly, and aged another year.

"Now?" he whispered, desperate.

"Now. You, do the same," I said, gesturing with the gun at the bomber. "Put his clothes on."

The bomber looked less surprised. I watched as the two men began to undress, the old man stumbling on his trousers.

"Hurry," I said, trying to keep things tight. The bomber was being too compliant, too cool. I watched him put on the guard's black, chevroned jacket. It was large for him, ridiculous in its bagginess. He looked up, checking to see if he was meant to fasten all the buttons. I nodded. "And the hat."

I didn't insist on shoes. Time was running out.

"Oxford Street, 22nd December, was that you?" I asked.

"Does it matter?"

"Don't fuck about. Was it you?" I shouted.

"I was there."

"With Samantha West?"

"Was that her name? We were never introduced."

"Was there anyone else?"

He scrutinised my face.

"We're all going to die, pal," he said.

"Just fucking tell me," I yelled.

"Okay, okay. It was me, and her. No one else."

"What did she do?" I asked.

"Do? She got herself killed. Did you know her or something?"

I wanted to shoot him and he knew it. He was taking me to the edge.

"Before that," I said, closing my eyes, trying to remain composed. "What did she do before she got killed?"

"She picked up the Semtex."

I felt a pang of relief, but I still needed to know more, to hear it for myself.

"And did she detonate it, too?" I asked.

"Why does it matter?"

"Tell me."

"No. She handed it to me. Then she died. It was an accident. She got in the way."

Walter had been right. I hoped he knew that.

"Today," I continued, "you picked up the Semtex and were meant to give it to someone else, right?"

He didn't answer.

"But they didn't show, so you had to do it all yourself. Risky, but there was no choice. The same thing happened at Moorgate. Someone else said they would pick it up. Me, as it happens. You waited and waited but I never arrived, did I? Thanks but not for me. So you did it all yourself. The bomb was an hour late, but it worked, re-drew the A to Z."

"What a waste," the bomber said. "So much satisfaction, so little time to enjoy it."

He had a point.

"You, by the hatch," I said to the guard. Walking towards the bomber, I pushed him backwards. His cap slipped forward over his eyes.

"Hey, steady," the bomber said, tilting the peak back on his head. "Easy now." He held his hands up in front of him.

I pushed again, harder, watching him stumble. I could feel Annalese tugging at my sleeve, pleading with me to stop. I felt then that I wasn't going to survive, but it didn't trouble me. If I went, he went, and so much had already been resolved. Slowly I raised the gun.

"Go ahead, shoot me," the bomber said, standing his ground. "Then pull it on yourself, him too if you're feeling kind. We've run out of time. Bombs, they can be untidy things, really messy. Just look at Samantha. Hey, give me the bullet any time."

I saw the man's blue lips moving but I was no longer listening. I didn't even notice his uniform. All I could think of was the study, years ago, where my world had stopped and another had started. I was back there, smelling the furniture polish, listening to other boys playing in the street. My housemaster had never touched me before, except to beat me. But suddenly he was ushering me into a chair, resting rigid, pianist's hands gently on my shoulders, comforting, preparing me.

"I've got some very bad news to tell you," he had said, steepling his finger tips together, as if in prayer. "Very bad. Your mother died in the night. A heart attack. The doctor said she would have felt little pain. Like a bee-sting, nothing more."

Like a bee-sting? The words fell on to the floor, deadened by the thick carpet.

"Your father will meet you off the train. We'll say prayers for you tonight, at assembly."

From that moment on the world outside had looked just the same, but I knew it had cracked beneath the surface, slipped and separated in two.

I saw myself now, from the side, pointing the gun at the bomber, my arm unsteady. Two men pretending to be brave, about to die. In that snapshot I knew I couldn't pull the trigger. The bomber knew it, too. Imperceptibly he moved towards me, eyes locked on to mine, his hand rising tentatively. This is what I had rowed with Annalese about. If you didn't retaliate first, you died. But I could do nothing about it. Annalese felt very close, stretching out under my skin. I felt my fingers go limp. We were doing things her way now, but it wasn't Annalese's hands sliding down the barrel, taking the gun from my grip.

Then I noticed the bomber's eyes widen and crease.

He fell easily, his indignant face twisting with pain. I turned at the sound of gunfire and saw Charlotte's head and arms in the hatchway, a hand-gun in front of her. She fired again, loosing bullets into the luminous void. Silhouetted, the bomber was a simple target.

I looked at her for a second, then glanced at the guard, still shivering in his shirt and Y-fronts. I turned and stared at the bomber's leaking body, crumpled on the floor.

"The bomb," I muttered, "there's no time."

Charlotte's gaze lingered on the bomber as she slid back down through the hatch. She had intruded, made a decision for me. Stirring, I walked over to the corner, nodded at the guard. The old man fell to his knees and climbed through the hole, slipping on the rungs. I followed. There was a strong smell of urine.

"Come on, come on!" Charlotte shouted from the narrow door of the service lift. The guard was a sobbing heap on the floor. I jumped the last few rungs, grabbed his arm and dragged him into the lift. The doors rattled shut and we started descending. A second later the lift shaft shook with a deafening blast. I tried to imagine how the pyramid would look now, smoking as usual, but with a little more conviction. Charlotte glanced up at the ceiling. We were still descending at a steady pace.

CHAPTER 28

Dawn was breaking when I finally arrived in the Kenidjack valley. I had hitched a lift the night before from Plymouth to Penzance, but the final twelve miles I had walked, hiding in the hedgerows whenever cars passed. I was tired and had been travelling for four days. The place was much as I remembered it, ochre soil and dead gorse, marinated in reds and browns. The skyline to the right was dominated by the rig of an old tin mine, the chimney like a Norman tower, sheer and impregnable. Ahead lay the sea, salty but still out of sight.

I walked down a pockmarked track, following the course of the stream. It had recently flooded and the puddles were deep. I passed two rundown stone farm buildings, boarded up and empty, and startled a goat. It was hidden behind a corrugated shed, chewing at grass growing up through the carcass of a 2CV. Another car had been abandoned on the far side of the stream, its rusting metalwork blending in with the gorse.

On the corner, where the last farm building stood, I climbed around the edge of a vast puddle, more of a lake, deep enough to warn off innocent walkers, and made my way on up the bleak hillside, leaving the stream below me. Cape Cornwall was on the other side of the valley, St Just behind me. A group of boulders and small islands tailed off from a shoulder of rock into the sea. A thin plinth stretched up from one of them. Ten years earlier, long before I had lived here, there used to be a bender village down at the water's edge, near a small quarry. They lived like Stone

Agers and it had become a tourist attraction until a local councillor took umbrage and decided to evict them in the middle of winter (the coldest night of the year, as it turned out).

I neared the top of the hill and stopped. In the dim charcoal light the Atlantic stretched out before me. My eyes were drawn to the distant horizon, where the sea blurred with the sky. A myriad lights were shining, dots of white littered across the black water like glow-worms. Some of them were from tankers, waiting to enter the Channel, but most of them were fishing boats, beamers from Newlyn and Normandy.

I breathed in deeply and looked around. The tops of a few caravans were visible above the hedge to my right. Everyone would be asleep. It was over a year since I had left here with Annalese for London. I wondered who would still be about. Tricky, probably, and Snap. There were fewer caravans than I remembered. The National Trust had been threatening to buy the land. Perhaps some people had left already, too cold to fight.

I knew I could live here for a while, provided I collected firewood and water from off the moor. I had never been close to any of them, apart from Annalese of course, but I liked their attitude. They never asked questions, and had offered sanctuary to any number of people on the run. (Once, according to Tricky, the M11 gunman had even spent a few days with them.)

I climbed over a gap in the hedge and walked quietly amongst the caravans. Tricky's was still there, the only one looking cared for and painted. I saw a burnt-out shell by a pick-up truck near the cliff edge and went over to it. It had been stripped of aluminium and somebody had tried unsuccessfully to incinerate the remains. It would do for the night, breaking the cold wind coming in off the sea. I lay down in one corner, resting the crystal beside me.

"Sleep in that one tonight," Tricky said, nodding at another caravan. "You should have woken me."

I watched as Tricky went over to a van brought up the valley by the pick-up earlier in the morning. The sound of the truck's asthmatic exhaust had woken me. I had slept deeply despite the gaping wound in the ceiling and the broken windows.

"You heard about Annalese then," I said, wandering over to him.

"Yeah. We went to the funeral."

I didn't know where to start, how to explain. "I couldn't face it," I said weakly, hoping that would do for now.

"Snap sang a few songs."

"Is he still around?"

"Cutting cabbages."

"Anyone else?"

Tricky shook his head. He was wearing a woollen hat, glasses and a lumberjack shirt. A man of few words, he had lived here longer than anyone, and felt stronger for it. The site was located on top of an old uranium mine, and possessed a rare energy. (Aleister Crowley, another Kenidjack regular, had believed there was a serpent coiled up beneath the rock.)

"They're moving us on," he said.

"Where you going?"

"Other side of town. Snap found it. There's porridge if you want some." His head was now hidden under the bonnet.

I sat in my new caravan, a marginal upgrade from the previous one, and spooned down breakfast. It had a wood-burning stove, and a car battery to power a small radio, but the window facing the sea had been blown in. The seam joining the walls and ceiling also looked split. That was the problem with old caravans. If a wind found a way in during a storm it could pop the whole thing apart.

We had pushed the security guard out on the twelfth floor and descended in silence, not knowing what to expect. Outside in the sunset as sirens approached, the scene was one of confusion. A police officer helped us to safety as we walked innocently out of Canary Wharf station, mistaking us for shaken victims.

The tower had been evacuated, it seemed, and hundreds of people were standing around on the dockside boulevards, looking upwards, talking on mobile phones, chatting to police who had formed a loose cordon around the complex. Using loudhailers, they were trying to get people to move further away, but either people weren't listening or didn't know where to go. A few tactical punches, and it had the makings of a healthy riot, but I had other things on my mind.

I managed to thank the officer, explaining that I hadn't heard the alarm, and in the confusion I lost myself quickly in the densest part of the crowd. I wanted to get away from Charlotte as much as anything. I heard her calling but I kept going until her voice was lost in the throng. Only once did I allow myself to stop and look back. A plume of black smoke was rising from the top of the tower, the pyramid pierced by a neat hole on one side. Charlotte was nowhere in sight.

Cornwall felt reassuringly far from Docklands. The distance gave me a breathing space, time to think. All I wanted was a few days on my own. I felt close to Annalese here. I needed to go where we had been together, to Treen beach, to the Merry Maidens. I should have come straight away, as soon as she had died, but I had gone to Walter instead. I felt ready to mourn now.

Would anyone come after me? It depended on whether Charlotte could find people to listen. I didn't know what I felt about her. In my defining moment I had been shown up, by the bomber, by her. I had to believe that I would have shot him, and I resented her interference. She had saved my life, though, and I hoped she was alive.

For the next week I pulled my weight on the site, cooking stews and gathering firewood. Tricky talked honestly with me about Annalese but it was more difficult with Snap. Perhaps he had been in love with her. A lot of people were. I stood on the cliffs at Treen, looking down at the beach, wrapped in mist, and I walked along the coast to the Minack theatre. In Penzance I listened to a band playing badly on Causeway Head. For a moment I thought I saw Leafe, but it was someone else. When I rang Annalese's mum from a phonebox, there was no answer.

Eight days after I arrived, I was walking early with Tricky towards St Just. We were going to cut cabbages in a field near St Buryan. It was hard work when the ground was frozen, and there were the inevitable problems with the DSS, but on a good day it was £35 in the back pocket. As we dropped down the hill towards the track we looked up and saw a black Daimler in the distance, pushing around the corner towards the farm buildings.

"Who the fuck's that?" Tricky asked.

I didn't answer. My mind was racing. We both stood still and watched as the car pulled over and stopped, still five hundred yards away from us. A woman got out of the back seat and started walking up the track.

Tricky turned to me. "Friend of yours?" he asked.

It was Charlotte.

Tricky decided not to be introduced. Presuming it was someone from the Social, he climbed back over the hill and cut across a field, hidden from the track below. I sat down on a rock and waited. I suddenly felt very tired, too exhausted to think, to react. Charlotte was picking her way carefully through the puddles, carrying a black case in one hand. She saw me and gave a wave.

"Hello Dutchie," she said, five yards below me. "I thought I'd find you here."

I said nothing. She was dressed in tight red jeans and an Aran sweater. She looked relaxed, healthy.

"What a view," she said, looking beyond me towards the Atlantic.

"I don't imagine you're here on a sight-seeing trip," I said. "Are you arresting me?"

"Arresting you? Why would I be arresting you?"

"You tell me."

I looked at the Daimler and wondered who was employing her now.

"You look thin," she said. "Are you alright?"

I didn't answer. She was holding the case in front of her with both hands, like a schoolgirl with her books.

"I've come to give you your file back. It's the least we could do."

"Who's we?"

"The government. Number Ten."

I smirked.

"You've done the country a great service."

"Please, cut the crap."

"Really. You have."

She went over to a gate and rested the case on one of the bars. Opening it, she pulled out a thick file, boxed and ring-bound.

"Stella wanted to meet you herself," she laughed. "She took a great interest in all this. I told her you probably weren't so keen. Everything's here. Photos, newspaper cuttings, confidential reports. You should read it all some day. Not now, a few months' time."

She passed me the file.

"Thank you," I said. It was pleasantly heavy. But I couldn't believe she was just here to give me my file back. Too much had happened. "Have the bombings stopped?" I asked, indifferently.

"Completely. Touch wood. They were old school MI5, much as Walter suspected." She paused awkwardly. "I've got to be getting back to London. If you ever need anything, give me a call. The number's in there, at the front."

We were silent. I looked up at her, standing confidently against the bright sky. I was pleased she had come.

"You went without saying goodbye," she said quietly.

"I know."

"I was worried."

"Were you?"

"Yes, I was. We went through a lot together."

"Not by choice."

"No."

She hesitated, then leant forward and kissed me gently on the lips. "Thanks, for everything."

I watched her walk back down the hill, breaking into a run where it was steep. It still didn't add up, her coming all this way. Before she reached the car I had picked up the file and opened it. There were photos resting on the top, pictures of me and Annalese on the barge. Charlotte must have developed the film left in the camera. I sifted through some other photos, riot shots, the ones Walter had blackmailed me with at the house in Clapham. I wondered when the funeral had been, if my dad had gone. There was also a small bag of blow. I smiled as I read the label attached to it. "Lot number 48." Charlotte was alright, in her way.

Then I saw a sheet of paper, covered in red italic ink. It was Annalese's handwriting. There were more sheets below it. I pulled one out, curious, grateful for another souvenir. But I began to read and my mouth went dry. I read on, more about myself, my politics, my friendship with Leggit, background information on Class War, addresses of South London houses where I had once got drugs and bats for riots. Every sheet had been stamped with "Confidential – Metropolitan Police", and then the date. I sifted through them relentlessly. They were in chronological order and I soon found the first report. It had been written shortly after we had talked outside the Minack theatre. My face flushed hot and cold. But I had approached Annalese, hadn't I? I tried to think back through the sequence of events, but already my memory of them was confused, corrupted by the knowledge I was holding in my hands.

Were they genuine? It was her handwriting, no question. They must have blackmailed her. I heard Leggit's words in the pub: "Old Bill are all over us." Standing up, I felt nauseous and swallowed hard. Then I leant against the gate and vomited. My stomach was empty, the painful contractions yielding nothing but yellow bile. I looked around, wiping my mouth with my sleeve. Charlotte had reached the car. She glanced up before opening the door.

"Charlotte!" I yelled, but the car was turning around on the grass next to the stream. My cry echoed down the valley. I picked up the file and ran down the slope, slipping and falling as I went. When I reached the track I stopped, shoulders heaving. The Daimler had already disappeared around the far corner. The valley fell quiet. The barren gorse-land seemed less reassuring now, threatening even. Annalese had so often talked about this place, thick with uranium.

Annalese. The name was already resonating differently, a metallic hiss tarnishing its softness. *You were the only woman I have ever loved, the first person to betray me.* I felt very cold as I walked back down the track to the cliff edge, cold and hollow. Far beneath me the Atlantic was boiling. Seagulls were riding the up currents, close enough to touch.

Using fingers clumsy with cold, I pulled out a photo taken on the barge, and looked at it for a moment, searching her face for an explanation, for something to tell me it wasn't true. "She was left with no choice," Charlotte had said. "It's important you hold on to that." I screwed the picture up into a ball, so tight my nails dug into my palms. Slowly, one by one, I pulled out the other sheets and photos, ripped them up, and threw each one to the wind and sea.